Second Time Around

KATHERINE ALLRED

Cerridwen Press

What the critics are saying...

5 Blue Ribbons "Since this is one of the most moving stories I have had the privilege to read and review in a long time I could not resist giving it a much deserved 5 Blue Ribbon Rating." ~ *Romance Junkies Reviews*

4 Angels "*Second Time Around* is an emotional love story. It gives us some very memorable characters and each one will leave an indelible mark on the reader. Ultimately it is a "second" chance at love story which works on all levels, from the characters to the storyline, *Second Time Around* is a definite winner!" ~ *Fallen Angel Reviews*

A Cerridwen Press Publication

www.cerridwenpress.com

Second Time Around

ISBN 9781419954870
ALL RIGHTS RESERVED.
Second Time Around Copyright © 2005 Katherine Allred
Edited by Pamela Campbell
Cover art by Syneca.

This book printed in the U.S.A. by Jasmine-Jade Enterprises, LLC.

Electronic book Publication September 2005
Trade paperback Publication October 2008

With the exception of quotes used in reviews, this book may not be reproduced or used in whole or in part by any means existing without written permission from the publisher, Ellora's Cave Publishing Inc., 1056 Home Avenue, Akron, OH 44310-3502.

Warning: The unauthorized reproduction or distribution of this copyrighted work is illegal. Criminal copyright infringement, including infringement without monetary gain, is investigated by the FBI and is punishable by up to 5 years in federal prison and a fine of $250,000.
(http://www.fbi.gov/ipr/)

This book is a work of fiction and any resemblance to persons, living or dead, or places, events or locales is purely coincidental. The characters are productions of the author's imagination and used fictitiously.

Cerridwen Press is an imprint of Ellora's Cave Publishing, Inc.®

Second Time Around

Trademarks Acknowledgement

☙

The author acknowledges the trademarked status and trademark owners of the following wordmarks mentioned in this work of fiction:

Band-aid: Johnson & Johnson Corporation

Formica: The Diller Corporation

Jeep Cherokee: Daimler Chrysler Corporation

Resistol: RHE Hatco, Inc.

Rolodex: Berol Corporation

Stetson: John B. Stetson, Company

Volvo: Volvo Personvagnar AB Corporation

Chapter One

The hum of refined voices sent butterflies skittering through Lanie's stomach even as she located her target. And he'd seen her, too. In spite of her good intentions, the hair prickled erect on her arms, and her heart thundered in her chest as she took a step toward him.

"Do you have an invitation?"

"No." Lanie surveyed the woman who had stepped in front of her, halting her progress through the room. "I'm only here to speak with Quinn McAllister and then I'll be going." Her gaze went back to the man in question. He was moving in their direction through the crowd of richly dressed people occupying the museum reception room.

"I'm Judith French, his fiancée. What business could you possibly have with Quinn?"

"I'm his wife." She tried to keep her voice lowered.

"That's impossible."

She flinched at the redhead's elegantly belligerent tone, and her glance flicked to Quinn. The only indication that he'd heard her was a slight narrowing of his amber eyes as they moved over her.

"Ex-wife." Casually, he handed one of the drinks to the auburn-haired beauty before draping his free arm around her shoulders. "Nothing to worry about, Judith, my dear. You can pull your claws back in."

Trying to ignore his companion, Lanie faced the man she hadn't seen in five years. "Quinn, we need to talk."

"Call my secretary and set up an appointment."

The anger she'd been holding in since she'd crashed the museum fund-raiser erupted. "I've been calling your secretary since the minute I got to Chicago and you know it. If you hadn't been avoiding me, I wouldn't be here now. Either we go somewhere and talk in private, or we can do it here in front of your fiancée and all your fancy friends." Sarcasm laced her words as her gaze ran over the woman's chic black dress.

He took a deliberate drink from the glass, his eyes meeting hers over the rim.

"Fine," Lanie snapped. "Just remember it was your choice. I have a little piece of news I thought you might be interested in. Our divorce? It was bogus. We're still married. Which means you and Judith," contempt dripped as she spoke the woman's name, "can forget your upcoming nuptials."

She spun, her ankles almost buckling in the unfamiliar high heels, and marched toward the door. She'd told him what she had to. Her conscience was satisfied. The next move was up to him.

It didn't take him long to make it. His hand shot out and closed around her arm, his long fingers secure enough to prevent her escape. The force of his grip spun her to face him.

"What the hell do you mean, it's bogus?"

A lock of hair had fallen onto his forehead at the sudden move, almost obscuring the thin scar that ran from his temple into that wild mane of hair. The last time she'd seen him, no white had marred the ebony mass. Now, the streak stood out starkly from the surrounding blackness like lightening on a dark night. Even though she was mad enough to spit, she had to stop herself from brushing the lock back. Old habits died hard.

"Take your hand off me," she hissed, yanking away from his grasp. Every well-groomed head in the room turned in their direction. "I've wasted all the time I'm going to waste on you."

"Lanie, wait."

She ignored the order, pausing only long enough to pull open the heavy glass doors before rushing out onto the street. He could have his damn charity events, his fancy women, and all his money. She leaned down and yanked her shoes off, letting them dangle from her fingers as she breathed a sigh of relief. She'd get her own divorce, and this time she'd make sure it was the real thing.

The museum door opened behind her as she flagged a passing cab. A muffled curse escaped her when it kept going.

"How many times have I told you, if you're going to curse, do it out loud?" There was a hint of arrogant amusement in Quinn's voice.

She kept her gaze on the traffic, praying for another cab. "Stay away from me, Quinn."

"If you'll remember, I have been. For five years. You're the one who showed up here tonight."

"My mistake. For a while I forgot who I was dealing with. Believe me, it won't happen again."

"Where are you going?"

She waved at another cab, barely stopping her mumbled curse when it also ignored her. "Not that it's any of your business, but I'm going to the motel to get my things, then I'm taking the first plane back home. You remember Wyoming, don't you Quinn?" The sarcasm was back as she turned and stared at him. Somewhere under that tux had to be the man she'd fallen in love with, but he was buried so deep little evidence of him remained. Oh, he still looked the same. Tall, with a body that made women stop for a second look and prompted fantasies of hot nights and sweat-slicked skin. A body she'd made love to, and that still had the power to make her heart beat faster.

"Barefoot?" The amusement was back, one corner of his mobile lips lifting slightly. "Even with the expensive dress and new hairdo you haven't changed, Lanie."

"That's where you're wrong. I'm not nearly as stupid as I used to be." She glanced back at the street.

"Meaning when you married me?"

"Exactly."

"Come on." He took her arm again, just as firmly but without the bruising force. "It looks like we need to talk and I'd rather not do it out here on the street."

Lanie pulled back against the pressure until she realized it was either give in or get dragged down the sidewalk. "What about your fiancée?"

"Judith and I have an agreement. She keeps my father off my back, and in return she gets lots of nice green money to play with. She won't miss me."

Lanie caught only a glimpse of a shiny black car before he opened the door and guided her into the plush leather seat. The odor of expensive perfume still lingered in the air. His fiancée's, or someone else's? Before she could get the safety belt fastened, he slid under the wheel. "Still a gentleman, I see."

He glanced at her before pulling smoothly into the flow of traffic. "I don't remember ever claiming to be one. It didn't seem to bother you before."

It hadn't. She'd loved his confidence as much as she had his body, as much as she'd loved him. Loved that he'd treated her like an equal instead of a helpless female. At least he had in the beginning. There'd never been another man like him. Thank God.

"I've been staying at the motel on Franklin. You can drop me there and I'll get a cab to the airport." She braced for the right-hand turn, only to be thrown against the door when the car turned left. "This is the wrong way! Where are you taking me?"

"To my apartment. Where else would I take my *wife*?" His lips curled in a sneer as he placed emphasis on the word "wife."

She reached for her seat belt. "Stop the car this instant. I'm getting out. If you think an illegal divorce gives you any rights, you're dead wrong."

"Afraid to be alone with me?"

"You certainly have a short memory, Quinn. I *tried* to get you alone tonight and you refused." Anger oozed from every pore in her body. Another five minutes and she'd slug him.

"That was before I knew what you wanted."

"If you'd bothered to answer my calls you'd have known what I wanted. A divorce. A real one this time, and the faster the better."

He turned again, this time into a parking garage, and pulled the car to a stop. "We can talk about it upstairs."

She hesitated briefly, wondering if she shouldn't make a run for it, then gave a mental shrug. This was what she'd come for. It was better to get it over with now.

Picking up her shoes and purse, Lanie hurried to catch up with him as he held the elevator door with one hand. No doubt about it. Jared had spoiled her. He was as different from Quinn as daylight from dark. She'd gotten used to having doors opened for her, to being treated like something rare and precious.

The ride up was a silent one, Lanie watching the floors tick off on the digital counter. It figured. He lived in the penthouse. Just one more thing to point up the differences between them, the reasons why their short-lived marriage could never have worked.

"How's your father doing these days? Still the same S.O.B. he used to be?" The elevator doors slid open soundlessly and she stepped onto the cold marble floor of an ultramodern foyer.

He didn't answer, just gestured down several steps into the living room.

Her battered feet sank into plush white carpet as she dropped her shoes and walked to the bank of windows overlooking the city. A shiver ran over her, goose bumps popping erect on her arms. How could he stand to live in such a cold, sterile place?

There was no color in the room, everything done in shades of black and white, with chrome providing the only relief. The Quinn she'd known would have died in a place like this. He'd loved color as much as she had. Here, even the air had a cold metallic smell.

She watched him approach in the wide expanse of glass, his reflection stopping mere inches behind her own. Stomach coiling into a hard knot of tension, she moved a few steps away and saw his mouth curve up again.

"What makes you think the divorce was bogus?"

Reaching into her purse, she withdrew an envelope and passed it to him. "I got this two weeks ago. The lawyer you hired wasn't a lawyer. He conned hundreds of people. The papers were never filed. After he was arrested the court confiscated his records. That's where they got our names."

Face expressionless, he scanned the letter. "Why didn't I get one of these?"

"I don't know. Maybe they didn't know where to find you. But your address is listed as the McAllister Ranch in Wyoming, and we both know you haven't been back since..." Her words trailed off.

"Since the accident," he finished for her. He lifted his hand, his fingers tracing the scar on his face. "You can say it."

"I was going to say since the night you left, but have it your way." She kept her tone curt. "The problem is, I need that divorce as soon as possible. I thought maybe one of us could go to Vegas and get it done. Doesn't it take about six weeks?"

He folded the letter and stuck it back in the envelope. "Why the rush?"

Lanie hesitated then took a deep breath. "I'm seeing someone. Someone very special. He's asked me to marry him."

His gaze fastened on hers, and she wasn't sure she liked what she saw there. The clear amber of his eyes had been replaced with the sharp yellow flames of anger.

"So who's the poor sap you've roped in this time?"

Her chin went up and her body stiffened. "Jared is not a poor sap. He's a wonderful man. He's kind and smart and caring and he loves me. In other words, he's everything you're not."

"Sounds boring as hell. Does this paragon have a last name?"

"His name is Jared Harper. You don't know him. He set up practice after you left."

"Practice?" He took a step closer his gaze still holding her captive.

"That's right. He's a vet."

"And he loves you."

"Yes."

"He loves you so much that he let you come out here to face me alone?"

The air didn't smell metallic anymore. It smelled hot and electric with the scent of his aftershave. A tingle ran along her spine as he picked up her hand, and she knew how a snake must feel as it swayed to the siren call of the charmer's pipe. She couldn't move, couldn't look away.

"He wanted to come." She forced the words through numb lips. "I wouldn't let him."

"If I'd been in his shoes, you couldn't have stopped me."

She shouldn't have let him bring her here, should have insisted on going somewhere public. She knew how dangerous he could be. He seemed to have the uncanny ability to turn that animal magnetism on and off at will. He always had.

"Jared isn't like you."

"Right. He loves you." His mouth hovered over hers. "The question is, do you love him?"

His breath was warm and lightly scented with wine. Her mouth went dry, her heart pounding so hard it echoed in her ears. "Of course I do."

"You don't sound too sure of that, Lanie."

From somewhere she found the strength to step away from him, praying her legs would hold her up. "Then maybe you should listen closer. I love Jared and I plan on marrying him."

Quinn looked down at the envelope again. He didn't know why the surge of anger should surprise him. He'd known he was in trouble the second he'd seen her walk through the door tonight. In trouble and shocked right down to his soul.

Of all the people who could have shown up at that stupid fund-raiser, Lanie was the last one he would have expected. And she'd been here several days if her words were true. His anger became a boiling, helpless rage. It would do no good to fire his secretary. She'd only been following his father's orders.

Wearily, he rubbed the scar, a gesture that had become second nature to him after five years. "I'll need to keep this to show my lawyers. I can have them send it back to you after they make a copy."

"Thank you. You'll be going to Vegas, then?"

"Looks that way. I'll know more tomorrow."

Her head bobbed once, the dark brown curls, held by an elaborate gold clip, shinning in the overhead light. "I need to be going. I've already been away from home longer than I'd planned. You can call me there as soon as you find out anything."

"I'll drive you back to your motel."

She hesitated only a second. "I think it would be better if I took a cab. Can I use your phone?"

"That's not necessary." He stepped to an intercom and pushed a button. "Duncan? Bring the car around to the front. A lady in a red dress will be down shortly. Take her wherever she wants to go."

He watched as she slipped the shoes back on and draped her purse strap over her shoulder, his gaze soaking up the feminine curves revealed by the clinging red silk. A dull weight settled on his chest. He had been denied the chance to tell her goodbye five years ago, and now she was walking out of his life again, this time straight into the arms of another man. He would have sworn he'd put her betrayal behind him, but seeing her again brought all the old hurt surging back to the surface.

"Well." She straightened. "I guess this is goodbye, then."

"Lanie?" He made himself smile, even though it felt fake, unnatural. "You look great. I always said you'd clean up good."

A tiny smile curved her lips. "We both know I don't belong in clothes like these, Quinn. I never will." She paused before pulling the door open, casting one last look in his direction. "Take care of yourself."

* * * * *

Quinn stared at the closed door, wondering if he'd imagined her being here. He undid his tie and slid it from his neck, heading straight for the wet bar. Seeing Lanie again after all these years had rattled him. She was a part of his life he'd thought gone forever. A part he had tried desperately to convince himself he no longer wanted or cared about. And he'd succeeded to some extent, burying himself in his work between the rounds of surgeries and physical therapy. Entire weeks went by when he didn't think about her, wonder what she was doing or if she were involved with anyone. Now he didn't have to wonder anymore.

His hand trembled slightly as he poured a scotch straight up. The limp he went to great lengths to hide was more pronounced as he turned down the hall, the pain in his thigh a burning spasm. Even if Lanie hadn't shown up, he wouldn't have stayed at the fund-raiser much longer. He needed a long soak in the whirlpool.

The phone rang as he went by his office and he turned in the door, easing down onto the padded chair before lifting the receiver.

"McAllister."

"I hear you had a visitor tonight."

Quinn leaned his head back and closed his eyes, taking a sip of scotch before he answered his father. "I see Judith didn't waste any time calling you."

"Why should she? You walked out and left her stranded. That's no way to treat your fiancée."

"Drop the crap, Edward. We both know Judith would have gone home with one of her 'friends' whether I was there or not."

"Judith comes from an excellent background. Good family, good connections. If you treated her the way she deserved, maybe her attitude would improve."

"Sorry. Not interested. She was your idea, not mine."

There was a moment of silence from his father's end of the line. "What did Lanie want that was important enough to make her come to Chicago? If it was money, she can forget it. She's gotten everything from us she's going to get."

"If you'd bothered to let me know she was here you might have found out sooner. Why wasn't I told she'd been calling?"

"Because I didn't think it was important enough to disturb you. We have some big deals coming up and you need to focus on those, not the past."

"Well, this time you screwed up royally. It would appear the lawyer you hired to handle our divorce wasn't really a lawyer after all. Lanie and I are still married. The good news is, that means I don't have to marry Judith."

A shocked silence greeted his statement. When his father finally answered, his words sounded gritty, as though spoken through clenched jaws.

"That's impossible."

"No, it's not. I've got the letter from the court to prove it. I'm going to fax it over to Franklin. You might want to do the same with the rest of the divorce papers. Give him a chance to look them over before tomorrow."

There was another pause from his father's end of the line. "Is she still there?"

"No, she left a few minutes ago. I got the impression she was in a big rush to get back to her fiancé. She'll probably take the first plane out."

"This divorce business is all you talked about?"

Quinn couldn't keep the sarcasm out of his voice. "What did you expect me to do? Reminisce about old times and then drag her to bed?"

"Just don't get any of your crazy ideas. We'll get this mess straightened out as soon as possible and everything will get back to normal. You and Judith will have to move the wedding date but that shouldn't be a problem. I'll give Franklin a call and explain what's going on. You just send him that letter."

Quinn dropped the phone back into its cradle, glad for once that his father was taking over. He was too tired to think about legal ramifications right now, and he could feel the first dull throb of what he knew would soon become a crippling headache.

He levered himself out of the chair and put the letter in the fax before continuing down the hall. Stepping into the gym, he turned on the whirlpool and stripped, leaving the tux in a wrinkled heap on the floor.

The jets of hot water massaged his thigh, bringing blessed relief from the bone-deep ache. The scar there was much wider than the one on his face, standing out in stark, ugly contrast from the bronze of the surrounding skin. After the accident, it had taken months of physical therapy and numerous operations before he could walk again. And even after that had been accomplished, there had been several more surgeries to make his leg as normal as possible. The final one had been just a few months ago. But he hadn't complained. The hard, painful workouts had helped keep his mind off Lanie. All for nothing. They were still married. And she was in love with another man. The spurt of anger that hit him was hotter than the water in the tub.

He was still trying to get his emotions under control when he heard the front door open and the sound of footsteps in the hall. Opening his eyes a slit, he watched Duncan scoop his clothes off the floor and hang them neatly in the closet.

"Did you take her to a motel?"

Duncan nodded. "I offered to take her to the airport, but she refused. What are you drinking?" He pointed toward the glass perched on the edge of the tub.

"Scotch."

"How much have you had?"

"Only what's missing from the glass."

Duncan eyed the contents, apparently satisfied that he wasn't half soused. "How about water and a couple of muscle relaxers instead?"

"Scotch," Quinn repeated firmly. "You know I hate those damn pills."

"Why the hell do you pay me if you aren't going to listen to a thing I say?" Ignoring Quinn's words, he went to a small fridge in the corner and took out a bottle of water. On his way back, he snagged a bottle of pills. "Take them and stop being stupid. You know the scotch isn't going to help, and there's no one here you have to put on an act for."

Quinn eyed them warily, but finally held out his hand and let Duncan drop the medication into it. After five years, he knew better than to argue. There may have only been a slight difference in their ages, but Duncan took his job seriously. He could be a real tyrant when he thought Quinn was overdoing it. That Quinn let him get away with it spoke volumes about their relationship. If it hadn't been for Duncan, he would probably be in a wheelchair now. Or worse. He was the physical therapist who bullied, browbeat and forced Quinn into walking when all he'd wanted was to die. He owed Duncan a lot more than the hefty salary he paid him.

"How long have you been in there?" Duncan gestured at the whirlpool.

"About twenty minutes." He swallowed the pills and washed them down with the cold water, letting his head fall back on the tub rim as he waited for the drug-induced floating sensations to begin.

"Why don't you climb out and let me massage that leg. It might help."

"Help?" Quinn opened his eyes. "I'm afraid the only way you'll be able to help this time, Dunc, is if you can change the past."

Chapter Two

Quinn swiveled his chair restlessly as the lawyers went over the papers yet again. They had been at it for hours now. Even his father was making impatient noises.

"This is a disaster." Franklin Delaney, Chief Counsel for McAllister Pharmaceuticals, raked a hand through his thick brown hair.

Light sparked from the gold etched pen Quinn toyed with, casting tiny rainbows across the ceiling. "I don't see why I can't hop a plane and get a quick divorce. No muss, no fuss."

"Use your head, Quinn. Five years have passed. You're the CEO and one of the largest stockholders of a major corporation. If Lanie wants to make trouble it's conceivable she could wind up owning half the business."

"How?" He glanced at his father, sitting silent at the other end of the table, gnarled hands curled around the head of his cane.

"You haven't cohabited for five years. She can claim abandonment, and that's not all. There hasn't been a week your picture hasn't shown up in the newspaper with some woman or other. How hard do you think it will be for her to prove infidelity? I'm telling you, if she takes this to court, she'll win, and she'll win big."

"What about her infidelity? She told me she was in love with this guy, for God's sake."

"One man." The lawyer held up a finger to emphasize his point. "We'd have to prove she's sleeping with him, and that he's not the first."

"Lanie wants a fast divorce. Why should she fight it?"

The sound of Franklin grinding his teeth together was audible throughout the room. "You aren't listening to me, Quinn. There's just too much of a legal tangle that has to be ironed out before the divorce can even get started."

Edward McAllister stirred, his gaze fixed on Franklin. "What about the McAllister Ranch? It was given to her free and clear when the divorce became final. Can't we take it back if she doesn't cooperate?"

Franklin shuffled through the papers and pulled one off the bottom. "According to the wording on the agreement, and since the divorce never became final, we *could* say the place still belongs to Quinn. That doesn't mean she couldn't make a lot of trouble in court. After all, the deed is registered in her name. It would be a long battle with an uncertain outcome. And that's just one example of the mess this has caused. There are hundreds of others."

He looked back at Quinn. "I know you want to get it over with, but there are too many problems. At this point, a fast divorce is out of the question. We'll be lucky to have it all sorted through before the end of the year. And that's only if the lady *does* cooperate."

John Dempsey, one of the junior counselors who'd been making notes on a yellow pad, glanced up. "Don't forget the publicity. The newspapers will have a field day when they get hold of this. The stockholders aren't going to be happy. We can't afford any adverse publicity with the launch of the new drug scheduled in a few months."

Quinn suppressed a groan. In all the emotional turmoil he'd virtually forgotten their breakthrough new drug, which could reverse damage done by coronary artery disease. "So what do you suggest I do?"

"For starters, you're going to have to go to Wyoming and talk to her. We can't do anything until we know what she'll agree to." Franklin held up a hand as Quinn started to protest. "John and I will draw up some papers that you'll need to take with you. If she'll sign them, we can at least get things started. It will also serve the purpose of getting you away from the press while we take care of the legal end here. Edward can step back in and handle the business while you're gone. That will placate the stockholders."

Edward lifted his bulk from the chair using the cane for balance, and walked to the window, his back to the room. "It's out of the question. He can't go back there."

Franklin shook his head. "Edward, he has no choice. This woman could destroy McAllister Pharmaceuticals. She's holding all the cards."

"Why can't you simply send her the papers?"

"Because right now, there's a chance she doesn't realize what she could do to us. If we start sending release papers and asking her to sign them, it might put ideas into her head." The lawyer shook his head again. "No, we need Quinn to handle it, to handle her. He knows her better than anyone else here."

Quinn tensed as his father remained silent. Every line of the rigid back spoke of righteous indignation. He knew the old man well enough to sense a storm brewing. When his father faced the room again, his eyes were filled with a hard determination. Whatever he'd been debating, he had reached a decision.

"If she refuses to sign the papers or makes one move toward the business, we'll sue her."

Every eye in the room was suddenly fixed on Edward.

"Sue her for what?" Both lawyers spoke at once.

Edward stared at Franklin, his gaze avoiding Quinn. "Sue her for custody of my grandson. She'll agree to anything to keep the boy."

Franklin dropped his head to the table with a groaned, "Oh, God," but Quinn barely heard him. A roaring filled his ears, blocking sound while blackness threatened the edges of his vision. In his hand, the gold pen snapped, spattering smears of ink over the table.

A son. He had a son. The boiling rage he'd felt last night was nothing compared to the black fury that hit him now, eating away all vestiges of shock in its need for release. One more lie. One more betrayal in a viper's nest of many.

"Get out."

The words directed at the lawyers were soft, but Franklin knew a command when he heard it. Both men stood and quietly left the room, not even bothering to gather their papers.

Quinn waited until the door close behind them, his hot gaze never leaving Edward's. "You bastard. How long have you known?"

"From the beginning." Edward pulled his chair out and sat back down.

As though Edward's action galvanized him, Quinn leaped to his feet, his leg screaming in protest. But for once, he welcomed the pain, focused on it. Anything to keep him from wrapping his hands around his father's neck and squeezing the life out of him.

He flattened his hands on the table to still them and leaned toward his father. "Would you care to tell me why this is the first time you've mentioned it? Why you didn't seem to feel I had the right to know about my own child?" A blood vessel on the side of his face pulsed in time with the anger he couldn't control.

The cold mask of Edward's expression never changed as he studied Quinn. "Because I knew what you'd do. You'd have thrown away everything I've created, everything I've done for you. Someday you'll have a son worthy of taking over the company, one that's accepted by society the way I never was. You've got your foot in the door, thanks to me, but they'll never accept a child born to a woman of Lanie Stewart's standing. They'd eat both you and the child alive. You were better off not knowing."

"Any son of mine is worthy of succession, you son of a bitch. How dare you presume you could pick and choose my heir based on his mother?"

Edward's fingers tightened on the cane, the blue veins standing out in stark relief under the paper-thin skin. "I had no choice in the woman I married. You do, and by God you'll take advantage of it! You made a mistake when you married Lanie Stewart, and my company isn't going to suffer because your hormones overrode your good sense."

"I married Lanie because she did things for me that none of your blue-blooded little debutantes could."

Quinn's lip curled at the look on his father's face. "No, I don't mean in the sack. Jesus Christ. She made me feel alive, she made me laugh."

"And then she betrayed you, divorced you and wound up with your ranch. Now she's after the rest and you're going to let her get away with it. You may as well hand her the company on a silver platter."

He ran a hand through his hair, trying to get himself under control. "Your company, Edward. Your son, your grandson, your bloodlines. That's all this comes down to, isn't it? The ultimate ego trip."

"The only ego involved is yours. You're weak, Quinn. You always were. There's no place in business for emotions, but you're too much like your mother. I've tried to drum it out of you, to give you a chance to succeed, but her blood keeps pushing you, making you rash and impulsive. Any child of Lanie Stewart's will be even worse. The woman has no breeding, no class."

"That child is my flesh and blood and you hid him from me. You deprived him of a father, and you deprived me of my son."

"The boy has a father. Lanie's fiancé. The man is the only father he's ever known. I would have told you about him when I judged the time was right."

"When you judged the time was right." Automatically, Quinn's hand lifted to the scar on his face. "And just when was the time going to be right, Edward? When he showed up at my door in twenty years and demanded to know where the hell I was when he was growing up? Would you 'judge' that soon enough? Or were you planning to use him to keep me under your thumb for the rest of my life?"

Quinn stared at his father. "That's it, isn't it? He was your ace in the hole. A carrot to dangle in front of me if I got out of line."

He straightened. "The truth is you've been controlling my life since the day I was born and I've let you. Well, this is where it stops. You aren't using my son the way you did me even if it means I leave the company."

"You're not thinking with your head, Quinn. We both know you'll never let the company go. It's in your blood as much as it's in mine."

Quinn swept the papers off the table with one vicious movement, then stabbed a finger in Edward's direction. "I've spent my entire life putting up with your schemes and manipulations because I thought you were doing what was best for the business. But this time, Edward, you've gone too far." He turned his head to the door. "Franklin!"

The door to the boardroom opened immediately, almost as if the lawyer had been leaning against it, and he stepped back into the room, his eyes going straight to Quinn.

"I want you to draw up a legal document. A trust fund for my son that he'll receive when he's twenty-five. All my assets, including my shares of McAllister Pharmaceuticals are to go in it with myself as trustee until that time." He started toward the door.

"Wait! It's perfect," Franklin said excitedly. "I don't know why I didn't think of it. She can't touch anything if it's tied up in a trust fund. You can go ahead and get a quick divorce." He hesitated. "The only problem is, you won't be able to get it back after the divorce."

Quinn stopped with one hand on the glossy knob. "There's not going to be a divorce. At least, not unless she gives me custody of my son." His eyes closed in pain. "God, I don't even know his name."

He speared his father with another angry glare. "You disgust me, old man."

Edward stood slowly. "Where are you going?"

"Wyoming," Quinn snapped. "I think it's time I got to know my son."

"You'll be back."

"You're damn right I will. I'll be back to make sure my son owns this company in spite of your machinations. You lose this time, Edward. And before I'm done, you'll lose it all."

Without waiting for a response, he went out the door, his limp more pronounced than usual as he strode down the flat gray expanse of carpeted hall. Desperately, he fought off the blinding arc of pain that started in his temple and shot through his head like an assassin's bullet. There was too much to do, too many things to think about. He couldn't give in to the headache now.

His secretary was absent from her desk as he swept through the outer office. Probably hiding, if her fearful attitude this morning was any indication. And the way he felt now, she was smart to vanish. He would no longer tolerate Edward's spies.

Inside his office, the gray carpet was broken by a deep maroon circle edged in black that matched the marble of his desk. All of it was as stark and cold as his apartment, both done by the same decorator, compliments of Edward.

He hated the lifeless color scheme, but at the time it hadn't seemed worth the effort to change it. His energy had been focused on walking again. Walking and trying to forget that his wife didn't care enough to visit him while he was desperately ill, had in fact taken the opportunity to divorce him and claim the ranch he loved.

Had Lanie known she was pregnant when he left that night? Even if she hadn't, she must have known by the time the divorce was final. Known and chosen not to tell him. But then, what was one more betrayal among the rest?

Quinn moved into the adjoining bathroom and took a bottle of aspirin from the cabinet. In spite of the headache, a sense of exaltation crept over him. He had a son. A child that he and Lanie had created together. Finally, here was a part of her he could love without reservation, a part that no one was ever going to take away from him again.

He swallowed the aspirin, questions swirling through his mind as he headed for the phone. What was the boy like? Did he know who his father was? Where did he think Quinn had been all these years? Did he look like Lanie?

Rapidly, he punched in his home number and waited impatiently for Duncan to pick up. He got the answering machine and glanced at the gold clock sitting on his desk. Duncan must be running errands.

"Dunc? It's me. Listen, something's come up. I'll tell you about it later, but for now, I want you to start packing. We're leaving for Wyoming first thing in the morning. I don't know how long we'll be gone, but it could be for quite a while."

He looked up as the door opened and Franklin slipped in, then continued with his instructions. "Also, call the airport and have them get the plane ready, then arrange for a car to be waiting on us when we get to Wyoming. See you when I get home."

"Did Edward send you?" Quinn dropped the phone back into the cradle.

"No." The lawyer sank into one of the leather chairs positioned in front of the desk. "He doesn't know I'm here. We need to talk, Quinn. I don't want you walking into that situation blind."

"Blind?" He shook his head then winced as the movement sent fresh pain streaking from his temple. "I think this may be the first time in my life I see everything clearly."

"Not if you think you can stop your wife from divorcing you."

Quinn smiled. "Oh, I know she can divorce me. But I also know I can drag it out for a year or more. And I won't stop until I have custody of my son."

Franklin hesitated. "That's another thing. You can keep her from getting anything with this trust fund, but what about you? How will you survive if you put all your assets into it?"

"My mother's blood may not have been blue enough to suit Edward, but she was smart. She left me enough money to live comfortably, and she tied it up so no one, not even Edward could touch it. I suspect she'd approve of the use I'm going to put it to."

He began gathering up papers and shoving them into his briefcase. "How long will it take you to get the trust fund set up?"

"A few days. Week at the most. I'll need your signature on several documents before it goes into effect."

"I'll see to it there's a fax at the ranch. You can send them to me there."

"You're sure this is what you want to do?"

"Positive."

Franklin stood. "In that case, good luck. I hope it works out for you, Quinn. If you need me for anything, I'll be here." He held out his hand and Quinn shook it.

"Thanks, Franklin. I'll be in touch."

As soon as the attorney was through the door, Quinn picked up the phone again and dialed the number for his stockbroker.

"Tom? Quinn McAllister. I've got new orders for you. I'm going to deposit a large amount of cash into my account. I want you to start buying up every share of McAllister Pharmaceutical stock you can get your hands on."

Chapter Three

Quinn watched the Wyoming mountains loom large as the plane banked and began a slow descent in the bright mid-morning sun. Not a single cloud marred the pristine blue sky and he wondered if it were a good omen.

Duncan appeared from the cockpit, his wide frame taking up most of the space in the passageway. With a relieved sigh, he sank down beside Quinn and fastened his seat belt.

"Almost there. Pilots have clearance to land. How are you doing?"

He gave him a wry smile. "No headache, but I'm scared spitless. What if my son hates me on sight? Or worse, what if he's afraid of me?" His hand touched the scar that ran from his temple into his hair.

Duncan shrugged. "The scar's not that bad. If he's like most kids that age, it'll fascinate the hell out of him for about five minutes, then he'll forget you've got it."

"Kids that age," he mused. "That's the problem, Dunc. The last time I was around preschoolers was when I was one, and I wasn't taking notes back then. I don't have a clue how to treat him. Maybe I should have picked him up a gift."

"No." Duncan shook his head. "You're bringing him the only gift he really needs. His father. All you have to remember is not to push him. Let him set the pace. I promise, he'll be curious enough that it won't take you long to get to know him. My sister's youngest is about that age, and the kid never meets a stranger. He can talk the paint off the walls."

"Well, since you're the expert, poke me if I start to do something wrong."

"Just relax and be yourself. Kids can spot a phony attitude a mile off."

"Oh, thanks. That really helps boost my confidence."

Quinn was silent, staring out the window as the plane settled to the ground. Five years. He couldn't stop his heart from proclaiming he'd finally come home. Would the ranch be the same, or had Lanie changed it to the point where he wouldn't recognize it anymore?

He glanced around at the click of Duncan's seat belt being unfastened. "Did you rent a car?"

"The only thing they had was a Jeep," Duncan said. "It should be waiting on us." He reached into the overhead and pulled out several bags. "You know, being on a ranch will probably be good for that leg. Might even see some improvement. No matter how many hours you spent in the gym, sitting behind a desk most of the day wasn't helping."

"So you told me." Quinn stepped into the aisle and lifted out several more bags. "At least twice a day, if I remember correctly."

"For all the good it did." Duncan paused as the pilot appeared and opened the door, then went past him into the warm sunlight.

Quinn stopped the pilot as he turned back toward the cockpit. "Jack, when are you heading back to Chicago?"

"In the morning. It'll take most of the afternoon to service the plane. Duncan booked a room for us at a motel near here."

He nodded. "Have a safe flight back."

"Thank you, sir. And you have a pleasant vacation."

Duncan was waiting at the bottom of the stairs, and Quinn glanced at his watch as he joined him. "Let's grab something to eat before we head out. I don't want to get there right at lunch time."

"Sounds good to me."

* * * * *

"I've never been to the mountains before," Duncan commented as they headed north on Antelope Flats Road, leaving the town of Jackson behind them. "It's a good thing I'm not claustrophobic. It kind of feels like they're falling on you."

"I think most people feel that way at first. You get used to it." Quinn looked out at the majestic peaks of the Grand Tetons, Rendezvous Mountain towering in the distance. Snow still covered the higher slopes, the sun causing the white powder to glimmer with sparkles of light.

"I guess you spent a lot of time here when you were growing up. Strange, but Edward never struck me as the type of person who would enjoy a place like this."

Quinn smiled sardonically. "He didn't. It was my mother who loved it. My grandfather bought her the ranch as a wedding gift. Until she died, we stayed here every summer and holiday."

"And this is where you met your wife?"

His wife. A strange tickle of emotion ran through Quinn. He'd spent every day since the accident trying to make himself believe that Lanie was no longer his wife. But she had been, even if they hadn't realized it, and Duncan's words brought all those possessive instincts surging back to life. His wife, his child.

"Yeah." He traced his scar with one finger. "Although at first she was just a pest. She was only fourteen. I was eighteen. Her parents had died a few months before and she'd moved in with her grandparents, the Howells. Their place was next to mine, so we were neighbors." For the first time in years, he let himself remember the night he'd met Lanie, and a smile played around his lips as he related the incident to Duncan…

~ ~ ~ ~ ~

Who would have thought prim, proper Susie Morsten would be so hot, so uninhibited? Or maybe she just got her rocks off because they were practically in public. He knew some women did, had even participated with a few of them, although he personally preferred privacy.

Yeah, it sure looked to be a good summer, even if he'd had to blackmail Edward into letting him spend it here in Wyoming. His father thought he should work at the company, waste his last few months of freedom before college started in the fall.

For once, Quinn had stood up to him, threatening to withdraw from college if he weren't allowed to spend summers at the ranch. And for once, Edward had realized he wasn't bluffing. He'd meant every word. His father hadn't given in gracefully, but he had given in and that was the only thing that mattered.

Trying to ignore the burning ache in his groin, he glanced around the dark balcony of the only theater in town. There were only a few couples scattered through the seats, most preferring the bottom floor. As far as he could tell, no one was paying any attention to them.

While Susie's panting breath slowed, he kept his hand cupped on her. Her head was buried in his neck, his free arm around her shoulders, his hand inside her blouse as he teased a plump nipple.

As soon as he was sure she'd recovered enough, he let his fingers do the walking. Instantly, she arched into his hand, another moan quivering from her lips.

"God, Quinn. Are you trying to kill me?"

"If you want me to stop, just say the word," he murmured.

"No," she gasped. "Don't stop. There. Oh, yes, Quinn. Yes."

A high-pitched, mocking voice came from right behind them. "Oh, yes, Quinn. Yes. Don't stop, Quinn."

Quinn froze.

"Man, you two are so disgusting. Why don't you get a room? Hasn't it occurred to you that some people would actually like to watch the movie?"

He turned his head enough to identify the small figure as female. From her size, a very young female, although her words indicated she might be older than she looked. "Go play with yourself, kid."

"At least, if I feel the urge, I'll do it in private," she shot back. "Watching that kind of stuff could warp my delicate psyche, you know."

In spite of his irritation, Quinn couldn't stop his lips from twitching. The kid had a smart mouth on her, that was for sure.

"Come on, Quinn. Let's get out of here." As they stood Susie shot a glare at the girl. "You breathe one word of this, Lanie Stewart and I'll know where to come looking."

Even in the dark, he could see the girl's gray eyes widen in mock innocence. "Leaving on my account, Susie? You sure 'Studly' here can walk with that boner?"

Damned if the kid wasn't right. He could barely walk. He didn't need to look down to know the bulge in his jeans was really obvious. Trying not to hobble, he followed Susie down the aisle, still chuckling over the kid's remarks. He pitied the man who had to handle that one when she was full-grown...

~ ~ ~ ~ ~

Duncan was laughing out loud by the time he finished the story. "When Lanie found out I lived next door, she spent the rest of the summer driving me nuts. Followed me everywhere, always smarting off about something. Almost ruined my love life, popping up at the damnedest times. But we wound up friends. Maybe because she didn't know anyone else," he mused.

Friends right up until the time he'd realized that Lanie had done something no other woman had ever done to him before. She'd made him fall in love with her. It hadn't been a stunning revelation, captured in a single instant of time. It had been a gradual thing, building up over the years as she'd matured. Looking back, he suspected a part of him had fallen in love with the flat-chested, skinny-as-a-rail kid he'd met that first summer.

Now they had a child together. A child he was on his way to meet for the first time.

* * * * *

Lanie braced herself, leaned down, and snagged Zack around the waist as he darted past her, heading for the back door. "And just where do you think you're going, cowboy?" She lifted him onto her hip in spite of his struggles to get free, and inhaled the sweet little boy aroma.

"Mama!" His bottom lip extended in a pout. "I want to play with the puppies."

"Nap first, puppies later." She ran a hand through the black hair that was so like Quinn's.

"But I promised Daisy I'd be back."

"I'm sure Daisy will understand. She's probably got the puppies asleep by now, anyway."

His pout increased. "I could wake them up."

"That's some lip you've got there. Think I need to help you hold it?" When he nodded, she gently grasped the bow shape with her thumb and index finger, causing Zack to collapse in giggles. It was a game they had played since he was a baby, and it never failed to make him laugh.

She deposited him on the floor, giving him a playful swat on his tiny jeans-clad bottom to head him in the right direction. "Upstairs with you, sir."

"But I'm not sleepy."

Lanie smiled, knowing he'd be out like a light as soon as his head hit the pillow. "Tell you what. If you don't want to sleep, you don't have to, but Mr. Jingles is tired and he can't rest without you. Why don't you lie down with him for a few minutes and then you can get back up."

Mr. Jingles, a colorful harlequin made from parachute silk, was one of the first toys he'd ever had, and was still one of his favorites. When Zack had started walking, she'd only had to listen for the sound of the bells on the dolls shoes and hat to know where her son was currently located.

Zack looked at her suspiciously. "You promise?"

"Cross my heart." She made an X on her chest.

They had reached the stairs when the sound of a vehicle on the driveway drifted through the open windows at the front of the house.

"Company!" Zack yelled with glee, making a U-turn and racing out the front door.

Lanie sighed as she followed at a more sedate pace. She'd never get him to take that nap now. Unless it was Jared. He could get Zack to do almost anything. She hadn't been expecting him until later tonight, but maybe he'd decided to stop in between calls.

She heard the motor die. It didn't really sound like Jared's truck, she decided. For that matter, it didn't sound like any of the vehicles she was familiar with. She quickened her pace and pushed the screen door open.

Zack was standing uncertainly halfway between the porch and the black Jeep Cherokee, and a tingle of anxiety ran over her as she moved closer. Her son tended to be way too trusting of strangers.

"Zack."

He ignored her, his gaze fixed on the Jeep as the passenger door began to open. The windows were tinted, and she could barely make out the shape of two people inside, but suddenly she knew. Even as Quinn unfolded his body from the seat and stood, her heart slammed into her throat.

Zack. Oh, god. He wasn't ready for this. *She* wasn't ready for this. Somehow she kept her feet moving until she was standing behind her son. Shakily, she rested a hand on his shoulder, as much to comfort herself as him.

"Quinn. I didn't expect to see you here."

Quinn felt like he was drowning. Each breath was labored and he'd broken out in a sweat. One hand gripped the top of the door so tightly his knuckles turned white. He couldn't take his eyes off the little boy in front of him. Zack. Lanie had called him Zack. His hungry gaze devoured every detail from the miniature boots to the thick mop of black hair. He didn't look like either Lanie or himself, Quinn realized. Instead, he was a mixture of both. His wide gray eyes and firm chin were definitely Lanie's, but that dark hair and straight nose mimicked Quinn's own. He ached to hold him, to just touch him, but he knew instinctively it would be the wrong thing to do right now.

Zack studied him just as intently, and Quinn fought for control. Leaning down slightly, he smiled. "Hi there, Zack. Do you know who I am?"

The little boy nodded. "You're my daddy. Aren't you busy anymore?"

"Busy?"

"Mama said the reason you never come to see me is because you're real busy."

A wave of dizziness swept over him, threatening to bring him to his knees. "No," he said softly. "I'm not busy anymore. I don't plan on being busy for a long time. As a matter of fact, I thought I'd hang around here for a while, if that's okay with you."

"I have to ask Mama before I invite guests to stay." He was leaning back against Lanie's legs. "Who's he?" He pointed at Duncan, who had come around the Jeep.

"This is a good friend of mine. His name is Duncan."

Duncan held out his hand for Zack to shake. "Hi, Zack. How's it going?"

"Okay." Zack released his hand and stuck one finger in his mouth before suddenly remembering his earlier mission. He looked back at Quinn. "I've got puppies. Want to go see them?"

Lanie cupped his cheek. "Not right now, sweetie. I need to talk to...your father...first. Why don't you take Duncan to see them?"

The little boy looked up at Duncan. "You want to see my puppies?"

"You bet I do. Puppies are my favorite things in the whole world." He shot a quick glance at Quinn. "Are you going to be okay?" he murmured softly. "You're white as a sheet."

Quinn merely nodded, his gaze still on his son.

Zack took Duncan's hand, then turned back to Quinn. "Are you going to leave again?"

"No, Zack. I'm not going to leave."

Apparently satisfied, Zack headed around the house, dragging Duncan with him.

"Quinn? What's going on? Why are you here?"

"He's beautiful, Lanie."

"He always has been." Her tone could have frozen salt water. "If you'd ever bothered to come see him, you would have known that."

Chapter Four

Feeling as though he'd aged twenty years, Quinn sank back onto the edge of the passenger seat. "And how the hell was I supposed to come see him when you didn't bother to let me know we had a child?" Tiredly, he rubbed his face. The shock and turmoil of the last two days was finally starting to hit home. "I didn't think even you could do something like keep my son's existence from me."

Her eyes narrowed, anger turning the gray to a flashing steel color. "Right, Quinn. You expect me to believe you didn't know about him when you've been sending him presents every Christmas and on his birthday?" Indignation rang in her voice.

Slowly, he shook his head. "I don't even know when his birthday is. Edward must have sent the gifts."

"If this is supposed to be some kind of joke, I don't think it's funny. Or is this your way of finding an excuse for ignoring him all this time?"

"I wasn't ignoring him. What I said is the truth. And if you hadn't shown up with that letter from the court, Edward would have never told me."

"But— He promised— You signed the custody papers!" She took a shaky step forward and gripped the Jeep's door as if it were the only thing keeping her on her feet. "Oh, God. I don't know why this surprises me, but it does. I didn't believe even Edward could be that cruel." Her gaze searched his face. "You honestly didn't know?"

"If I'd known, nothing could have kept me away, and I sure as hell wouldn't have given up custody of my child." He pulled himself to his feet. "Can we go inside? There's a lot we have to talk about."

"I think we'd better."

When she turned toward the house, Quinn fell into step beside her. His gaze swept the ranch, noting the white fences, the horses grazing here and there. "It still looks the same," he murmured.

"I had a new stable built last year," she answered absently. They climbed the steps onto the porch and Lanie opened the front door. "Let's go into the office. We'll have more privacy there."

Before they reached the office there was a flurry of footsteps at the end of the hall, and Quinn suddenly found himself enveloped in the arms of a sobbing woman.

"Mr. Quinn! Land sakes, I can't believe it's you. I didn't think you was ever coming back."

He returned the hug, nearly lifting the stout woman off her feet. "Martha, my love, you should have known I could never stay away from your cooking. Every time I think about your lemonade my mouth waters."

She stepped away from him, swabbing her eyes with a corner of the apron she was never without. "Now look what you've gone and made me do. I must look a fright."

"You always look beautiful to me."

"Still got that smooth tongue, I see." The cook beamed up at him. "And that boy of yours is just like you. He reminds me of you when you were that age. Always wanting to know 'why.' It's enough to worry a body to death." She barely paused for breath. "I'm going to cook all your favorites for supper tonight. You will be here for supper, won't you?" She looked hesitantly at Lanie, but his wife's gaze was fixed on the floor, bottom lip clenched between her teeth.

Their conversation barely impinged on Lanie's consciousness when he answered, her thoughts in a frantic whirl. All these years of pain and resentment, thinking he cared nothing for their child, and he hadn't even known Zack existed.

"I'll be here, Martha, and I brought a friend with me. His appetite is even worse than mine so cook plenty."

"Now don't I always, Mr. Quinn? When has anyone left my table still hungry?"

Fighting twin urges to either collapse in hysteria or wail with the injustice of it all, Lanie pushed the office door open. "Why don't you get started on that, Martha? Mr. Quinn and I have some things to discuss. And would you call down to the barn and ask Sherry to keep an eye on Zack for me? He's supposed to be showing Quinn's friend the puppies, but he's just as likely to have him in the pen with Gator."

"Reckon you got some talking to do, at that." The cook tucked a strand of gray hair behind her ear and waddled back to the kitchen, still mumbling to herself. "Man gets better-looking every time I see him. Ought to be a law against things like that. 'Bout time he showed up. That youngun' needs his daddy..." Her voice faded as she vanished into the kitchen.

"Come in."

Lanie waited as Quinn went by her. He headed straight for the black leather sofa and sat on one end, carefully stretching his leg along the entire length of the couch.

"Who's Gator?"

"Our bull." She closed the door and turned. "He's not one you want to be around on foot, but for some reason Zack is fascinated by him."

She perched on the front of the desk, so many problems streaking through her mind she didn't know how they would ever sort them out. Mentally, she reached up and grabbed one thought from the maelstrom. "If I'd had any idea that Edward wouldn't tell you, I would have found a way to let you know, Quinn. It was never my intention to keep Zack from you." Her tone was as tense as the rest of her body.

Pushing away from the desk, she paced across the room in agitation. "I should have known, should have realized something was wrong. No matter what happened between us, you aren't the type to ignore your own child." Her eyes closed briefly. "I can't believe I was stupid enough to trust Edward with something this important. I know what he's like."

"Yes, you do."

"You don't understand, Quinn. I blamed you for not being here when Zack needed you. I blamed you for not caring enough to be here when he was born, and when he was a year old and I thought he was going to die from pneumonia, I hated you because you couldn't even call the hospital to ask about him." She swiped angrily at her eyes. "I tried to convince myself it didn't matter, that I loved him enough for both of us, but it wasn't true. It did matter. For Zack and me both. Do you know what his favorite video is? The one we made at the lake right after we got married. He's almost worn it out rewinding and playing the parts with you in them."

"So that's how he recognized me." Quinn put both feet back on the floor and leaned forward, elbows on his knees as he rubbed his face. "You could have made him hate me. I expected it."

She shook her head violently. "No, I couldn't. I refused to do that to my son. It was bad enough that I knew, that I hurt for him. I couldn't have stood hurting him, too."

When he lifted his head and looked at her his eyes were full of the same pain she was feeling. "I came as soon as I knew. I know it doesn't make up for the last four years. They're gone and I can't get them back. But I'm here now. I want to know everything about him, and from here on out, I *will* be his father."

With his last words the pain in his eyes was replaced with what she could only describe as challenge. A shiver of apprehension ran down her spine as the words he hadn't spoken hung in the air between them. He, not Jared, would be Zack's father.

"I would never stop you from seeing him, Quinn." She hesitated, then took a deep breath, praying she had misunderstood him. "He's still a little young to be away from the ranch, but I'm sure we can work out a visitation schedule. The bunkhouse isn't in use most of the year. You can stay there when you want to see Zack. When do you have to go back to Chicago?"

Quinn rose and moved across the room until there was a bare inch separating them. Her breath caught in her chest when he gripped her shoulders and looked intently into her eyes.

"I'm not going back to Chicago. And I'm not going to Vegas to get a divorce. I'm staying right here. I just found my son, Lanie. No one is taking him away from me again, and I won't settle for 'visitation rights'. I want him all the time."

"No." She twisted away from him, anger lending strength to the movement. "You can't do this, Quinn. You can't take him away from me. I won't let you. He's my son. If you force me, I'll call the sheriff and have you thrown off the ranch."

The smile that curled his lips was sardonic. "You can try. But since the ranch is still mine, I don't think you'll succeed."

"What do you mean, the ranch is yours? I have the deed. It's in my name."

He turned and walked to the window, staring out at the barns. "When you filed for divorce the ranch was your settlement, but you could only claim ownership after the divorce was final. Since it never was, the ranch still belongs to me. And there's another little item everyone seems to be forgetting. I never signed the agreement. Under the circumstances, forgery shouldn't be too hard to prove."

"You bastard." Her fists clenched so tightly the nails dug into her palms, every line of her body rigid. She caught back a sob of rage. "I never wanted the ranch. You were the one who insisted I take it. But to blame me for the divorce? That's pretty low even for you."

The laugh that escaped her was bitter. "Is that one of the lies you're going to use when you try to take Zack away from me, or are you just planning on buying the judge? Do you have any idea what it was like for me, Quinn? I'd just found out I was pregnant. All I wanted to do was talk to you, to share my excitement and joy with the father of my child. Instead I got slapped with divorce papers and a restraining order. You're damn right I took the ranch. For our child, not for myself. But if you think I'm going to give you Zack in exchange for a few acres of land then you've underestimated me. I'll pack our clothes and live in a car before I'll let you take him."

He turned to face her, his skin suddenly pale under its bronze tint. "I didn't file for divorce. You did." Even though the words were spoken softly, there was a tense edge to them that he couldn't hide.

"I did not! Do you think I'm so stupid I wouldn't remem…" Her words trailed off as she stared at him. She'd always been able to tell when Quinn lied to her. He wasn't lying now. He believed what he was saying.

"Oh, my God," she whispered. "Edward." Her hands flew to her cheeks as she shook her head violently. "It doesn't matter. He just speeded up what we both knew was coming. The only important thing right now is Zack."

She was wrong, Quinn thought dazedly. It did matter. It mattered a hell of a lot. He felt as though someone had tied his feet to the floor, bound his arms to his sides while shock after shock ripped through his body. Unable to move, all he could do was try and control the emotions that were threatening to tear him apart. Lanie hadn't wanted the divorce any more than he had. He closed his eyes as the realization pounded through his head straight to his heart. Edward had tricked them both. Not only had he deprived Quinn of his son, he'd taken away the life he and Lanie should have had, a life together. No matter what she thought, they would have worked things out.

Because he knew something she didn't. The night he'd had the accident he hadn't been going to Chicago. He'd been coming home. Home to her and the ranch.

The rest of her words washed over him like a wave over rocks as she continued to talk. He was aware of them on some level, but they had no effect on him. This changed everything. He'd come here to claim the son he'd never known he had. Was it possible he could reclaim the wife he'd never wanted to lose? The wife who was engaged to another man? Would he be able to live with himself if he didn't at least try? The answer to that one was easy. No, he wouldn't.

"Have you heard a single word I've said?"

He opened his eyes and looked at her. The elaborate curls she'd worn in Chicago were gone, her glossy hair pulled into a braid that reached the middle of her back. Her face was pale, but the light of battle still raged in her eyes. She looked like a warrior princess who had exchanged her regal garb for faded jeans and worn boots.

Sweat beaded his forehead and palms at what he was about to do. It probably wasn't fighting fair, but he never hesitated. He'd use any weapon, any advantage he had to make this work. "Sit down, Lanie."

Her hands went to her hips. "Don't tell me what to do. I've never taken orders from you and I don't intend to start now."

He took a deep breath. "Fine. Then stand there." Restlessly, he moved to the desk and picked up a picture of Zack. It must have been a recent one because he looked just as he had earlier, in the front yard.

"Fighting isn't going to solve a thing." He traced Zack's face with one finger. "You want a divorce, and we both want Zack." Replacing the picture, he looked at her over his shoulder. "There's a way we can work this out."

"How?" Her eyes had gone all dark and wary. "I'm not going to let you take Zack no matter what."

This time it was Quinn who rested on the desk, crossing his arms over his chest as he studied her. "I want three months. Three months to see if there's any chance we can make our marriage work. Three months to get to know my son. I don't think that's too much to ask, under the circumstances."

"Too much to ask?" She stared at him as if he'd lost his mind. "I'm supposed to be married in six weeks, for God's sake!" She threw her hands up in the air and resumed her pacing. "This is crazy." Abruptly, she came to a halt. "What if I just say no?"

He shrugged. "Then you leave me no choice. I'll fight the divorce, and I'll sue you for custody of Zack. Either way, you aren't getting married in six weeks, Lanie. It'll be long and messy, and Zack will be the one who gets hurt. Is that really what you want?"

"And what if I agree and it still doesn't work out? It won't, you know. I love Jared and have every intention of marrying him, no matter how long it takes."

"Then you don't have anything to worry about, do you? If you still feel the same way after three months, I'll get that quickie divorce you want, and we can work out a custody agreement. I won't give Zack up, either, but maybe we can reach a peaceful solution where he's concerned."

Quinn could see the "no" trembling on her lips and interrupted before she could utter it. "You don't have to give me an answer right now. Think about it. You may even want to talk to your lawyer first."

"Why are you doing this? I don't understand! In Chicago you were all ready to hop the next plane out to get that divorce."

"That was before I knew about Zack." He lifted his hands and massaged his temples. "But Zack isn't the only reason. Maybe you're right. Maybe we would have ended up getting the divorce anyway. However, I'd like to know for sure that it's our decision, not something we were tricked into. Thanks to

Edward, we've lost five years. Will three more months make that much difference?"

He hesitated, and when he spoke again his voice had softened. "We were best friends for a long time, Lanie. There wasn't anything we couldn't talk about, no problem so big we couldn't handle it together. I've missed my friend. If nothing else, I'd like her back. Give us the chance to work this out. For our sakes, and for Zack's."

Her eyes squeezed shut for an instant before she looked at him again. "This is blackmail, you know."

"I know."

"But you're going to do it anyway, aren't you?"

"I'll do anything I have to do." He smiled. "I'm no gentleman, remember?"

She jammed her hands into her front pockets and looked down at the floor, to all appearances icy calm. But he knew her too well not to recognize the signs of inner turmoil. The tightened mouth, the stubborn set to her chin, the stiff shoulders.

Suddenly she looked up. "You're right. I need time to think about this, and I need to talk to Sara."

The sound of Duncan's deep voice followed by Zack's giggles drifted through the tightly closed door and Quinn stood.

"Sara?"

"Sara Carson. You should remember her. She's my lawyer now."

"I remember her." He moved to the door. "Just let me know what you decide. I'm going to put my things in one of the guest rooms upstairs, and then I want to start getting acquainted with my son."

* * * * *

Lanie waited until the door closed behind him, then moved around the desk and collapsed onto the chair, burying her face in both hands. Damn him. He knew exactly what buttons to push where she was concerned. The truth was, she had missed their friendship as much as he claimed to, had grieved over its loss.

She'd lost count of the times she'd turned to share something with him, had reached for the phone to call him before she remembered he wasn't there for her anymore. As much as she loved Jared, she hadn't been able to bring herself to let him get that close. True, they had been friends first, but not the kind of friendship she'd had with Quinn.

Jared. Dear God, he was coming over tonight. Lanie reached for the phone. He wouldn't be home this time of the day, but she could leave a message.

Waiting for his recorded voice to end, she began. "Jared, there's been a change of plans. Instead of you coming over tonight, I'll drop by your house after I get Zack in bed." She rubbed her eyes. "I need to talk you. Quinn is here, Jared, and I don't know what to do." A sigh escaped her. "I'll tell you about it when I see you. I love you."

She dropped the phone into the cradle, waited a beat, then picked it up and dialed another number.

"Doris? It's Lanie McAllister. Is Sara in?"

"Hi, Lanie," the motherly voice replied. "No, I'm sorry. She's in court this afternoon. Can I give her a message for you?"

"Please. Will you ask her if she can meet me at Jared's tonight? About eight. Tell her it's very important, Doris."

"You bet I will. Is it anything I might help with?"

"Thanks, but I'm afraid not."

She hung up and stared fixedly out the window. How was she going to tell Jared that Quinn wanted to give their marriage another chance? It was going to kill him.

Chapter Five

Lanie climbed into the pickup and pulled the door closed behind her. It felt as if every muscle in her body had contracted into one huge painful knot. The feeling was becoming familiar to her. She'd been fighting tension since she'd first opened the court's letter and discovered that she and Quinn were still married.

With a sigh she leaned her head against the steering wheel and closed her eyes. For Zack's sake she had to get a grip. Quinn was his father, and her son's curiosity had been obvious all evening. But to her, what was more apparent were the wary glances Zack had been giving her. Even though his eyes had bubbled with hope, happiness and a thousand questions when he looked at Quinn, her normally exuberant son had, for the most part, remained silent. There could only be one explanation. Zack sensed her anger, her frustration, and he didn't know how to react.

She had to find a way to keep his world stable, even if it meant pretending she was happy to have Quinn on the ranch. There was nothing she wouldn't do for Zack. He was her life, her baby, the only thing in the world that mattered to her. Which was why she'd finally agreed to marry Jared after four years of dating. He loved Zack as much as she did. Jared would make a wonderful father. He had all the qualities she wanted Zack to learn, qualities that would make her son a strong, honest man.

And Jared loved her. Maybe she didn't feel that flash fire of heat when he held her, but she'd changed since Quinn. Matured. She no longer expected or wanted fireworks. Jared made her feel safe, secure. He never raised his voice, never deliberately prodded her into anger. Jared would never leave her. He was steady as the Rock of Gibraltar, as eternal as the stars in the sky.

Putting the truck in gear, she headed down the driveway. Not once since she'd been dating him had Jared tried to coerce her into sleeping with him. He respected her wish to wait until they were married, even though she knew he wanted her.

He hadn't even shown any irritation with her after she'd gotten the letter from the court informing her she was still married to Quinn. The letter shouldn't have made any difference in her relationship with Jared, but it had. No matter what her head was saying, her heart was telling her she still had a husband and seeing Jared while married to Quinn was wrong. And it would stay wrong until everything was settled and the divorce became real.

A niggling sense of uneasiness tickled the back of her mind, but she pushed it away. The fact that she'd refused to sleep with Jared had nothing to do with Quinn. It was her damn conservative upbringing, that was all. Jared understood. He'd continued to stop by for visits, but he hadn't pressured her to be alone with him.

She felt so guilty. She had seen the hurt lingering behind Jared's smile when he looked at her, and knew she was the cause. Hurting him was the last thing she wanted to do. And now she would have to tell him that Quinn was demanding a chance to make their marriage work. Thank God Sara would be there. She wasn't sure she'd have the courage to face Jared alone.

The lights from her truck swept the yard as she turned up Jared's drive, and picked up a reflection from the blue Volvo parked near the house. Relief rippled through her. Sara was already here.

Jared must have been listening for her, because the front door opened before she turned the motor off, and he started down the steps toward her. He looked so familiar, so dear, that she had to fight the urge to break into tears. His thick blond hair was still a little damp from his shower, falling over his forehead in a shaggy mop. In the light spilling from the house she could see the concern etched on his ruggedly handsome face.

Without a word, he opened his arms. Lanie threw herself into them, and they closed around her, warm and tight. His lips brushed her hair as she buried her face in his neck.

"Sweetheart," he murmured. "I've been going out of my mind since I got your message." His big hands stroked her back, gentle and soothing. "Are you okay?"

She nodded. "As much as possible under the circumstances."

He tilted her chin up and brushed a strand of hair away from her face. "You sounded so upset that I almost headed straight for the ranch. What's he doing here, Lanie?"

A tear trickled down her cheek. "He wants Zack, Jared."

His slim body stiffened for an instant, then relaxed. "He can't get him. No judge would take Zack away from you. You're a wonderful mother."

She swiped at the tear. "Zack isn't the only thing he wants."

Silence descended over the yard and his hand stilled on her back. "I see." His tone was soft. "Want to tell me about it?"

"I don't think I can explain twice and I need Sara to hear it, too."

Lanie felt a sigh lift his chest. "I'm not going to like this, am I?"

"No," she whispered.

He hesitated a moment longer. "Okay, let's get it over with." Jared dropped his arms and stepped away from her, taking her hand in his large, warm one.

A shiver rippled across her. If only it were simple enough that they *could* get it over with tonight. But she knew they couldn't.

Sara looked up as they came in and deposited her coffee cup on the table beside her. She was still wearing one of the trim suits that were her standard uniform at the office, and her black hair was pinned up in an elegant twist.

Lanie leaned over and hugged her. "I'm sorry for dragging you out tonight. I know you're probably tired."

"Don't be silly. It's not like I had any plans, and Doris said you sounded upset." She smoothed her skirt. "After hearing the message you left for Jared, I can understand why. Having Quinn suddenly show up after all this time must have been a shock. And knowing him, he wants something."

"He does." She sank onto the couch and felt Jared's solid weight settle next to her, one of his arms slipping around her waist. "You see, he didn't know about Zack until a few days ago. I know that sounds strange, but you have to know Quinn's father to understand."

For the next hour and a half she told them everything, Sara interrupting occasionally with questions. She couldn't look at Jared, couldn't stand to see the hurt in his eyes when she told them that Quinn wanted three months to try and make their marriage work. By the time she finished, her body felt limp, exhaustion draining all emotion until there was nothing left but numbness.

"Can he do this, Sara? Can he force me into a trial marriage?"

The lawyer cleared her throat. "Of course he can't." She leaned forward and took both of Lanie's hands. "I'm going to give it to you straight, kid. You've got a choice to make, and you're the only one who can make it. Say the word and I'll file your divorce papers tomorrow, right along with a petition for custody. But—" She shot a quick glance at Jared. "There's a chance Quinn could win. Knowledge of Zack was kept from him, even if you weren't aware of it. The courts are big on father's rights these days. And if he can prove what he told you about the ranch, you'll certainly lose it. Furthermore, he could drag this out for years. Especially the custody battle. I know of cases that lasted eight or more years with the child in question going back and forth like a ping pong ball. As your friend and as your lawyer, my advice would be to take his deal. This could all be settled in three months. If we go through the system it will take longer than that anyway, and Zack will ultimately be the victim."

"She'll do it."

Jared's voice was harsh, raw with pain that sent an answering echo into her heart. "Jared, no. I need to think about it."

His hand moved up her back to cradle her nape, one thumb caressing the skin below her ear as he forced her to look at him. "No, you don't. We both know you can't do that to Zack." He paused, his gaze searching hers. "Do you love me?"

Lanie swallowed the lump in her throat. "You know I do."

"Do you plan on sleeping with him?"

"No." Tears welled in her eyes. "God, no."

"Then we can get through this."

"But I don't want to hurt you," she whispered.

The smile he gave her was forced. "It hurts me more to see you torn in half like this. As long as I know you'll come back to me when it's over, I can survive. And you know I'll be here if you need me. I'm not going to vanish just because McAllister wants me to."

"Lanie?" Sara was watching them both. "Is that what you want to do?"

"No, but it seems I don't have much choice after all. I'll give Quinn his three months. For Zack's sake."

* * * * *

Jared stood on the porch, one hand propped above him on the post as he watched Lanie's truck follow Sara's sedan down the drive. An agony of fear knotted his stomach until he thought he was going to be sick.

It had sounded so easy when McAllister offered him this chance. Just keep an eye on the man's ex-daughter-in-law and grandson, make sure they were okay and didn't need anything. In return, all his college loans were paid off and he got a practice handed to him on a silver platter. Easy.

Until he'd seen Lanie McAllister for the first time, and known instantly that she was the woman he'd dreamed about his entire life. Known he'd found the woman he wanted to grow old with, to have a family with.

And suddenly the job wasn't easy anymore. Because Lanie had still loved her ex-husband. It had taken Jared four long, slow years of watching his every step before she'd finally agreed to marry him. Now, God help him, he was terrified that he was losing her. Because as much as she denied it, part of her loved McAllister and always would. He had been willing to accept that, even if it meant being second best. He loved her too much to live without her.

But now McAllister was back. Lord, how he'd wanted to tell her to refuse McAllister's deal, to fight the man until the end. He took a deep breath and turned back toward the house.

Lanie was right. Even if it meant losing her, they had to protect Zack, the child he'd come to love to as his own. And he wasn't going to simply step aside and make things easy for McAllister. He'd see Lanie every chance he got, remind her what they had together.

And pray like hell she never discovered why he'd moved to Wyoming in the first place.

* * * * *

Quinn let the curtain drop back into place as the taillights from Lanie's truck vanished down the drive. She'd stayed locked in the office most of the afternoon, only coming out when Martha had announced supper was ready. And even then, she'd ignored him, answering only when he'd asked her a direct question.

A soft patter of bare feet and the sound of bells came from behind him and he turned. Zack was standing in the door, clutching a doll and watching him warily. His expression made Quinn's stomach clench. He didn't want the tension between him and Lanie to affect his relationship with his son.

"Hi." He kept his voice even. "I thought you were in bed."

"Mr. Jingles isn't sleepy." The little boy glanced around the room. "Where's Duncan?"

"He's in the office setting up some equipment we brought." Quinn moved to the couch and sat down. "Since Mr. Jingles isn't sleepy, why don't you come in and talk to me? I'm not sleepy either."

Zack didn't need a second invitation. He ran across the room and climbed onto the couch beside Quinn, staring up at him in fascination. "Does your mama make you go to bed, too?"

"She used to, when I was about your size. I think most moms do."

Zack edged a little closer. Apparently with Lanie gone, his curiosity had overcome his divided sense of loyalty. "Billy's mom makes him go to bed."

"Is Billy your friend?"

"My best friend in the world. Besides Daisy." He rose up onto his knees and leaned forward. "Does that hurt?"

"This?" Quinn pointed at the scar. "Not anymore."

"Can I touch it?"

"Sure, if you want to."

Zack scrambled into his lap like he'd been doing it all his life and lifted one tiny finger to trace the line of scar tissue. Quinn desperately fought off the need to crush him in a hug, the effort sending a tremor through his body. He settled for running a tentative hand over the mop of dark hair.

"How did you get hurt?"

"In a car accident."

Gray eyes, so much like Lanie's, looked at him seriously. "Is that why you never came to see me before, 'cause you had an accident?"

Pain worse than any he'd felt in his life streaked through him and his eyes closed in reflex. "No." He could barely get the words out. "The accident happened before you were born."

He opened his eyes and looked at his son. "The truth is, I didn't know about you until yesterday. Zack, if I had known you were here, I never would have stayed away."

Zack studied him for a moment. "You didn't know I was borned?"

"No."

"Are you going to stay here and be my daddy now?"

"I'm going to be your daddy from now on, no matter where we are."

"Does that mean I'll have two dads? 'Cause Mama said Jared was going to be my daddy."

How could he answer a question like that when he planned on doing everything in his power to keep Lanie from marrying her fiancé? "Do you like Jared?"

Zack squirmed until he was leaning back with his head on Quinn's shoulder. "Jared is great." His mouth gaped in a huge yawn. "He comes over and plays with me, and sometimes he takes me with him to work on sick animals. He says I'm the best helper he's ever had."

Quinn let his arms close around the small body and buried his face in Zack's hair. "It sounds like he loves you a lot, and you know something? You can never have enough people around who love you."

"Do you love me?" His eyelids were beginning to droop.

Involuntarily, Quinn's arms tightened. "More than anything else in the whole world," he whispered, his voice scratchy.

"Can I call you Dad?"

"I'd like that."

"Okay." He snuggled tighter in Quinn's arms and his eyes drifted shut. "You smell good," he murmured. Abruptly, his body went limp and relaxed.

Quinn took a deep, shaky breath, not even bothering to hide the tears that coursed down his cheeks. He knew he should take Zack back to bed, but he couldn't bring himself to let go. Not yet. They had lost too much time already. Time that had scarred Zack as surely as the accident had scarred him. Both of them had a lot of healing to do. No, he amended, looking down at his son's face. All three of them had a lot of healing to do. He only wished it could be as easy with Lanie as it was turning out to be with Zack.

But he knew it wouldn't. Even if Jared Harper weren't on the scene, she wouldn't trust him. She had been hurt too badly. Somehow, he was going to have to find a way to make it up to her. A way to convince her she still loved him as much as he did her. And he knew she did. She may have buried it so deep that she'd forgotten, but the kind of love they'd shared didn't just fade with time. God knows, his hadn't, no matter how hard he'd tried to kill it.

A movement in the doorway caught his attention and he looked up as Duncan stopped.

"That didn't take long." He nodded his head at Zack.

"It's a start, Dunc. I'm afraid it's going to take a while before he really believes I won't leave him again." He kept his voice low enough not to disturb the child in his arms.

"He will." Duncan hesitated. "I couldn't help overhearing part of the conversation. You did great with him, Quinn."

"I hope so. I don't want to hurt him anymore that he already has been."

"You handled it just right. Well, I'm done in the office. I'd like to start unpacking. Are you sure your wife won't mind me staying in the house?"

Quinn smiled ruefully. "She'd prefer both of us completely off the ranch and out of the state right now, but it's not going to happen. Put your things in the room next to mine. I'm going to stay down here for a while."

"Okay. If you need me just beat on the wall or something. See you in the morning."

"Goodnight."

The house grew quiet around him as he examined his son, trying to memorize every minute detail. Zack's pajamas were soft white cotton, sprinkled with images of horses and dogs. The pants were twisted around his waist, one leg bunched up around his knee to expose a sturdy shin with a small bruise in the middle.

Even in sleep, the cleft in his chin, a legacy from his mother, was prominent, and Quinn smiled. He'd be willing to bet the boy was just as stubborn as Lanie, too. He didn't know much about four-year-olds but he suspected Zack was tall for his age.

Gently, he picked up one small hand and inspected it. The fingers were perfect, long and slender in spite of their babyish quality. A Band-aid with big yellow birds and blue monsters was wrapped around his thumb.

The sound of the truck returning impinged on his consciousness, and he listened to Lanie's steps crossing the porch. Had she made a decision? He braced himself as the front door opened.

She came down the hall and into the room, making it halfway across before she came to a sudden stop, her gaze fixed on Zack. "What happened?"

"Mr. Jingles couldn't sleep, so Zack and I had a talk instead." He was tempted to smile, but a glance at Lanie's face changed his mind. She was pale and it looked as if she'd been crying.

"A talk about what?"

"Why I haven't been around the last four years."

"Oh, God." She shut her eyes briefly. "What did you tell him?"

"A short version of the truth. I think he needs to know that I wasn't just ignoring him, Lanie."

She exhaled a short burst of air. "I know. I was going to tell him myself." Moving closer, she leaned over and reached for Zack. "I'll take him back to bed."

"I'd like to do it, if you don't mind." She was close enough that he could see her pupils dilate when their gazes met, close enough to catch the scent of her light perfume. "I think it's my turn," he added softly.

The hesitation was scarcely noticeable before she nodded. "I'll be in the kitchen. When you're done, we need to talk."

So the verdict was in. Now it was time for the delivery. Quinn slid to the edge of the couch and stood carefully, disregarding the protest of his leg while he shifted Zack's weight. "I'll be right back."

The blankets on the twin bed were still turned back, and he slipped Zack under the covers, tucking them in around the small body. For a moment longer he watched his son sleep, the muted sounds of running water drifting up from the kitchen below. In the dim glow of the night-light, he brushed the hair back from Zack's forehead and kissed him.

The trip back downstairs felt like the longest of his life. When he reached the kitchen he paused in the door before moving to the table and pulling out a chair. Lanie was leaning against the countertop, staring out the window.

Quinn cleared his throat. "I had Duncan set up a fax machine and another computer in the office. I'm expecting some papers from my lawyer in a few days."

She turned to face him, arms crossed over her chest. "You can tell your lawyer not to bother. I've decided to give you the three months."

Elation surged through him. It was all he could do to remain seated and keep his expression neutral. "The papers I'm expecting don't have anything to do with a divorce or custody suit."

"Oh." She suddenly became busy taking out cups, adding tea bags, and pouring water. When she was done, she carried them to the table, placing one in front of him then taking the seat across from him. Her chin firmed and lifted as she watched him. "I think we should set up some ground rules right now, before we go any farther."

He took a sip of the tea. "You're right. And here's the first one. If you think you're going to spend the entire three months pretending I'm not here, then the deal is off. I want part of your time every day, above what we spend together with Zack."

Her jaw clenched. "I have a ranch to run. I can't just drop everything on a whim."

"I'm assuming the people working for you are competent or they wouldn't be here. Let them do their jobs. If you need more help, hire extra people. I'll pay their wages."

"I don't need your money. If I hire anyone, I can pay them myself." She looked down at the cup cradled in her hands and a flush of red climbed into her cheeks. "I'm not going to sleep with you, Quinn. Sex isn't part of this agreement."

He shrugged. "I wasn't planning on forcing you. Making love to an unwilling partner takes the fun out of it. However, since you agreed to the deal, I do expect an honest effort from you to make this work. Can you do that much?"

Lanie took a deep breath, then nodded. "I'll try."

Quinn toyed with the handle on the cup. "And what about Harper? Am I going to be tripping over him every time I turn around?"

Her head shot up and she glared at him. "I said I'd try, damn it! But I'm not going to hurt Zack by keeping Jared away from him. He loves Jared."

He studied her silently, one brow arched. "I don't want to see Zack hurt either, so I'll make this easy. I won't try to stop Harper from seeing him, but when he's around, you won't be alone with him. And there's one more thing, Lanie."

"Of course there is," she muttered sarcastically. "Okay, let's hear it."

Slowly Quinn reached across the table and took her left hand, noting the goose bumps that erupted on her skin with a great deal of interest. "I think it's time you took that off," he tilted his head at the diamond engagement ring on her finger, "and put your wedding rings back on."

Chapter Six

Quinn kept his eyes closed, a smile playing around his lips as he drifted on the edge of waking. The bed was warm and comfortable, the scent of breakfast teased his nostrils. Waking up on the ranch again after all this time had memories flooding his mind, but he pushed most of them away, only interested in the ones involving Lanie. He settled a little deeper into the bed, thinking about the second time he'd seen her. It had been the day after that wild date with Susie Morsten...

~ ~ ~ ~ ~

Depositing his Stetson on the ground beside him, Quinn settled back on the grassy bank and let his eyes drift shut. He wasn't crazy about fishing, but it had been the only way he could think of to escape Ethan's incessant questions about his date with Susie. His friend had tried to get her to go out with him for years with no success. The fact that Quinn had managed it in less that a week had his nose out of joint.

Fishing had also been a way to evade Jonesy. Even though it was Saturday, the ranch foreman hated to see idle hands. He'd have found something for Quinn to do, and he was just too sleepy to spend the day shoveling manure or mending fences. It had been well past dawn before Susie had let him go, and his body felt like an old sponge with all the water squeezed out.

There certainly was a lot to be said for older women. A smile tilted one corner of his lips. It had been his experience that girls his own age or younger didn't offer half the pleasure women like Susie did. Maybe he'd continue to see her while he was there.

The hot, midmorning sun soaked into him and soothed him toward sleep. From the tree above came the hypnotic drone of bees busily gathering pollen from the new buds. Three months before college started. Three months of freedom without Edward breathing down his neck, lecturing about his duties and obligations. Three months on the ranch he loved.

He was almost asleep when the first drop of water hit him on the chin and rolled down his neck. His brow furrowed. It couldn't be rain. The sun was still shinning. He opted to keep his eyes closed and ignore it.

A whole minute passed before another drop hit him in the exact same place. Reluctantly, he opened his eyes a slit and discovered he was no longer alone.

It took him a second to place her, but when he did, he almost groaned. It was the kid from the movies last night. How she'd gotten that close without him hearing her, he didn't know, but she was sitting beside him on the grass, long coltish legs crossed Indian style.

A pair of flowered cotton shorts covered a one-piece, hot pink tank suit that sagged on her skinny frame. Not a single curve marred the straight lines of her body and her chest was flat as a board. Her long, dark brown hair was pulled into a ponytail, lighter streaks of auburn highlights running through it. She had fished an ice cube from the glass in her hand, and was holding it positioned over his chin.

Another drop of water swayed precariously from the end of her fingers as she watched his face intently. Just before it dropped, Quinn's hand shot out to circle her wrist and push it aside.

Instead of flinching in surprise, she grinned and gestured toward his fishing pole. "Your bobber has been underwater for the last five minutes."

"Do I look like I care?" He let his eyes close again. "Beat it, kid."

"Whip it out."

An involuntary snort of laughter spurted from between Quinn's lips. Casually, he propped his elbows behind him on the ground, lifting the upper half of his body as he surveyed her. "How old are you? Ten? Eleven?" She certainly didn't look old enough to be coming up with sexual repartees.

Her chin squared, a tiny cleft appearing in the center. "I'm fourteen."

"Bull. You're too scrawny to be fourteen. You're still practically a boy." He grinned as fire kindled in those clear gray eyes.

"I'm fourteen. My birthday was last week. And all the women in my family are late bloomers."

"Well, go bloom somewhere else. I'm busy."

"Yeah, I could tell by the way you were snoring."

"I wasn't snoring."

"You were, too. Besides, you're in my spot. If anyone leaves, it should be you."

"I don't see your name nailed to any of the trees."

"It doesn't have to be. This is my grandparents' land."

"Like hell. This is my land."

Her eyes widened. "You're a McAllister?"

"That's right. And I happen to know the people who own the land that adjoins mine are named Howell, not Stewart."

"The Howells are my grandparents. Guess that means we're neighbors."

"Wonderful. That really makes my day." He lay back down. "Look, don't you have any little friends that you can go play with?"

"Not really." She shrugged. "I haven't been here long."

Quinn turned his head and looked at her, curious in spite of himself. "Where have you been?"

"Montana. That's where I'm from. I came to live with my grandparents two months ago."

"Where are your parents?"

For the first time, her eyes clouded and there was a quiver in her voice when she answered him. "Dead."

A twinge of sympathy hit him. "Sorry."

Her bony shoulder lifted in another shrug as she gazed toward the water, blinking rapidly. Suddenly she bounded to her feet. "I'm going swimming. Want to come?"

"No, thanks. I want to sleep."

"Susie wore you out, huh?" There was a smirk in her voice. "You should feel privileged. Normally she only dates college seniors." The elastic band on her shorts slid down over nonexistent hips as she tugged on the material.

"Now how do you know that?"

"Watson is a small town. Everyone knows everyone else's business. But don't worry. I won't tell anyone about the little show you were putting on last night."

"Brat."

"Jerk." With a loud war whoop she ran for the water, leaping over his forgotten fishing pole as she dived into the lake headfirst…

~ ~ ~ ~ ~

Lanie's remembered yell became real as a small body landed in the middle of his stomach, knocking the air out of him with a woosh and effectively bringing him back to the present. His eyes popped open like they were attached to springs, only to find Zack's gaze fastened on him, his face intent.

"Hide me," the little boy whispered.

Carefully, Quinn pushed himself up to lean against the headboard, blankets sliding to his waist as he steadied Zack. "Hide you from what?" he whispered back.

"Mama says I have to go to daycare, and I want to stay home today."

Before Quinn could formulate a reply, footsteps echoed down the hall. "Zachary Quinn McAllister, when I get hold of you…"

Lanie's words faded as she reached the door of Quinn's room and stopped. A pink flush slowly covered her cheeks as she stared in at them.

"Uh-oh." Quinn smiled at Zack. "She used all three of your names. I think she's serious."

The little boy's chin firmed, jutting into the air as he eyed his mother. "I won't go. I'm gonna stay with my Daddy today."

Taking a few hesitant steps into the room, Lanie stopped again. "Zack, Kelsey is waiting to drive you. Your Daddy will still be here when you get home."

Part of him wanted to agree with Zack. He'd missed four years, what would it hurt for Zack to stay home today? But he also didn't want his son playing him against Lanie. "She's right, you know." Quinn reinforced her words. "I'll still be here, and maybe when you get home you can show me the puppies."

"There are four." Zack was instantly distracted. "But I like the black one best. It's the littlest. You can have one if you want."

"Thank you. I'd like that," Quinn declared solemnly.

"Okay." Lanie took another step closer. "Now that it's all settled, you need to get downstairs. And tell Kelsey you're sorry you made her wait."

"Yes, ma'am."

Zack scooted off Quinn's stomach, the toe of his boot digging in, causing Quinn to wince. The little boy paused in the doorway to look back at the bed. "Promise you won't go see them until I get back?"

"Promise."

"Cross your heart," the little boy commanded.

Quinn lifted an eyebrow at Lanie, nodding with understanding when she made an X on her chest. He repeated the gesture. "Cross my heart."

Beaming, Zack darted out the door, leaving him alone with Lanie. She looked nervous, he decided. That could be a very good sign.

"I'm sorry." She waved a hand vaguely in the direction Zack had gone. "He usually loves daycare. I think he was afraid you'd leave if he didn't stay home today."

Quinn gave a short nod. "I know. He'll have to get used to the idea that I'm not going anywhere." He hesitated, and when he spoke again, his voice was softer. "You named him after me."

She dropped her gaze to the floor. "Yes. I thought he should have a part of you, even if it was only your name."

"Thank you." He hesitated. "You know, I wouldn't mind if he stayed home from daycare a few days. It would give me some time with him."

"I thought about it." She lifted a hand and tucked a stray lock of hair behind her ear. "But I don't want to disrupt his routine. With everything that's going on, he needs the rest of his life to be as normal as possible right now."

"I understand."

"Good." Her shoulder lifted in a shrug as she turned toward the door. "Breakfast is ready. We eat in the kitchen these days. It saves Martha from making so many trips back and forth to the dinning room."

"I'll be down in a minute. And Lanie?"

She paused, her back stiff.

"It's nice to see your wedding rings back where they belong."

* * * * *

Lanie closed his door behind her then leaned weakly against the wall. Her whole body was vibrating like a violin string that had been harshly plucked. It was the sight of him in bed, of course. In bed with his hair tousled, chest bare. She shut her eyes, trying to push away the image of other mornings. Mornings when he'd smiled down at her, amber eyes drowsy with desire. Mornings they'd forgone breakfast for the joy of being together, of staying in bed to make slow sweet love.

She didn't want to remember, couldn't allow herself that luxury. Not if she wanted to survive the next three months. He'd made it clear she couldn't avoid him, but she'd make sure she stayed out of his room from now on.

Pushing away from the wall, she continued toward the kitchen. Why was he having this effect on her? And she couldn't fool herself. He *was* having an effect. Even in Chicago she'd felt it, that flush of heat racing through her at his nearness.

Maybe it had been too long since she'd been with a man. She shouldn't have held Jared off. If they had made love then the mere sight of Quinn wouldn't be able to set her blood racing this way.

But Jared had never set her on fire with a simple look the way Quinn could.

Rapidly, she suppressed the troubling thought.

Duncan looked up as she entered the kitchen, and Lanie made herself smile at him. "Quinn said he'd be down in a minute."

She didn't know quite what to make of Duncan. In Chicago, she'd assumed he was Quinn's butler, or houseboy maybe. But he certainly didn't look like a servant, or act like one either. He was as tall as Quinn, with dark brown hair and eyes, and the body of a professional athlete.

Now he nodded at her statement before lifting a cup of coffee and taking a sip. "Good. We've got a lot to do today."

She reached for the chair at the head of the table, then hesitated. When they were married, Quinn had always sat there, and last night he'd unconsciously picked up the habit again. Her chin lifted. Well, things had changed and the sooner he realized that, the better. Defiantly, she pulled the chair out and sat down.

"What exactly is it that you do for Quinn, Mr...."

"Call me Duncan. I do whatever he needs done."

"Which is usually a lot more than he gets paid for." Quinn's voice came from behind her, sending her pulse racing anew. "But he won't let me give him a raise."

Duncan grinned, his brown eyes sparkling as Quinn took the seat across from him. "What do I need money for? You pay for everything."

"Don't get used to it. One of these days I'll get tired of you ordering me around and toss you out on your ear." Quinn's smile made his words sound like a long-standing joke. Duncan, at least, seemed to think it was funny. He threw back his head and laughed.

Quinn's gaze moved to her. "Duncan is more than an employee. He's one of the best friends I've ever had."

An honor that used to belong to her. Lanie was startled at the tiny stab of jealousy she felt, and grateful when Martha interrupted, filling first Quinn's cup, then her own.

Silence fell while they loaded their plates and dug in. Quinn was the first to break it.

"What are your plans for the day?"

Lanie kept her gaze on her plate. "I've got three groups scheduled this morning for riding. Since there hasn't been time yet to hire additional help, I'll have to take care of them."

"I thought you had several people working for you?"

"I do." She finally met his eyes. "But only Sherry helps with the riders, and she has groups scheduled, too. Of course, you're welcome to come with me if you'd like."

He seemed to consider it for a moment, then shook his head. "Maybe another time."

She saw Duncan give Quinn a speaking glance before he went back to eating, and wondered what was going on.

"When did you start taking people riding?"

"Zack was a few months old, so I guess it's been about four years now," she mused aloud. "Raising cattle and horses simply doesn't pay enough anymore. It's the tourists that keep us going. Jackson Hole has gotten very popular. Not only do we take groups out riding daily, but once a month we have a trail ride and campout. They're our biggest draw, booked solid weeks in advance."

"What about during the winter?"

She took a drink of coffee before answering him. "It slows down a little and we don't do the campouts, but there's always the people who come to ski and snowboard. They like our sleigh rides."

"Sounds like you've got a good operation going."

Her brows lowered. "We aren't hurting, if that's what you're implying. The ranch makes a good living."

Quinn straightened, his voice quiet when he replied. "I wasn't implying anything. I was just curious about the ranch."

Of course he was curious, she realized. This had been the only real home he'd ever known. That's why it had surprised her so much when he'd offered her the ranch as part of the divorce settlement. Although apparently he hadn't. Her lips thinned and she glanced at her watch before pushing her plate aside.

"I have to go get the horses ready. If you need anything, ask Martha."

He gave her a lopsided smile. "I think can still find my way around."

Doing her best not to look like she was bolting, she escaped through the back door.

*****

Quinn closed the office door and turned to Duncan. "Did you get a chance to check out the bunkhouse?"

"Yes. It'll take some work, but it should be okay as a gym. The hot tub will have to go outside, though. I figured we could put a deck in the back with a fence around it to keep Zack from falling in."

"Are you sure all this is really necessary?" Quinn frowned. He hated the thought of Lanie finding out about his leg.

"You know it is. You've only been off the crutches six months. You can't afford to let that leg go at this point. Not if you want to keep seeing improvement."

Quinn sighed. "Okay, why don't you start calling around and find someone who can do the work?"

"In a few minutes. First I want to know something. You aren't actually planning on getting on a horse, are you?"

"Not in front of Lanie." Quinn smiled ruefully. "I know my limitations. But sooner or later, I will ride again." He held up a hand when Duncan started to protest. "I promise, I'll start slow, and only when you're around."

"Quinn, your leg is still too weak. It hasn't been that long since your final surgery."

"And it won't get any stronger unless I start using it. You just told me so yourself. Now make those calls."

"Fine." Duncan moved to the desk. "But I don't see why we can't have the equipment moved from the apartment. It would save a lot of money."

"I don't care about the money. I'd rather spend twice what it's going to cost than take anything from that apartment. It never belonged to me anyway. It was my father's."

"You're the boss." He reached for the phone. "Why don't you start the warm-up exercises while I'm on the phone and get them out of the way? Guess we can do the massages on the floor until the new equipment arrives."

With a sigh, Quinn started stretching to loosen his muscles, only listening with half an ear to Duncan's conversations. What was Lanie going to say when she found out they were transforming the bunkhouse into a personal spa? Better yet, what would he say? He wasn't ready to tell her about his leg. Not because he thought she'd be put off by it, but because he didn't want her pity. He could take almost anything but that.

His mind wandered back to earlier, in his room. Yes, she had definitely been nervous. Did she remember that he slept naked? Probably. Last night she'd told him that sex was out of the question, but he knew her too well to mistake the look he'd seen in her eyes this morning. And it hadn't been the look of a woman well-satisfied with her love life.

He didn't doubt for a second that she'd fight what she felt. Hadn't he done the same thing for all these years? But denying his feelings hadn't changed them. It would be the same for Lanie.

Right now she was angry and resentful. He'd have to work hard to make her trust him again. And to make himself trust her. Five years of betrayal and pain, true or not, wouldn't go away overnight for either of them. But if this morning was any indication, Lanie still wanted him. He could work with that.

"Tough luck, Harper," he whispered. "It's only a matter of time until she's back in my bed." He could almost feel sorry for the man. Almost, but not quite. Harper wanted his wife and that was something Quinn couldn't allow. He had one last chance to set right the lives Edward had destroyed, and he would fight tooth and nail to make sure it worked.

Chapter Seven

Leg still aching from his morning workout, Quinn stood at the back door, watching as the first of the contractors removed the old beds from the bunkhouse and tossed them in a waiting dump truck. Luckily, they had arrived after Lanie left with her second group of riders. It would give him another hour or two to think up a good explanation for the renovations.

He was contemplating going out to join them when he saw Duncan detach himself from one group and head for the house. Impatiently, Quinn pushed the door open for him.

"Well?"

"They said the building is structurally sound, and the changes we need are fairly simple. It shouldn't take them more than a week, tops. Fortunately, the contractor has a plumber and an electrician he works with on a regular basis, so that won't hold them up."

"Good. That's faster than I expected."

"He's got two separate crews working. One has already started on the deck for the hot tub, and the other is working inside."

Before Quinn could respond, the phone on the wall next to him rang, and without thought he picked it up.

"Hello?"

There was a slight hesitation from the person on the other end. "Quinn McAllister?"

"Speaking."

"This is Jared Harper."

Every muscle in Quinn's body tightened and his jaw went rigid. When he answered his voice was clipped. "Sorry, Harper. My wife is out working, but I'll be sure to tell her you called."

"I wasn't calling to speak with Lanie." There was another hesitation. "I think we need to talk, McAllister, but not over the phone. Would you meet me at the Spotted Horse in an hour?"

"I'll be there." Quinn dropped the phone into the cradle.

Duncan was leaning against the counter, one eyebrow arched. "You'll be where?"

"He wants to meet me at the Spotted Horse. It's a combination bar and restaurant in Watson."

"Want me to go with you?"

"Thanks, but I doubt it will come down to throwing punches. Besides, one of us needs to be here in case the contractor has any questions."

"And what if Lanie wants to know where you are?"

Quinn started out of the room. "Tell her the truth."

* * * * *

Watson had changed, Quinn realized as he drove through the town. He had seen two new hotels and several fancy restaurants that hadn't been there five years ago. Most of the stores along Main Street now catered to tourists instead of residents. A huge banner spanned the roadway, proclaiming the start of Frontier Days in a few weeks.

The Spotted Horse hadn't changed, though. It still looked exactly as it had when he was eighteen and spent most of his weekends at the bar. There were only a few vehicles in the parking lot, but it was midway between breakfast and lunch. He knew it would fill to capacity in an hour or so. During the day the bar section was closed, the business catering to families. At eight on the button, the families left and the bar opened. It was a system that worked well for the owner, Buck Denton, and customers alike.

Buck himself, sitting behind the checkout counter, glanced up from the newspaper he was reading when Quinn entered, a grin splitting his face.

"Dang, McAllister. I thought we'd seen the last of your sorry hide around here. Do I need to get my ball bat out from under the bar?"

Quinn returned his smile and shook hands with the older man. Buck had put on a little weight, but for the most part, he still looked exactly the same. Like a slab of solid granite.

"No need, Buck. My fighting days are over. Guess we all have to grow up sometime."

"Speak for yourself. That's a disease I never plan on catching. Just ask Ruby. She'll vouch for me. How long are you here for?"

"I'm back for good."

"Well, that's the best news I've heard in weeks. You always were one of my most regular customers. Tell you what. How about I treat you to a welcome back breakfast?"

"Thanks, but maybe next time. I'm here to meet someone."

Buck glanced toward the dinning room, a slight frown on his face when he turned back.

"I'm beginning to get the picture."

And if Buck got it, everyone in town would know what was going on before the day was out. Quinn stifled a sigh.

"I'll talk to you later."

Since only three tables were occupied, it didn't take him long to identify Harper. The man was sitting alone near a window, his gaze fixed on Quinn. Warily, the two men assessed each other as Quinn crossed the room, and he wasn't sure he liked what he saw. He didn't know what he'd been expecting, but Harper was too damn good looking for his peace of mind.

The veterinarian stood as Quinn reached the table and gestured to the booth across from him. "Thanks for coming. I wasn't sure you would."

"Why wouldn't I?" He slid onto the seat.

Harper shrugged as he sat down. "You have to admit this is a little awkward."

They both paused as Buck stopped by the table and filled two cups with coffee, his gaze shifting between them warily. He moved on quickly, not bothering to ask if they wanted to order.

Quinn ignored the cup, keeping his gaze on his rival. "Did Lanie ask you to try and talk me out of this?"

"No. She'd probably be upset if she knew I called you."

"Then why did you?"

"Partly curiosity, I suppose." The man's expression didn't change. "I wanted to see what I'm up against. Lanie never told me much about you."

Quinn curled a hand around his cup, forearms propped on the Formica top of the table as he studied the man who wanted to marry his wife. Lanie couldn't have found anyone more opposite from Quinn if she'd searched deliberately. And he wasn't just opposite in appearance. Harper exuded a calm steadiness that was palpable. Would anything shake him up, rattle that placid exterior? Maybe it was time to give Harper a dose of the truth.

"Lanie still loves me, you know. She may not be ready to admit it yet, but she does."

"You're right. Part of her does love you. You're Zack's father, after all." Harper lowered his gaze to the table. "I met Lanie when Zack was a month old and I rented her grandparents' place. For me, it was love at first sight, but it took over a year to convince her to go out with me. It was another three years before she agreed to marry me."

Exaltation surged through Quinn but he kept it out of his voice. "Why are you telling me this?"

Harper looked up, his eyes narrowed. "Because I want you to understand a few things. I'm a patient man when it comes to something I want, McAllister. I've already waited years for Lanie. Three more months isn't going to make that much difference. In spite of what you think, she loves me, too."

Quinn leaned back, straightening his leg a bit. "I'm going to fight for her, Harper. And I'm going to win. There's nothing you can say that will make me change my mind."

"I can't blame you for trying, even if you are wasting your time. If I were in your shoes I'd be doing the same thing." He ran a hand through his shaggy blond hair. "As much as I hate to admit it, maybe it's a good thing this happened. I don't like seeing Lanie upset and hurting, but at least now she'll have to make a choice. A bed can get awfully crowded when there are three people in it. When this is over, the only people who'll be in mine are me and Lanie." He shrugged again. "Better get used to the idea."

"I suppose that means you'll still try to see her?"

Harper gave him a cool smile. "You aren't the only one who plans on fighting for what he wants. I'll see her every chance I get."

"Too bad," Quinn commented. "She's already promised me she won't see you alone."

"You may be able to keep her away from me, McAllister, but you can't force her to trust you again. You had your chance five years ago and you blew it." He hesitated. "There is one more thing, though. Zack. I promised him he could go on some calls with me Saturday. I'd still like to take him."

Quinn nodded. "I told Lanie last night I wouldn't stop you from seeing Zack. Having me show up suddenly is enough trauma for him. I'd like to keep the rest of his life as normal as possible."

"I appreciate that."

"And now that we've drawn the lines, you might as well call me Quinn."

Harper arched an eyebrow.

"We're never going to be friends, Harper—" Quinn paused to smile. "But we do have one thing in common. We both have great taste in women. And it will make it easier on Zack if we can keep this civil."

"Quinn." Harper nodded. "And you can call me Jared."

"You aren't going to win," Quinn told him quietly. "Lanie and I have too much tying us together."

"And Lanie knows that at the end of these three months I'll still be here waiting. I'll always be here for her. Can you honestly say she believes the same thing about you? Don't count me out yet, McAllister. You may have won the first battle, but the war is just starting."

* * * * *

Jared stayed at the table after McAllister left, finishing off his coffee and thinking. A frown creased his brow. From Edward's description, he'd expected Lanie's husband to be the nerdish type, more interested in business than people.

Nothing could be further from the truth. He was going to have to be very careful with this man, maybe keep his distance from Lanie for a while. At least until he came up with a legitimate excuse for seeing her. Lanie wouldn't break a promise easily.

He paid Buck then stepped out onto the wooden sidewalk. For the last four years, he'd followed Edward's orders. They hadn't seemed demanding at the time, and he owed the man a lot. Now he was beginning to wonder if Edward had told him the entire truth about Lanie's past with McAllister.

Second Time Around

With an inward sigh, he walked to his truck and climbed in. Even if Edward had been lying through his teeth, it was too late to back out of the deal. It had been too late the first time he'd seen Lanie.

* * * * *

"What do you think you're doing?" Lanie stood with her hands on her hips, glaring at the horde of men who had come to a standstill at her barked question. One of them, obviously the crew chief, finally stepped forward.

"Mr. McAllister hired us. I have the order right here." Tentatively, he held out a yellow piece of paper.

She yanked it out of his hand, rapidly scanning the list with growing disbelief. A weight room? A sauna? A hot tub and deck? But that was undeniably Quinn's signature on the bottom. Was he trying to turn her ranch into a spa, for God's sake?

So furious her hair was prickling erect, she shoved the slip back at the confused foreman, spun on her heel, and ran smack into a hard male body. When she lifted her gaze it was to meet Duncan's calm brown eyes.

"Where's Quinn?" she spit the question through clenched teeth.

"In the kitchen. He just got back."

She paused suspiciously at the wicked gleam in his eyes. "Got back from where?"

"From town."

Something was up. Duncan looked at her speculatively, and she could see he was waiting with great interest for her next question. For a second she contemplated ignoring him, but curiosity won out.

"Okay, what was he doing in town?"

"Meeting Jared Harper."

The anger left her like a deflated balloon, replaced by fear and a hollow ache in the pit of her stomach. Without a word, she headed for the kitchen.

Quinn looked up and smiled as she stomped through the door. "Perfect timing. Martha just finished making us lunch. I noticed the picnic table is still under those trees out back. I thought we could eat there."

"How dare you?" She wanted to yell, but her voice wasn't cooperating. The words were barely a whisper. "I agreed to your terms, Quinn, but they didn't include you going after Jared. I won't have him hurt anymore than he already has been. He doesn't deserve this, and if you persist, our deal is off. We can fight this out in court."

His smile faded before he reached for the picnic basket on the table. "We can talk about it while we eat."

"I'm not hungry."

"Then you can sit and watch me." His grim gaze met hers, flickers of yellow anger shooting through the amber depths. He reached around her and pushed the door open. "After you."

"Quinn—"

"I said we'd talk about it while we eat."

Her lips thinned to a straight line as she followed him across the yard. His back was stiff, his gait jerky. From his body language, he was as upset as she was. Puzzled, she let her gaze sweep over him again. There was something odd about the way he was walking, something she couldn't put her finger on.

Mentally, she shook her head. He was only compensating for the weight of the picnic basket. And she wouldn't allow anything to distract her.

"You really have a low opinion of me, don't you?" Quinn took a cloth from the basket and spread it over the table before removing dishes of food.

"If I do it's because you've given me good reason." Her chin squared defiantly.

"I suppose I have." He sat down and filled two plates, pushing one across in front of her. "But for your information, Jared Harper called and asked to meet me, not the other way around."

"What?" She sank onto the bench. "Why would Jared want to meet you?"

A half-smile lifted one corner of his lips. "He wanted to see what he was up against. I have to admit, I was curious myself."

"And now that you've met him?" She reached for the chicken leg on her plate, absently noting he'd given her the part she liked best.

"Let's just say he wasn't what I expected. Is he always that stoic? I've seen statues with more emotion."

Lanie stared at him, guilt curling in her stomach. Hadn't she thought the very same thing from time to time? But she wasn't about to admit that to Quinn. "He's not stoic, he's dependable. Everyone loves him."

Quinn continued to eat. "I don't. There's something strange about him."

"There is not. You only think that because I'm engaged to him." She picked up a fork and dug into the potato salad. "What did you talk about?"

"You. Zack."

"Zack?"

"We agreed to keep everything civil for Zack's sake. I told him the same thing I told you. I don't want to disrupt Zack's life any more than necessary. It's obvious he cares about Jared, and I won't do anything to hurt him."

She dropped the piece of chicken back onto her plate. "That's it?"

"Pretty much."

Relief flowed through her, but it was short-lived.

"Were you sleeping with him?"

Her gaze snapped to Quinn's face. "That's none of your business."

"You're still my wife, Lanie. Anything you do is my business." His voice softened. "You weren't, were you?"

"No." She kept her gaze steady in spite of the heat suffusing her cheeks. "I wanted to wait until we were married and Jared agreed with me."

Satisfaction gleamed from his eyes as he reached across the table and took her hand. "Maybe you wanted to wait because you were afraid it wouldn't be as good as it always was for us."

She yanked her hand away from him, trying desperately to stop the tingle his touch sent coursing up her arm. "There's more to a relationship than sex. I think you and I proved that."

"If you're implying sex was all we had together, Lanie, then you're lying to yourself. We loved each other." He focused on his food again.

She couldn't do this, couldn't have this conversation with him. Not yet. She wasn't ready to dissect their marriage. It was time to change the subject.

"What are you doing to my bunkhouse?"

He glanced up, amusement flickering across his face as though he knew exactly what she was doing.

"Turning it into a gym."

"Why?"

He shrugged. "Working out is kind of a hobby for me these days."

"Damn it, Quinn. You should have asked me first. I'm going to need that bunkhouse later this month."

"By the time you do, we'll have another one built."

"I can't afford to have another one built. You'll just have to put it back the way it was."

"I'm paying for the new bunkhouse."

"No." She stood, hands clenched at her side. "This is still my ranch. You have no right to start changing things without asking me first."

Carefully, Quinn put his fork beside his plate, his eyes glinting with tawny sparks. "The ranch wasn't part of our deal. I'm keeping it however this turns out. This is my home and I'm not leaving it again."

A chill ran over her at his tone, but she wouldn't let him know he'd upset her. "I'll fight you, Quinn. There's only your word that you didn't sign it over to me."

"Really?" He stood abruptly, anger clear on his rugged face. "You might want to take a look at the date on that signature and then compare it to my hospital records. I'll even have them delivered to you. It's pretty damn hard for someone in a coma to sign his name on the dotted line."

Shock held her still as he stalked away. A coma? For how long? Why hadn't she been told?

Oh, God. Edward.

Slowly, she repacked the basket, her mind spinning. She hadn't been told because Edward didn't want her to know. He had wanted her to believe the divorce was Quinn's idea. And no doubt he'd seen a chance to kill two birds with one stone when he'd offered her the ranch. Not only did he see it as a way to keep her quiet, he'd wanted to get it away from his son. He had always hated the time Quinn spent here.

If it were true, she couldn't keep the ranch. Rightfully, it belonged to Quinn. She needed more information, needed to know exactly what happened the night Quinn left her, and during the months following. Only, who could she ask, who could she believe? There had been so many lies, so much pain.

She took a deep breath. Maybe she should take Quinn up on his offer to get her his medical records. It would take a few weeks to get them, but at least she'd finally know the truth.

Chapter Eight

Quinn paced the length of his room, cursing softly. He'd planned to spend the afternoon with Lanie, getting to know her again, letting her get used to having him around. Instead, he'd let all the old bitterness and pain rise to the surface.

He paused at the window, watching Lanie walk toward the house. Her steps were slow, head down as though lost in thought, and he cursed again. How could he expect her to trust him again when he couldn't let himself trust her?

Somehow, he had to put the past behind him, forget about his time in the hospital. Remember that it hadn't been her fault because she hadn't known. It was the only way to give them another chance. And he wanted another chance. A chance to hold her, love her, make a life with her and their son.

She went out of sight onto the back porch, and from below he heard the door close. With a deep breath, he headed downstairs. He had to apologize before it was too late.

Lanie was in the kitchen, standing at the sink staring out the window, so deep in thought she didn't hear him. He put his hands on her shoulders and turned her to face him.

"I'm sorry," he murmured. "I shouldn't have gotten mad. If you need the bunkhouse, I'll tell them to leave it alone."

Her gray eyes widened, turned the color of slate, and he felt her tremble under his hands. It was enough to send desire rippling through every inch of his body.

Slowly, she shook her head. "The bunkhouse isn't important. I can hire some high school kids from Watson for the summer instead of the college kids I usually hire. They'll be able to go home at night."

"Are you sure?"

"Yes." She moistened her lips then hesitantly lifted a hand to the scar on his face.

Quinn went still as she traced the line with her fingertips. Her gaze shifted to his, and abruptly she lowered her hand.

"I'm sorry, too, Quinn. I never should have jumped to the conclusion that you were out to get Jared. It's just..."

"You don't have to explain. We've both been through a lot in the last five years. A lot of pain and a lot of lies. I guess it would be asking too much for the past to go away overnight." He shifted his hand to cradle her nape, his thumb caressing the soft skin below her jaw.

"As much as I want this to work, Lanie, we don't have a chance if you're only suffering it out for the three months. Zack deserves to have both his parents, and we deserve a shot at the life we should have had. But if you're going to fight me every step of the way, tell me now and we'll forget the whole thing. I can't do this alone."

Quinn held his breath as she gazed up at him intently. He'd taken a horrible risk, giving her the opportunity to back out of their deal.

"You're right." She sighed and closed her eyes briefly. "I guess part of me did think I could wait out the time and then get on with my life. That wasn't very honest of me. I agreed to your terms and it wouldn't be fair not to live up to my end of the deal. So I'll try, Quinn. I can promise you that much."

"That's all I'm asking." He'd never wanted anyone as much as he wanted her right then. "Will you let me kiss you?" he whispered. Normally, he wouldn't have asked permission. But nothing about this was normal. Pushing her before she was ready would only drive her farther away.

Her pupils expanded until only a thin rim of gray remained before her eyelids drifted shut and she lifted her face in silent acquiescence. It was hard to determine who was shaking more now, her or him. And he really didn't care.

His hand tightened on her nape as he drew her closer, and lowered his mouth to hers. Afraid she'd bolt, he kept the kiss soft, gently parting her lips, but when her tongue hesitantly met his, he nearly lost control. How many nights had he imagined this? So many it was impossible to count. Even when he'd spent every waking moment trying to hate her, his dreams had betrayed him.

Without thought, he deepened the kiss, desperately soaking in her taste, her scent. Part of his mind was aware that Martha had entered the kitchen, but he didn't let that stop him. He'd waited too long.

By the time he eased up, both of them were breathing in ragged gasps. At some point, Lanie had twined her arms around his neck and her hands were still buried in his hair. For a second longer they stared at each other, then a red flush rose to color her cheeks. Hastily, she moved her arms and stepped back.

Martha was standing with her hands on her hips, beaming approval. Lanie shot her an embarrassed look as she edged toward the door. "I...I have to get back to work."

Quinn smiled as she darted outside. His body might be aching, but his heart felt better than it had in ages. He hadn't been wrong. Lanie still loved him, still wanted him, even if she didn't want to acknowledge it yet.

He turned his grin on the housekeeper. "Martha, my love, it's a beautiful day."

She chuckled. "From what I just saw, it's not the day that's got you in such a good mood."

"I always said you were a very perceptive woman."

"Does this mean you're back to stay?"

"Yes." His smile faded. "This is my home, Martha. I'll never leave it again."

* * * * *

Lanie came to a halt at the first stall and leaned her forehead against the partition, ignoring the curious mare who inhaled gently against her cheek. She never should have let Quinn kiss her. Yes, she'd promised him to try, but that kiss was a big mistake. It had reminded her body of things she'd rather not have it remember right now, made it ache with a hungry intensity that still had her rattled. One she had no intention of giving in to.

One kiss and she'd forgotten her name, forgotten where she was, forgotten...Jared. Dear God. Guilt streaked through her. Sweet, wonderful Jared. He loved her, trusted her, and yet the first time Quinn touched her she'd been ready to rip his clothes off. Was she really that desperate?

"Lanie? Are you okay?"

She straightened, turning to stare at Sherry. The blonde had been her foreman since Jonesy, Sherry's grandfather, retired two years earlier. She was also a friend.

"Sure." A low laugh escaped her throat. "I'm just great. My ex-husband, who's no longer my ex, shows up after five years and demands another chance to make our marriage work. My son is confused. And my fiancé—" She rubbed her eyes. "I can't begin to imagine what this is doing to him. Yeah, life is a real bowl of cherries."

Sherry put a comforting hand on her arm. "You know, I was just a kid during the summers Quinn spent here, but he always treated me great. Even back then I knew how much he loved you. And he is Zack's father. Maybe he deserves another chance."

"You don't understand. There's nothing Quinn loves more than that damn company. Zack will get used to having him around, then Quinn will leave again. Do you know what that will do to my son?"

"To Zack, or to you?" Sherry arched an eyebrow.

"Zack. Believe me, I learned my lesson the hard way. The first time Edward calls with one of his schemes, Quinn will be heading back to Chicago."

"Now that he knows about Zack, do you really think Quinn will ignore him?"

She hesitated, then sighed. "Probably not."

Sherry shrugged. "Then if you really don't care about him, and he leaves, your problems are solved. Zack will still have his father and you'll get that divorce and marry Jared. That is what you want, isn't it?"

"Of course it is." Her brows lowered. Except she'd promised Quinn another chance. A promise she was honor-bound to keep, even knowing he'd leave again. Suddenly she felt like a high-wire walker, trying to juggle bowling pins while maintaining her balance. Or maybe a bone caught between two hungry dogs. Quinn or Jared. Jared or Quinn. Both pulling at her. Confusion had her dizzy. Confusion and the abrupt realization that she would have to choose between them. No one else could do this for her, and no matter what her decision, someone was going to be hurt. This wasn't a game or a nightmare she would wake from.

Somehow, she was going to have to make an honest attempt at this marriage without risking her heart or her son's. And that meant keeping Quinn at a physical distance, because she could no longer trust her traitorous body. She'd let her heart rule when she'd married Quinn, but now it was different. This was a decision she would have to make with her head, for all their sakes.

The sound of tires crunching on gravel brought her out of her thoughts to find Sherry studying her. "You still love him, don't you?"

Lanie gave her a wry smile. "He's Zack's father. I suppose a part of me can't help loving him. This would be a lot easier if I didn't."

"Hey, in ten years you'll look back on all this and wonder what all the fuss was about. Well, my next group is here. Are you going to be okay?"

"In ten years, maybe. Need some help saddling up?" Lanie made herself hold the smile in spite of her dismay. Would she be able to look back and know she'd made the right choice? God, she hoped so.

"Nope. Already got the horses ready. You might want to take a look at that cut on Clipper's leg, though. He keeps trying to chew the bandage off."

"It's probably starting to itch. I'll put something on it." She headed for the gelding's stall as Sherry went to greet the carload of guests.

* * * * *

Quinn walked down the front steps to meet the maroon van that had pulled to a stop in front of the house. Before he reached it the door opened and Zack tumbled out, turning to throw a taunt at the other back seat occupant.

"See? I told you my Dad was here!"

A pretty brunette rounded the front of the van, smiling. "You must be Mr. McAllister. Zack has been talking about you all day." She held out a hand. "I'm Kelsey George. I work for the daycare center. And this," she pointed back into the van, "is my son, Billy."

Quinn glanced at the child staring at him. There was something vaguely familiar about the red hair, one sprig standing straight up in the back, and the freckle-strewn face.

"Hi, Billy." He arched a brow at the woman. "George. Any relation to Ethan?"

Kelsey's smile widened. "He's my husband and he was thrilled to discover you're back. He's constantly telling Billy and Zack stories about 'the good old days' when you two were growing up. I suspect you'll be hearing from him soon."

"Great. I was planning on looking him up later this week."

"Dad." Zack tugged on his arm. "Can we go see the puppies now?"

"First, you need to go put your backpack up," Lanie answered his question as she stopped beside them and ruffled Zack's hair before he ran into the house.

Quinn's gaze met hers and he stifled a grin when her cheeks flushed. He'd made it a point to stay out of her way this afternoon, give her time to think about what had happened in the kitchen.

She looked away hurriedly. "Hi, Kelsey. How's Billy?"

"He's fine. The doctor said it was just a cold." The brunette climbed back into the van. "Don't forget, you promised to make some of your applesauce cookies for the kids tomorrow."

"I won't." Lanie waved. "They'll be ready in the morning."

"Cookies?" Quinn kept his gaze on her hopefully as the van left.

"Yes."

"Lots of cookies?"

She laughed. "Yes, lots of cookies. There will be plenty left after I box the ones for the daycare. You always did have a sweet tooth."

"Only where your cookies are concerned. Can I lick the spoon?"

"You'll have to fight Zack for it."

Both adults winced as the front door slammed shut with a loud bang. Zack careened down the steps and grabbed Quinn's hand, tugging him toward the path leading to the barn. "Come on, Dad. Let's go."

"Right behind you, champ."

Second Time Around

"I'll walk with you. I've still got a few things left to do in the stable."

"Need some help?" Quinn matched his steps to hers, watching his son dart ahead.

"No, I just have to turn the horses out to pasture for the night. Sherry usually does it, but I let her go home early this evening. Jonesy had a doctor's appointment."

"How is Jonesy?"

She smiled. "Cantankerous as ever. He lives with Sherry now that he's retired. Spends all his time fishing and talking with his friends about how ranching has gone to hell in a handbasket. He drops by occasionally to tell me I'm doing everything wrong."

"That's Jonesy." Quinn laughed. "He's another one I'll have to stop and say hello to."

"You'll probably see him at the Spotted Horse first. He's there every weekend."

"Yeah?" He glanced at her speculatively. "How about if we go Friday night? It might be fun."

"I don't know, Quinn. What about Zack?"

"Martha will be here. She can take care of him. We can ask Duncan and Sherry to go with us if you'd like."

She hesitated at the door of the stable. "Duncan doesn't like me."

"He doesn't know you yet and Duncan is always a little standoffish with strangers at first. Give him time." It wasn't exactly the truth, but Quinn had an idea what the problem was. Duncan knew his history, knew the kind of hell he had gone through. Now he was probably worried it would all start again if this attempt with Lanie didn't work out. Maybe he needed to have a talk with Dunc.

"Okay, Friday night, then." She shifted her weight from one foot to the other. "I'll ask Sherry tomorrow if she wants to go."

"Dad!"

The call came from a stall at the far end of the stable, and Quinn smiled. Would he ever get used to this rush of joy at being called Dad? He doubted it.

"On my way."

Zack was kneeling in a pile of straw, a mass of wiggling puppies crawling all over him. When Quinn stopped next to him, the mother, a Border collie mix, rolled onto her side, tail thumping gently as she eyed him. Leaning from the waist, he extended the back of his hand to let her catch his scent, then scratched behind her ears.

"I take it this is Daisy?"

Zack nodded. "She's the mama." He patted the straw. "Sit down so you can see the puppies."

Quinn hesitated. Getting down wouldn't be much of a problem, but getting back up might be. His leg tended to give out when he put too much weight on it.

Carefully, he checked to see where Lanie was. She had opened the pasture door and was freeing the horses from their stalls.

Making sure he was close to the stall partition so he could use it as a brace, he gingerly lowered himself to the floor, extending his left leg in front of him. He barely got settled before the puppies mobbed him. They looked about six weeks old and were a mixed lot. Daisy obviously wasn't choosy when it came to lovers.

Zack held one up for his inspection. "This one is mine. Mom said I could keep him." The pup was only half the size of his littermates, but just as energetic.

"Got a name picked out yet?"

"Spot."

Quinn eyed the solid black pup wryly. "Works for me."

"You can have this one." Depositing Spot in his lap, he picked up a brown and black ball of fuzz and thrust it at his father, giggling when the pup tried frantically to wash Quinn's face. "Now you have to pick out a name, too. How about Frodo?"

Quinn examined the pup critically. "There's just one problem with that. It's a girl."

Zack tilted his head, thinking, and Quinn's heart turned over. God, he looked so much like Lanie when he did that. It made him ache for all the time he'd missed with this child they had created together.

"Okay, how about Pippin? That could be a girl's name."

It was easy to tell who his favorite characters were. Quinn laughed. "Pippin it is." He glanced around as Lanie stopped at the stall.

"Five more minutes, guys. Martha will have supper ready soon."

"Aren't you going back with us?"

"I'll be there in a bit. I want to run over to the brood mare barn first. One of the mares has been acting restless all day and she had some problems with her last foal. Kenny is there, but I want to check her myself."

"Kenny?"

"Kenny Kelly. You don't know him. He and his wife, Barbara, moved here a few years ago. He helps me with my breeding program, and trains the colts."

Quinn nodded. "Guess we'll see you at supper then." He breathed a sigh of relief as she left the stable. At least it gave him a chance to stand up without her watching. He wanted her love, not her pity.

Chapter Nine

Lanie's boots clicked on the concrete floor of the barn as she made her way past the roomy box stalls, each filled with an expectant mare. A rustling noise came from half-way down the row and she saw Kenny's battered Resistol come into view as he stood.

"How is she?"

Lines of worry etched his weathered face. "Not good. I was about to come get you. She's definitely in labor. Near as I can tell, the foal is turned wrong."

"Damn," she muttered under her breath. Last year she'd spent a small fortune to buy an Andalusian stud. This would be the first of Cortez's foals and she didn't want to lose it or the mare.

Leaning against the stall door, she watched the obviously distressed bay. Sweaty lather coated her neck and her eyes rolled with each contraction.

"Okay, keep an eye on her. I'm going to go call Jared then come right back."

Kenny nodded. "Give Barb a call for me, too, if you don't mind. Tell her what's going on so she won't worry when I'm late."

Lanie nibbled her bottom lip as she headed for the house. Quinn probably wouldn't like her calling Jared, but he'd have to live with it. Jared was one of the only vets in the area that specialized in large animals.

Quinn was holding Zack at the sink, letting him wash his hands when she entered the kitchen. His welcoming smile faded as he gazed at her.

"Something wrong?" He dried Zack's hands and lowered him to the floor. The boy immediately joined Duncan at the table.

"The mare I told you about? She's having problems." Lifting the receiver to her ear, she punched in Jared's number, anxiety flowing through her when she got his answering machine instead of him. "Jared? It's me. Kadia is in labor and Kenny thinks the foal is turned wrong. Please come over as soon as you get this message."

She hung up and dialed another number. "Barb? It's Lanie. Kenny wanted me to let you know he's going to be late. We're having trouble with one of the mares."

Quinn was watching her when she turned. "Anything I can do to help?"

"Not really." She made herself smile at Zack before glancing at Quinn again. "You may as well go ahead and eat. I have to head back out to the barn. I don't how long this is going to take."

Martha was stirring something on the stove, but she paused at Lanie's words. "And when are you going to eat?"

"I'll grab something later. Oh, and Martha, I hate to ask you but I promised Kelsey I'd bake some cookies for tomorrow. Would you mind terribly stirring up a batch?"

"Don't bother yourself." The cook waved her spoon. "I'll take care of the cookies."

"Thanks, Martha. You're an angel."

Quinn followed her to the door. "Are you sure there's nothing I can do?"

Lanie shook her head. "There's really nothing even I can do except try to keep her calm until Jared gets here."

"Couldn't you page him?"

She blinked in surprise. This certainly wasn't the reaction she'd expected. Nor was it Duncan's if his frown was any indication. No matter what Quinn said, his friend didn't like her and she couldn't understand why. They'd barely spoken.

"I could, but the fact he's not home means he's already on an emergency call. He'll check his messages the first chance he gets."

Before she realized what he was going to do, he dropped a light kiss on her forehead and gave her a gentle push. "Then go. I'll keep an eye on Zack."

She held his gaze a moment. Somehow, during all the fights they'd had, with the pain of their breakup, she had forgotten that Quinn could be kind and compassionate. The man she saw standing here now was the one she'd fallen in love with, the one she'd married. And that made him even more dangerous, made her confusion even greater. It would be so easy to forget how he'd left her. Something she couldn't allow herself to do.

"Thank you," she murmured, lowering her gaze as she went out the door.

* * * * *

It was full dark by the time Quinn headed across the yard, a thermos of coffee in one hand and a bag of sandwiches in the other. Light spilled from the open doors of the brood mare barn, guiding his feet over the uneven ground. He paused to let his eyes adjust, then walked toward the low murmur of voices.

"How is she?"

Lanie looked up from her position next to the mare. "Not good. The contractions are coming faster." She gestured to the short, bow-legged man beside her. "Quinn, this is Kenny Kelly. Kenny, Quinn McAllister."

Tucking the thermos under his arm, he shook hands with the man. "Kenny."

"Nice to meet you," the trainer replied.

"Since you both missed supper, I thought you might like some sandwiches. Martha had plenty of roast left."

"Thanks." Lanie stood and stretched while Kenny took the bag. "Where's Zack?"

His heart rate sped up a notch when her breasts pushed against the fabric of her T-shirt. "Watching TV with Duncan." He tore his gaze away from her chest, hoping she hadn't noticed.

Luckily, her attention was focused on the food. She took a sandwich from Kenny and bit into it, leaning back against the stall door to keep an eye on the mare while she ate.

Crossing his arms on the top of the stall, he gazed down at the mare. "She's a beauty."

A frown marred Lanie's brow. "Yes, she is. One of Xan's daughters. If Jared doesn't make it soon, we'll have to try and turn the foal ourselves."

"You still have Xan?" Xan had been his horse and for some reason it surprised him that Lanie would still have the big black.

"Of course."

The sound of tires crunching on gravel had them all turning to the door. Lanie's frown eased to a look of relief when Jared appeared in the light, a black bag in his hand.

"Sorry it took me so long to get here. Seems like every animal in the county picked today to get in trouble." He gave Quinn a brief nod as the others made room for him. "Let's see what we've got."

Quinn touched Lanie's arm. "I'm going to head back to the house and put Zack to bed."

She gave him a distracted smile, her gaze on Jared as he knelt by the mare. "Thanks. Give him a kiss for me. And thanks again for bringing the food."

"No problem." With a sigh, he slipped out of the barn.

* * * * *

Lanie wiped her forehead with the back of her hand, watching the filly try to stand on wobbly legs. Kadia, the mare, had regained her feet, her efforts at nuzzling her daughter hindering the foal's attempts more than helping.

Jared stopped at the stall, drying his hands on a paper towel. "You can stop worrying now. They're both fine."

"Thanks to you." She smiled as she stepped out of the stall and closed the door.

"Just doin' my job, ma'am," he drawled. "Kenny leave?"

"I sent him home. Not much use in both of us staying here now that the danger is over."

"Tell me you aren't going to stay in the barn all night."

"I won't." She glanced at the mare and foal again. "I just want to check them again in a few minutes."

"Okay." He hesitated. "Can you walk me to the truck, or is that against the rules?"

She squared her chin. "Forget the rules. I'll walk you to the truck if I want to."

"That's my girl." He tossed the paper towel in the nearest trash can and picked up his bag.

Lanie followed him out, waiting while he put his things in the truck then turned back to face her. The light from the barn made a square on the ground just beyond where they stood, and she could clearly see the lines of pain on Jared's face as he lifted her hand and studied the rings she now wore.

"I thought I'd seen the last of these a year ago," he murmured.

"I'm sorry. I had no choice, Jared. We knew this wasn't going to be easy when I agreed to Quinn's terms."

He paused, his gaze moving over her face. "Maybe we were wrong, Lanie. It's not too late. We can still fight him. All you have to do is say the word."

"I can't do that to Zack," she said, softly. "You know what it would do to him."

"God, this is hard." He skimmed his knuckles down her cheek. "I miss both of you and it hasn't even been a week yet."

"We miss you, too."

"So how are you doing?"

"I'm fine." It was her turn to hesitate. "But there's something I have to tell you." She took a deep breath. "Quinn and I had a talk this afternoon and he made me realize something. I can't spend the next three months pretending he's not here just to get through it and get the divorce. The deal was to try and make the marriage work, to give it another chance. Jared, I gave him my word. I have to try."

The hurt glimmering in his green eyes made her want to cry.

"I've lost you already, haven't I?"

"No." She cupped his cheek. "It only means I have a decision to make. This isn't what I would have chosen, but it's what I agreed to. Three months is a long time." Her gaze drifted to the darkened house. "Knowing Quinn, he'll head back to Chicago the first time his father calls. If he does, our deal is off."

"Then I'll pray he calls fast." He took a step back. "Guess I better be going."

Lanie nodded. "I'll see you Saturday when you come to pick up Zack."

He climbed into the truck and started the engine before looking at her again. "Don't let him make you forget I love you, Lanie."

"I won't," she whispered, the lump in her throat nearly choking her. "I promise."

* * * * *

Wearily, Quinn closed his eyes and rubbed the scar on his temple, wishing he were any place but sitting on the back porch steps. If he could have left without letting them know he'd been there, he would have. But any movement on his part would have drawn their attention instantly.

He'd tried not to listen, not to watch. Unfortunately, sounds carried well on the night air, and the light from the barn had outlined them clearly. And now he felt like crap. He hoped Lanie would head back into the barn, but as soon as Jared's truck vanished down the drive he heard her steps moving toward the house. They stopped abruptly and he opened his eyes to see her peering uncertainly into the darkness of the porch.

"Quinn?"

"Yeah, it's me."

She moved closer and propped a foot on the bottom step. "How long have you been here?"

"Too long." He smiled wryly. "Sorry. I didn't mean to eavesdrop."

"You heard everything?"

"Yes."

Climbing the last few steps, she sank down beside him, remaining silent while she rubbed her eyes. "I had to call him, Quinn. He's the only vet in this area. And I owed him the truth."

"I know." Gingerly he put his arm around her, surprised when she leaned into his body. "I'm not blaming you. It's just not easy seeing you together." He let his thumb caress the skin on her arm. "You were wrong about one thing you told him, Lanie."

"What?"

"Me leaving. I'm not going anywhere."

"That's what you said last time."

"Last time I was an idiot. I won't make the same mistake again."

"What about Edward?"

Quinn's expression turned fierce. "He's my father, and part of me will always love him. But the rest of me hates him for what he's done. He made a big mistake when he broke us apart and kept my son from me. One he's going to regret. You have to believe me, Lanie. A second chance to be with you and Zack, for us to be a family, means more to me than anything Edward has to offer."

He put a finger under her chin and tilted her face to his. "Jared isn't the only one who loves you, Lanie. So do I. There was a time I fooled myself into thinking I didn't, but the minute you walked into that fund-raiser, I knew I'd been wrong. If anything, I love you more now than I did before. That's why I'm doing all this, why I want us to have another shot at making things right."

She lowered her head, rested it against his shoulder. "What about McAllister Pharmaceuticals? It's as much a part of your heritage as this ranch. I can't see you giving it up easily."

Involuntarily, his jaw clenched. "Let me worry about the company. I promise you, it won't interfere in our life."

A prodigious yawn stretched her features. "What were you doing out here?"

He lifted to gaze to sweep the ranch. There was a full moon tonight, its blue light creating familiar shadows. "Thinking. Soaking the place in. I used to do it a lot."

"I remember," she murmured. "I'd wake up and discover you weren't in bed. I'd always find you sitting out here."

"You never said anything."

"No. You seemed...I don't know, sort of untouchable. I didn't want to disturb you."

"You should have. It's a lot nicer with you here." He rested his chin on top of her head and put his other arm around her.

"I guess we both should have done some things differently." She paused for a moment. "Did Zack give you problems over his bath tonight?"

"Bath?"

She grinned. "Don't tell me he talked you out of it?"

"He never even mentioned it. Sorry. I'm still new at this father thing."

"It's okay. He can take one in the morning instead. You'll learn." She shifted, then straightened. "I need to go check Kadia one more time before bed."

"How is she?"

"Fine, now. The foal is a filly."

"Mind if I go with you?"

"No, I don't mind." She went down the steps, waiting for him at the bottom.

He'd forgotten about his leg. Stifling a groan, he rose awkwardly, well aware of Lanie's curious stare. He forced a smile. "Been sitting in one position too long." When he joined her, he took her hand. "I had a look at Gator earlier. That's about the ugliest bull I've ever seen."

"Now you know where he got his name."

"Why are you keeping him in the corral?"

"We moved him there about two weeks ago after he tried to gore Kenny. Luckily, he didn't get the job done, but I can't risk the same thing happening with one of our riding groups. Kenny knows what to do, these people don't." She glanced toward the corral that stretched between the brood mare barn and the stable. "I suppose I'm going to have to sell him. He's gotten too dangerous."

"Do you have a replacement?"

"A couple of his sons. They're still a little young, but I think they'll do."

"That's good. Oh, and I talked to the contractor. He'll start the new bunkhouse as soon as you show him where you want it."

She glanced up at him. "You don't have to do that, Quinn."

"I know, but I want to."

"Okay. I'll talk to him in the morning."

They admired the new filly for a while before heading back to the house. She was on her feet now, energetically nursing from her tired mother.

The spicy aroma of baking still filled the kitchen when Quinn opened the back door for her. "Want a cookie? Don't tell Martha I said so, but they aren't as good as yours."

She shook her head, smiling. "Thanks, but I'm bushed. All I want to do is take a fast shower then crawl into bed."

"It has been a long day."

He followed her up the stairs, pausing outside her room. "Lanie?"

With her hand on the doorknob, she turned.

"I know we've still got a lot of problems to work out. Things happened that neither of us will get over easily. But God, I've missed you. I want you so much I ache with it."

"Quinn—"

He put his fingers over her lips and smiled. "You don't have to say anything. I realize you're still confused and upset. I won't push you, but I wanted you to know I'm here if you ever decide you need me."

Slowly, he leaned over and replaced his fingers with his lips, kissing her gently. "Goodnight, Lanie."

He was halfway down the hall when her whisper reached him.

"Quinn? I've missed you too."

Heart leaping, he gazed back at her. "That's a start, Angel."

She nodded. "Goodnight."

Before he could say more, she stepped into her room and closed the door.

Chapter Ten

I've missed you, too.

The words continued to ring in his head the next morning as he sat in front of the computer Duncan had installed in the office. Through the window he watched Lanie talk to the contractor, gesturing occasionally to make a point.

Today, her T-shirt was white, tucked neatly into her jeans. The sun glinted on her hair, setting off deep auburn highlights in the darker brown strands. To his eyes, she looked no different than she had at eighteen, the summer she'd knocked him flat on his butt.

Until that year, she'd been his buddy, someone to take care of. She'd even been his pen pal, writing him newsy letters about everything that was going on in Watson during the winter months while he was in college. When he'd found out how much she loved horses, he'd convinced Jonesy to hire her each summer, paying her wages out of his own pocket.

But that particular summer…

~ ~ ~ ~ ~

Quinn hoisted his duffel bag with one hand to keep it from snagging on seats as he made his way off the airplane. He hoped Jonesy hadn't forgotten he was arriving today. An hour-long wait in the small terminal wasn't something he relished. He'd been in such a hurry to get home he hadn't even gone by Edward's, instead leaving straight from college.

A small crowd waited at the gate as he disembarked and he scanned the faces rapidly, looking for Jonesy. There was no sign of the older man, and he sighed. He should have called from the airport in Chicago and reminded his foreman that he was on his way.

"Hey, cowboy. What's your hurry?"

The voice was low and sexy, and he almost kept going. But there was something vaguely familiar about it. Abruptly, he stopped, turning to look at the crowd again.

She was standing in front of him, grinning from ear to ear. Her dark hair was pulled back in a thick braid, and she was wearing a skirt and blouse. A blouse that molded itself to her upper body, defining a shape that was about as far from childish as you could get. The skirt was full, some gauzy material that nipped in at her small waist and showed off legs a mile long below the hem.

"Lanie?" Stunned, he could do nothing but stare at her.

"It's about time."

Reflexively he dropped his bag as she launched herself at him, his arms closing around her.

"Welcome home," she murmured in his ear. "God, I've missed you."

He was still grappling with the fact that this woman was "his" Lanie when she kissed him. Not just a peck on the cheek, a real lip-lock. Combined with the feel of her curves pressed against him, her scent washing over him, his body reacted with a need that shocked him. This was Lanie. His best friend. He wasn't supposed to be feeling this way about her.

With a scowl, he pulled her arms away from his neck and glowered down at her. "Who taught you to kiss like that?"

Her grin turned saucy. "Who taught you? And don't try to tell me you didn't like it. I know better."

"We're in public, for gosh sakes."

She tilted her head. "Want to go somewhere private and try again?"

"Lanie!"

Laughter erupted from her throat. "Okay, okay. I was just teasing. But you should see your face." She reached into a pocket on her skirt and pulled out a set of keys, tossing them at him. "I brought your truck. I thought you might like to drive it home."

"Thanks. Is it still in one piece?" He couldn't stop looking at her and that scared him. This wasn't one of the women he took to bed without a second thought. Lanie trusted him, cared about him.

"Of course it's in one piece. I had a great driving instructor."

"Who still has gray hair from the experience."

"I wasn't that bad."

"Oh? What about the time you took the curve outside Watson on two wheels and nearly hit the ditch?"

"I was dodging a cat."

"Uh-huh. One I never saw."

"It's not my fault my eyes are better than yours."

They had reached the truck by then, and Quinn slung his bag into the back before opening it and pulling out a wrapped box. As soon as they were inside, he handed it to her.

"What's this?" She examined the colorful paper curiously.

"A graduation present. Open it."

He started the truck and pulled out of the parking lot, keeping an eye on her as she tore the paper off and opened the gift.

"Oh, Quinn. It's beautiful." She held the heart-shaped necklace by its chain, sunlight sparkling off the diamond in the center. "Thank you." She slid across the seat and kissed him, this time on the cheek.

To his horror, he realized he was disappointed that she hadn't really kissed him again. He cleared his throat. "So, going off to college now?"

She shook her head. "I'm not cut out for college. Jonesy gave me a full-time job at the ranch." There was a brief hesitation. "I moved into that cabin on the south part of the range. Jonesy let me have it as part of my salary."

"What about your grandparents?" He arched a brow in question.

"They threw me out," she said quietly. "You know how grandpa is. After the drunk driver who killed my parents got off with a fine and a suspended sentence, he thinks anyone with money is evil. My working at your ranch during the summers was bad enough. When I told him I'd been hired permanently he lost it." She shrugged. "I guess it's for the best. I never really felt welcome there anyway."

"I'm sorry, Lanie."

"It's not your fault." She smiled at him. "I love having the cabin to myself. It's so peaceful there."

"So, got a hot date lined up Friday night?"

"No. I haven't been dating much lately."

Relief washed over him. "Good. How about going to the drive-in with me?" The words popped out before he knew he was going to say them and his breath caught in his chest. He'd lost his mind. There was no other explanation. Carefully, he glanced at Lanie. She was staring at him intently.

"I thought you'd never ask," she said quietly.

~ ~ ~ ~ ~

Quinn smiled now as he watched her bend over a set of plans with the contractor, making a mark here and there on the paper. He'd managed not to let things go too far that summer, but just barely. It had been pure hell and sweet heaven working with her every day, spending every minute off together. By the time he'd gone back to college, he'd known he was in love.

The tone of their letters had changed his first year of graduate school. Neither had openly declared their love, but it was obvious. Never had a school year seemed so long. And he'd known deep down inside that the next summer he wouldn't be able to stop. He wanted her more than he'd ever wanted any woman before.

The phone beside him rang, interrupting his chain of memories. He snagged it before Martha could answer.

"Quinn?"

"Franklin. How's it going?"

"Thank God I caught you. Edward is driving me nuts. He wants me to stall the trust fund. I think he still believes you'll see the light and come back."

"Let Edward think whatever he wants. He'll find out the truth soon enough." Quinn picked up the sheaf of papers lying on the desk in front of him. "I got the papers you faxed. I've been looking them over. There are a few changes I want you to make before I sign them."

"What changes?"

"I'm going to be adding some stock to the fund." Quinn leaned back in the chair.

"Well, that shouldn't take long."

"Yeah, but I haven't finished buying yet. It could be a couple more weeks. I'll let you know when I'm ready."

He depressed the receiver and dialed the number for Tom Delaney, his stockbroker. The secretary put him right through.

"Tom, Quinn McAllister. How are we doing?"

"You aren't going to believe how well." The stockbroker's voice was excited. "It's like McAllister Pharmaceutical stock is falling from the sky."

A grim smile curved his lips at Tom's response. "Wonderful. How much longer do you think it will be before we have controlling interest?"

"We're getting close to the five percent mark. At this rate, I'd say another week."

Quinn paused and his smile widened. "That's better than I'd expected. A lot better."

"Are you going to inform Edward that you're making a takeover?"

"No, let the Security Exchange Commission tell him. It'll give Edward a taste of his own medicine."

Dropping the phone back into its cradle, he laced his fingers behind his head, satisfaction flowing through him. It was going to come as a big surprise when Edward discovered the company he lived for now belonged to the four-year-old grandson he hadn't considered good enough to acknowledge.

* * * * *

Lanie stopped in the stable door to let the first group of riders return to their cars before checking the booking schedule. Five more groups were down for today, which meant she and Sherry both would be in the saddle all day.

"Next week is worse," the blonde commented from behind her. "People are already drifting in for the Frontier Days Festival."

"I know. The newspaper is running our ad today and tomorrow. Maybe we'll have some help by Monday."

"Granddad can always pitch in if we need him."

"I hate to bother him." Lanie smiled at her foreman. "But that does remind me. Quinn is taking me to the Spotted Horse tomorrow night and he suggested you and Duncan come along."

"Yeah?" She glanced toward the bunkhouse where Duncan was standing and licked her lips with a great deal of exaggeration. "I think I can handle that."

"You're horrible." Lanie laughed out loud.

"No I'm not. But there are only three hunks like him in this county, and you're married to one of them, and engaged to the other. I've got dibs on this one."

Leave it to Sherry to remind her, Lanie thought ruefully. She closed the appointment book as her foreman went to get ready for the next group. She'd been trying not to remember how nice it had felt last night, sitting next to Quinn with his arms around her while they talked. Or about the dreams she'd had when she finally fell asleep. They made her feel like a traitor.

She pinched the bridge of her nose in confusion. How could she have dreams like that about Quinn when she loved Jared? There had to be something wrong with her.

Her next group had ten people in it, and she tried to think logically as she began saddling the horses. Quinn had not only been her first love, he'd been her first lover. The day they'd married had been one of the happiest of her life. She'd thought they would be together forever.

The night he'd left, her whole world had fallen apart. For weeks she'd waited by the phone, expecting him to call. But he never had. Edward had called instead.

And lied.

Lanie lifted her head and stared into space. That was it, of course. One minute Quinn had been there and the next he was gone. There had been no closure, nothing to tell her emotionally that their marriage was over. Part of her had always believed he'd come back. She simply hadn't expected it to take five years.

Now that she thought about it, she knew why she'd waited so long to take off her wedding rings, why she'd held Jared at arm's length for so long. In her heart she'd still been married to Quinn.

He was right, she realized. No matter how this turned out, they needed the chance to find out what might have happened if not for Edward. And if they wound up getting a divorce after all, then at least this chapter of their lives would be closed. They could both move on with no regrets.

"Need some help?"

She glanced over her shoulder to see Quinn watching her and her heart did a fast somersault. "Still remember how?"

"I think I can figure it out."

"Okay. I need six more saddled. We can split it."

"Which ones?"

She shrugged. "Doesn't matter. All the horses we use for riding are gentle and well trained. They have to be. A lot of the people we get have never been on a horse before."

He led a chestnut mare into the aisle. "Are the groups always this big?"

"It's about normal for early spring. They'll get larger later in the summer. There's only one other riding stable near Watson and their horses are nags. They rent them out for thirty minutes and pretty much just turn the people lose in a big pasture. Our rides are ninety minutes, and we take them to all the scenic spots on the ranch. Word gets around and we generally have more business than we can handle."

"I can see why you need to hire more people. I'm really sorry about the bunkhouse."

Critically, she watched him adjust the saddle as she tightened the girth on another. "Don't worry about it. I'm hoping for at least four local kids. And if it comes down to it I can always put a few college kids up in the cabin for the summer. Why don't you come with me this trip? You must be eager to look the place over."

He hesitated. "Maybe another time. They're installing the hot tub this afternoon and I want to be there."

"A hot tub." She grinned and shook her head in amazement. "The neighbors are going to think we've lost our minds."

"Wait until you try it. You won't care what the neighbors think. Did you get the plans for the new bunkhouse worked out with the contractor?"

"Yes. He'll start next week."

By the time they led the horses outside and draped the reins loosely around a hitching rail, people were starting to arrive. Quinn watched Lanie take the money, his mind doing a rapid calculation. One eyebrow rose as he finished. Even if the groups stayed this size, she'd make enough in four months to support the ranch all year. No wonder she'd never pushed for alimony or child support. Lanie had turned the ranch into a real moneymaking operation. And she'd done it on her own. A sense of pride filled him at her accomplishments.

She waved at him as the group headed out, already giving her guests a brief rundown on the history of Jackson Hole and the McAllister Ranch.

He waited until they were out of sight, then returned to the stable. Duncan was already there.

"Are you sure you want to do this?"

"Yes." Quinn went to the stall of a buckskin gelding and led the horse out. "She's already starting to wonder why I haven't been riding."

"You could tell her the truth."

"No." He settled a saddle blanket and saddle on the horse before glancing at Duncan. "I don't want her pity any more now than I did before."

"She'll have to know sooner or later. You can't hide those scars on your leg forever."

"I know that, Dunc. But I'm hoping by the time she finds out, it won't matter. Besides, I've missed riding." He untied the reins and looped them over the saddle horn. "I'll have to mount from the right. My left leg will never hold my weight. It might make him nervous until he gets used to it, so hold his head."

Duncan got a tight grip on the bridle as Quinn paused by the horse's right side. Curiously, the gelding turned his head as Quinn lifted his right foot to the stirrup, but made no effort to move out of the way.

Gingerly, he swung his bad leg over the horse's rump and lowered himself to the saddle before picking up the reins. "Okay, you can let go."

Duncan released his hold then walked beside him to the stable doors. "Thirty minutes this first time. No more. And stay where I can see you."

"Stop acting like a mother hen."

"Show a little sense and I won't have to," Duncan growled. "Even if nothing were wrong with you, it's been five years since you rode. You're going to be saddlesore at the least, and I don't want you re-injuring that leg."

"Fine. Thirty minutes."

He kept the horse at a walk as they went through the open gate that Lanie had taken a few minutes earlier. His heart pounded so hard it felt like he'd run a marathon. There had been many months after his surgeries when he'd doubted he would ever walk again. Now, he was back on a horse.

Automatically, the buckskin tried to turn in the same direction the riding group had gone, but Quinn held him straight. He didn't want to meet Lanie after telling her he couldn't ride today.

Taking a deep breath and clamping his teeth together, he let out on the reins. The horse trotted a few steps then broke into an easy canter.

Elation burst through him, and he had to stifle his yell of delight. Only a dull burning sensation centered in his thigh, not the sharp pain he'd been expecting. All those hours of physical therapy and exercise were paying off.

Duncan was leaning against the fence when he returned to the stable. He straightened as Quinn came through the gate.

"Well?"

Grinning like an idiot, Quinn slid off the horse. "It was fantastic. Hardly any pain at all."

"Then why are you sweating?"

"It's hot."

"Uh-huh. I think you'd better keep it to thirty minutes for the next week. If you're still doing okay, you can increase it to forty-five."

"Did anyone ever tell you you're too easygoing?"

"No. If memory serves, you usually call me a slave driver."

"And I'm usually right. Let me get the horse back in his stall and we'll go see how they're doing with the hot tub." He glanced at Duncan as they led the gelding back into the stable. "By the way. You have a date with Sherry tomorrow evening."

"The blonde?"

"Yep."

Duncan grinned. "Now I know why I put up with your abuse. It's the perks that come with the job."

Chapter Eleven

A crowd had already gathered at the Spotted Horse by the time they arrived. Lanie caught sight of Duncan and Sherry, saving a table near the dance floor, and wound her way through the mob, Quinn's hand resting lightly on her shoulder as he followed her.

"Did I tell you how great you look tonight?"

His warm breath tickled her ear and chill bumps erupted on her skin. Even with all the other scents in the room, she had no problem picking out his. It surrounded her like a cozy blanket, doing things to her insides she didn't want to think about.

She felt his hand shift, his fingers threading through her hair.

"It's been a long time since I saw your hair loose like this," he murmured.

A shiver ran over her. He'd loved having her hair loose when they made love, said it made her look wild and wanton. Had she subconsciously released it from its normal braid for that reason? Or worn her sexiest dress, a gauzy little number that floated around her and hit her mid-thigh, because she wanted his attention? At this point, she wasn't sure why she was doing anything, and she was tired of worrying about it. Tonight, she only wanted to relax and enjoy herself.

She glanced over her shoulder to meet those amber eyes smiling down at her. "You look pretty good yourself."

That was certainly an understatement. His white cotton shirt emphasized well-defined muscles, muscles that hadn't been quite so prominent when they were younger. But then, he said he worked out a lot. It was obviously paying off. It hadn't escaped her notice that every female in the room watched their progress toward the table.

Nothing new about that, she thought ruefully. Quinn had always attracted women. They were drawn to him to like steel to a magnet. She had to give him credit, though. Never once had he made her jealous. When they were together, he'd acted like she was the only woman in existence, totally ignoring anyone who tried to get his attention away from her. Maybe that was what made him so irresistible, she mused. There was something extraordinary about feeling like you were the center of a man's universe. Especially one who looked like Quinn.

When they reached the table, he pulled a chair out for her, keeping his hand on her arm until she was seated. Eyebrow arched, she smiled at him. "I thought you weren't a gentleman?"

He shrugged lightly as he pulled a chair closer to hers. "Maybe it's time I changed."

From across the table Duncan snorted. "I'll believe that when I see it. We almost decided you'd backed out of coming. What took so long?"

"Zack." Lanie made herself smile at the man. "He blackmailed us into two bedtime stories instead of just one."

"We ordered beers all around," Sherry told her. "Hope that was okay. In this mob, we figured we better get our request in fast."

"That's fine." Quinn almost had to yell to make himself heard above the noise. "I don't remember the Spotted Horse being this busy, even on a weekend."

"Tourists," Sherry explained. She pointed to an overweight man who looked as if he'd stepped off the set of a grade-B western. "You can always tell them from the locals."

A handsome, middle-aged woman stopped at their table and deposited four beers before turning to Quinn with a smile.

"Welcome back. Buck told me you'd been in the other day. Feels like old times."

"Thanks, Ruby. Nice to be here, but don't expect any excitement out of me. I've outgrown my wild ways."

"Well, thank heavens for that. It got tiresome replacing the mirrors behind the bar once a week." She winked before heading to the next table.

"Were you really that bad?" Duncan asked.

"Oh, he was." Lanie grinned at Quinn. "But he always paid more for the repairs than what they cost. It was the only thing that kept him out of jail. It was a running joke around here that he'd pay Buck for damages as soon as he walked in the door."

Quinn's gaze was fastened on hers. "And you'd always patch me up the next morning." He draped an arm over the back of her chair and ran a finger down her cheek.

"Someone had to. Couldn't have you bleeding all over the horses."

"If you two are going to start reminiscing, I'm leaving." Sherry stood and pulled Duncan to his feet. "Come on, city boy. Let's dance."

There was a line dance in progress and Lanie laughed as she watched Duncan's feet get tangled up trying to execute the moves. Sherry put her hands on his hips and slowly led him through the pattern, both of them looking down intently.

"Want to show him how it's done?" She looked questioningly at Quinn, but he shook his head.

"I'd rather wait for a slow song. It's a lot more fun."

"Okay." She let her gaze sweep the crowd, pausing on a woman with black hair who was making her way toward their table. When she reached them, she flopped into a chair and exhaled loudly.

"God. You can't even breathe in here tonight."

Lanie smiled. "Quinn, you remember Sara Carson, don't you?"

"Of course." He shook the woman's hand. "I believe you said she was your lawyer."

"That's right. And if you don't mind, I need to steal Lanie for a second."

"It can't wait until Monday?"

Lanie put her hand on his arm. "It's okay. I'll only be a minute."

He nodded. "Keep your seat. I see Jonesy at the bar. I'll go say hello to him."

When he was out of earshot, Sara leaned forward and propped her elbows on the table. "How's it going?"

"Well, we haven't killed each other yet, and Zack is ecstatic."

"It's you personally I'm worried about. This can't be easy. I keep expecting you to call and tell me you changed your mind, to start filing the papers."

"No, I won't do that." Lanie sighed and started to rub her face before she remembered the light makeup she'd put on. Her hand dropped back to the table. "I've been doing a lot of thinking, Sara. I agreed to this deal, now I have to live up to my end of it. No faking my way through the next three months. I have to try and make this marriage work."

"Have you told Jared?"

"Yes. That part of it anyway."

Sara tilted her head, her gaze going to the far end of the bar. "I guess that explains why he looks like he's one step away from Prozac."

"He's here?" Lanie swiveled in her chair to see better. Jared was sitting on the last seat at the bar, a glass of amber liquor in his hand. He looked tired, she realized. More so than she'd ever seen him, and her stomach twisted with guilt. He was watching her, but making no move to come over. "Oh, God. I've hurt him so badly."

"Lanie, this isn't your fault. You did what you had to do, for you and Zack, both. Jared should understand." She crossed her arms on the table. "What haven't you told him yet?"

Lanie took a deep breath. "That Quinn is right." She glanced up at the lawyer. "Everything happened so fast last time that I never really felt divorced. I think we need these three months."

"So, you've decided to stay with Quinn."

"No." She held up a hand. "Oh, no. I haven't decided anything yet except to wait and see." Her gaze moved to Quinn. He and Jonesy were laughing as they talked. "I'm not sure I can trust him. He left me so easily the first time. What's to say he won't do it again?"

"You still love him, don't you?" Sara was staring at her intently.

"Yes." She blinked back the moisture gathering in her eyes. "I suppose part of me always will. But I love Jared too. I'm so confused, Sara."

Sara reached across the table and covered her hand. "Then you're doing the right thing. It wouldn't be fair to either Quinn or Jared to make a choice until you're sure in your heart it's the right one."

"If I ever am." She made herself smile. "Would you do me a favor? Go talk to Jared. Everyone is avoiding him."

"They don't know what to say. You know how news travels in Watson. There's not a soul in town that doesn't know Quinn is back and plans on staying." She stood. "Don't worry. I'll keep Jared company, let him get good and drunk, and make sure he gets home in one piece. He'll feel better tomorrow."

"Thank you."

"No problem. Call me if you need me, or even if you just want to talk."

"I will."

* * * * *

Jared didn't look up as Sara slid onto the stool beside him. If he did, he'd have to watch McAllister sit back down with Lanie, and he didn't think he could stand watching them together anymore. Not when it felt like someone was ripping his heart out every time they smiled at each other.

God help him if she ever found out the truth about the last four years. Even without McAllister in the picture he'd lose her.

He downed the rest of his drink, pushing the empty glass across the bar for a refill. "Did she send you over here to babysit me?"

"Lanie is worried about you, Jared."

"Yeah, I can tell." He couldn't stop the sarcasm in his words.

"She is."

With a sigh, he ran a hand over his face. "I know. But that doesn't stop it from hurting."

"I'm curious." She turned to face him, tucking her feet under the wooden footrest on the bottom of the stool. "Why didn't you try to convince Lanie to fight him? She might have listened to you, and you wouldn't be going through all this now."

"No, I wouldn't." He stared into his drink. "I guess part of me thought that if she lasted through these months, it would prove once and for all she was over him. I've never been too sure she was, even after she agreed to marry me. And there's also Zack. I couldn't stand it if she fought McAllister because of me and lost her son. She'd grow to hate me if that happened."

"If she really loves you, Jared, there's nothing to worry about. And if she doesn't, it's better to find out now."

"What I advised her to do doesn't really matter, anyway." He shrugged, then took another drink. "Her mind was already made up when she came over that night, even if she didn't realize it. That's another reason I didn't argue. This way, there's still hope. When he leaves her again, I'll be around to pick up the pieces."

"What if he doesn't leave?" she asked quietly.

"He will." His gaze touched Sara then moved beyond her. McAllister had his arm around Lanie, leaning over to whisper something into her ear. "No one changes that much."

Lanie was smiling, but it faded as she looked up and met his gaze. There was so much sadness in her eyes that his breath caught in his chest, his head buzzing from the drinks he'd had.

"I've got to get out of here," he mumbled, tearing his gaze from Lanie's as he lurched to his feet.

"Hang on, there." Sara stood and steadied him. "You're in no shape to drive. I'll give you a lift."

He didn't even argue with her. He only knew he had to leave fast before he did something he'd regret for the rest of his life. Like drag Lanie away from McAllister and make love to her until she couldn't think of anyone but him.

On second thought, that didn't sound like such a bad idea. He knew Lanie. If he'd pushed a little harder to get her into his bed, none of this would be happening.

He took a step in their direction only to come up against Sara's hand on his chest. When he glanced down, she shook her head.

"It will only cause a scene, Jared, and hurt all of you even more. Don't do it."

The tension drained from his body as he stared at her, and finally he nodded. "Let's get the hell out of here before I change my mind."

* * * * *

Quinn leaned over, putting his mouth near Lanie's ear. "Do you want to leave?"

"You knew he was here?" Her gaze was on Harper.

"I saw him when we came in." He put a finger under her chin, turning her head until she was looking at him. "Watson is a small town, Lanie. Even if we try to avoid him when we're together it won't work. He may as well get used to it."

"God, I hate this," she whispered.

An intense stab of jealousy shot through him at the pain in her smoky eyes. Abruptly, he pushed his chair back and stood. "No one forced you to agree to my terms. But based on past performances, I should have known you'd never live up to them." He knew he was overreacting, but he couldn't seem to stop, couldn't lower his voice from a snarl. "He's leaving. If you hurry I'm sure you can catch up with him."

The noise level in the Spotted Horse dropped noticeably as he stalked across the room. He was almost at the door when she caught up with him. Instead of stopping him, she grabbed his arm and dragged him the rest of the way outside.

Hands on her hips, she faced him, her chin a stubborn square in the dim light. "Damn you, Quinn! I *have* been living up to your terms. I even talked myself into believing you were right, that we needed this time. But that doesn't mean I enjoy seeing Jared hurting. You have no right to accuse me of backing out of the deal."

His body relaxed, anger replaced by a strange mixture of remorse and elation. She really planned to try and make the marriage work. It was the first indication she'd given that she wasn't doing this merely to keep him from taking Zack.

From deep inside, hope flowered, tendrils spreading to warm all his extremities. Gently, he reached out and pulled her to him, burying his face in her hair as he wrapped his arms around her.

"You're right," he whispered around the lump in his throat. "I'm sorry I went off the deep end. But I love you, and it makes me a little crazy to see you hurting over another man."

Hesitantly, she slid her arms around his waist and rested her head on his chest. "I know. And I wish there was an easy answer to all this."

"There could be. All you have to do is make it a real marriage."

She tilted her head up and looked at him earnestly. "Quinn, I can't. There are just too many problems right now, things I have to be sure about before I make up my mind."

He started to protest, but she put her fingers against his lips. "No. You say you still love me, but it isn't enough. If we can't learn to trust each other again, this isn't going to work. You said it yourself. Too much has happened in the past. You proved that a few minutes ago."

She paused thoughtfully before speaking again. "These last few days I've been thinking I was the one who had a decision to make, but maybe you do, too. Because if you can't trust me, then you'd only be miserable if we stayed married. You need to think about that, Quinn."

"I don't have to think about it."

Her lips curved in a smile that nearly stopped his heart. "Typical McAllister pigheadedness. At least Zack gets it honestly. But I don't think trust is something you can force."

"Maybe you're right." He skimmed his fingers across her cheek. "Do you think we can start all over and learn it together?"

"We can try."

She leaned more heavily against him and his arms tightened reflexively. He could feel every lush curve, feel her warmth seeping though their clothing, and his body reacted accordingly.

"Want to go somewhere and neck?" His voice was husky in spite of his grin and she laughed.

"Not a chance in hell, McAllister. I know you too well. Besides, you still owe me a dance."

He curbed his disappointment with a dramatic sigh. "I guess that will have to do. For now." But not until he at least got a kiss out of the deal.

Lowering his head, he covered her lips, inhaling sharply when hers parted to allow him access. He kissed her slowly, savoring the caress of tongues, the taste of her mouth under his. The dull ache in the lower part of his body intensified until he groaned with need as she returned the kiss.

When they finally parted, both were breathing rapidly. He brushed her lips one more time before she stepped away from him.

"I think we'd better go back in now." Her voice trembled, seemed to keep time with the shaking of his own limbs.

His smile was rueful when he answered her. "Not for a few more minutes. If I go inside in this condition the gossips are going to have a field day."

Her gaze dropped to the front of his jeans and red flooded her cheeks. Delicately, she cleared her throat. "I don't suppose a few more minutes would hurt."

"Speak for yourself," he growled.

Lanie's laughter was the sweetest sound he'd heard in a long time. This was going to work, he promised silently. Even if it killed him.

Chapter Twelve

Lanie scanned the job application in front of her before glancing up at the young man patiently waiting. She'd already hired five high school kids today, but if only half what he'd listed was true, this guy was too good to pass up. And she needed him. Their first campout would be coming up the last weekend of Frontier Days. Because she kept the group size to ten per employee, they had been limited to fifty people. This year, they could increase that amount by twenty.

"You're looking for a permanent job?"

"Yes, ma'am."

She nodded. "Okay, Cody. You've got it. You'll take your orders from either my foreman or me, but I'm going to put you in charge of the kids I hired today. They start Monday so you can have the rest of the weekend to get settled and look around. Did you bring your things with you?"

"They're out in my truck."

"Good. There's an old cabin about two miles from here where you can stay. It's not fancy, but you'll have it to yourself."

"Sounds fine."

"Why don't we head out to the stable and I'll introduce you to Sherry. She can give you an idea of what you'll be doing and tell you how to get to the cabin."

Leaving his application on the desk, she headed out of the office. "Why did you decide to give up the rodeo circuit?"

He shrugged, twisting the brim of the faded Resistol in his hands. "I never planned on making a career out of it. It was just a way to make money until I finished junior college. I'd rather be working on a ranch."

She saw Quinn as soon as they stepped out the back door. He and Duncan had spent the day unloading equipment and setting it up in her former bunkhouse. Now, he fell into step with them as they walked toward the barn.

"All done?"

"Yes." She gestured to the young man. "Quinn, this is Cody Simmons. I hired him on permanently. Cody, this is my husband, Quinn McAllister."

"Mr. McAllister."

"Cody. Welcome aboard." They shook hands.

Sherry had just finished with her last group for the day, and Lanie gladly turned Cody over to her. She was more tired mentally than physically, but at least the interviews and hiring had kept her mind off Jared.

He looked so tired when he picked Zack up that morning, his eyes red-rimmed and his hair tousled. It looked as though he hadn't had a good night's sleep in days, and the guilt of knowing she was the reason ate at her.

Earlier, all his attention had been focused on Zack. He'd barely spoken two words to her, and ignored Quinn completely. It was a miracle Zack hadn't noticed the tension thickening the air, but he'd been too excited.

Her brow lowered at the thought of going through that again when he brought Zack home. Maybe she should find a way to talk to Jared alone.

"What's the frown for?"

"Nothing. Just been a busy day." She checked her watch. Jared had promised to have Zack home in time for supper, so they should be back soon.

Quinn reached over and brushed back a lock of hair that had escaped from her braid. "A day that didn't start out too great, at that. Worrying about it won't help, you know."

"Can you read my mind, now?"

"I don't have to. It's all over your face." He smiled as he traced the spot between her eyes with his thumb, smoothing out the frown line. "Lanie, last night was great. You don't have to feel guilty for enjoying yourself. If he can't handle it, it's his problem."

"Can't you put yourself in his place, Quinn, try to understand what he's feeling?"

"No," he said quietly. "Because if I were in his place I'd have convinced you to marry me years ago. No other man would get anywhere near you."

Her gaze shifted to the back of the stable where Sherry was showing Cody the door leading to Gator's pasture. "I know. But you and Jared are two different people." Her eyes met his. "Would you mind if I talked to him alone for a few minutes when they get here?"

"Why? There's only one thing you can say that will make him feel better."

She saw his jaw clench as she hesitated, but it relaxed when she slowly shook her head. "I can't tell him what he wants to hear any more than I could tell you last night. But I'd still like to talk to him."

"If that's what you want, I won't stop you."

"Thanks."

They both turned at the sound of Jared's truck on the drive. He pulled to a stop in front of the stable, stepping out before lifting Zack to the ground. The little boy ran across the space between them, practically climbing Quinn's leg in his excitement.

"Dad! Guess what? Mr. Robinson's mule got caught in a barbed wire fence and when he tried to get it loose it almost bit him and he said 'Damnitall' real loud." The words tumbled out so fast they ran together.

Quinn laughed. "Did you get him all fixed up?"

"Yep. Jared wouldn't let me get in the stall 'cause the mule was too mean, but I got to hand him stuff." He shifted his attention to Lanie. "Can I go see the puppies now?"

"Sure." She smiled at her son. He looked so cute in his red, western-style shirt and jeans. "But don't bother Sherry. She's busy right now. And don't go anywhere else. Just stay with the pups, okay?"

"Okay." He darted inside the stable, already calling the puppies.

When she glanced back at Jared, he was standing in the same spot, his gaze fixed on her. She tried to make her smile reassuring. "Do you have time to check Kadia for me? I think she's fine, but I'd rather be safe."

He shot Quinn a fast look before answering. "Probably a good idea."

"They're still in the brood mare barn." When she turned in that direction, he followed her.

* * * * *

Quinn watched them go, trying to stifle the tension that filled him. He hated seeing them together, hated the jealousy that burned inside his stomach every time he thought about Harper touching her. Why couldn't Lanie see that what she felt for the man stemmed from obligation and guilt when it was so clear to him?

The couple had almost reached the brood mare barn when hysterical barking impinged on Quinn's attention. Annoyed, he glanced into the corral, and abruptly, his blood turned to ice.

Zack was standing frozen twenty feet from the stable door, a pup clutched tightly in his arms. Facing him was two thousand pounds of enraged bull. The only thing keeping the animal from charging was the small mother dog between them. Barking furiously, she nipped the bull's nose, but Quinn knew it was only a matter of seconds before Gator ran her over.

"Zack!" His son's name ripped out of him. Heart in his throat, Quinn ignored the white-hot stab of pain in his thigh as he vaulted the fence. Lanie's terrified scream followed him as he raced across the pasture, praying harder than he'd ever prayed in his life.

Too far. Oh, God, it was too far. He'd never reach him in time. Even as he put on an adrenaline-enhanced burst of speed, the bull lowered his head. A bellow blistered the air as the animal shook its wicked horns, its beady eyes fixed on Zack. Flicking the dog away as though it were nothing more than a pesky fly, the bull charged.

Time slowed to a crawl as he sprinted toward his son, fear lending him strength in spite of the odds. The bull had only half the distance to cover that Quinn had.

Suddenly, a blur of movement flashed between Zack and the bull. Yells rent the corral as Cody Simmons, the young man Lanie had just hired, waved his arms and diverted Gator's attention.

The bull slowed, his head swinging from Cody to Zack, but it was all the time Quinn needed. Blood thundered in his ears, drowning all the other noise as he scooped Zack off the ground. Without stopping, he cut sharply left and dived through the stable door, rolling to protect Zack with his own body.

They had barely quit moving when Cody pounded through the door behind them, executing the same dive Quinn had, landing only an inch away before lunging to his knees to slam the door shut. A loud crash shook the building as the bull rammed it, his frustrated roars ringing off the walls.

Pushing himself into a sitting position, Quinn frantically ran his hands over Zack. "Are you okay?"

The little boy was crying, but he'd maintained his death grip on the pup. "I was scared." He sniffed. "Gator was going to hurt Spot."

Moisture filling his own eyes, Quinn wrapped his arms around Zack, rocking him gently. "I know," he soothed. "It's okay."

Cody stood and was dusting himself off when Lanie reached them, followed by Jared, Duncan and Sherry. She pushed the younger man aside in her efforts to get to Zack. Tears streaked down her cheeks as she lifted him from Quinn's arms.

"Oh, God, oh, God," she chanted, but her words faded into a buzzing drone as blackness threatened the edges of Quinn's vision. Pain screamed from his abused thigh, and he clenched his jaw against the nausea boiling up in his stomach, refusing to give in to it. He had to get on his feet while everyone's attention was on Zack.

Sweat darkened his shirt and dripped from his forehead as he struggled to rise. His left leg was useless, refusing to bear his weight, the pain blinding when he even tried.

Duncan appeared beside him, his face lined with anxiety. "We've got to get you to a doctor."

"No." Quinn's teeth ground together with effort. "Just help me up."

Cursing under his breath, Duncan moved to Quinn's left side. "Let me do all the work. You hang on and balance yourself with your other leg."

Once he was erect, Quinn released Duncan, swaying until he managed to lean weakly against the wall. He checked the group around Zack to make sure no one had noticed and met a pair of dark brown eyes watching him. Cody was frowning, but he kept his mouth shut, and that was all Quinn cared about at the moment. His gaze found Lanie and Zack, and he forced himself to focus on her words instead of the pain. Jared was trying to calm her, but to no avail.

"I said kill him. If you won't, I'll go get the gun and do it myself." Her glare could have formed ice crystals on the stalls.

"Lanie, he's a bull. He was only doing what instinct told him to do. Why don't you sell him to one of the rodeos?"

"And let him maim someone else, or even worse? No." She shook her head violently. "I should have done this weeks ago. I'm taking Zack in the house. When I get him settled down, I want to know exactly how something like this could happen."

She marched out of the barn still holding Zack in her arms, and everyone but Duncan and Cody followed her.

Cody took a step closer. "Hey, man. You okay?"

"I'm fine." The blackness was closing in again and he was desperately afraid he would pass out.

"No, he's not." Duncan contradicted him. "Can you help me get him to the house and upstairs?"

"No problem."

They stood on each side of him and wrapped one of his arms around their shoulders. "Front door," he gritted. If he had to be carried like an invalid, he damn well didn't want Lanie or Harper to see it.

They had made it to the stable door when Sherry returned. Her eyes widened in shock as she took in Quinn's appearance and her mouth opened. It closed again when Duncan shook his head. "Not a word. Can you go hold the front door for us?"

The trip across the yard and up the stairs seemed to last a lifetime to Quinn. Every movement sent a new wave of torment over him.

Sherry left them at the bedroom and Quinn closed his eyes in relief as they lowered him to the bed.

"Let's get these clothes off so I can check the damage."

Quinn opened his eyes to gaze at Duncan. "I suppose you're going to tell me what an idiot I am."

His friend pried a boot off before answering. "No. You didn't have a choice, and in your place, I'd have done the same thing."

Quinn shifted his head so he could see Cody. "Thank you. If you hadn't distracted that bull, Zack would be dead."

The sandy-haired man shrugged. "When you ride the critters as much as I have, dealing with them gets to be second nature."

"Regardless, you've got a job for life."

Cody grinned. "Thanks, but I'm kind of hoping to own a ranch like this one someday. Until then, I'm all yours."

Duncan had finally gotten Quinn's pants off and was making disgusted noises as he examined his thigh. "Damn it, you need to see a doctor. There's no way to tell how much damage you've done without X-rays. It's already swelling, red as blood, and the muscles are a solid knot."

"No doctor." He grimaced as Duncan continued to prod. "You can handle it."

"That's some scar," Cody commented. "Car accident?"

"Yeah. But do me a favor and don't mention this to anyone. Not even my wife."

"You got it." He settled his Resistol on his head. "Need me to do anything else?"

"No." Duncan answered, his attention still on Quinn's leg. "I'll take it from here."

"Guess I'll go see if they need help getting rid of that bull, then." He closed the door quietly behind him.

Duncan moved to the dresser and fished until he found two bottles in the top drawer. "Extra strength painreliever and two muscle relaxers," he commented, dropping the pills into Quinn's hand. "Best we can do since you won't see the doctor. I'll go get you some water, and a bag of ice for your leg."

"Dunc?" He swallowed the pills dry, unable to wait for the small relief they offered. "Make sure Lanie isn't in the kitchen first. And check on Zack for me."

Anger flashed across Duncan's face. "To hell with your wife. I'm not letting you lose that leg when we've worked so hard to save it. She can just wonder." The sound of the door closing was a lot louder than it had been when Cody left.

*****

"Eat your supper, sweetie. Spot doesn't like green beans." Lanie had been trying to coax Zack into putting the pup down since they'd returned to the house, but he wasn't buying it. The little scamp knew she could refuse him nothing right now. Every time she thought about that bull bearing down on him, her knees went weak and she had to sit.

"Can Spot sleep with me tonight?"

"Daisy will miss him if we don't take him back to the stable soon. You wouldn't want her to be sad, would you?" Jared had checked the dog after disposing of Gator, and luckily she'd only been knocked out.

"I guess not." Zack didn't look too convinced.

"Besides," she plucked a piece of straw from his hair. "You have to take a bath, and Spot would be lonesome all by himself."

He sighed. "Okay. Can I take him back?"

"No. Sherry can do it for you." She picked up the pup and handed it to her foreman.

The blonde was still visibly upset, blaming herself for not checking the door leading to the corral better. "It wasn't your fault," Lanie assured her again. "You had no way of knowing those weeds were caught in the threshold. It could have been me as easily as you."

"But it wasn't. I should have checked." She cuddled the pup closer.

Lanie put a hand on her arm. "Go home and get some rest. You'll feel better tomorrow."

Sherry nodded. She was going out the back door when Duncan entered the kitchen from the front of the house. Lanie's glance moved past him, then back to his face.

"Where's Quinn?" For the first time, she realized how odd it was that he hadn't followed them to the house.

"Upstairs." Duncan's reply was short and sharp.

Lanie hesitated. "Well, tell him supper is getting cold."

"He's not hungry."

Ignoring her, he moved to the freezer and filled a plastic bag with ice, twisting the top into a knot to hold the contents.

"Is he okay?" A flutter of anxiety curled in her stomach.

"He's just dandy." This time he snarled at her.

Eyes narrowed, she watched his stiff back retreat toward the stairs.

"Mom, why is Duncan mad at you?"

She ruffled Zack's hair. "I don't know, sweetie. Maybe he's still upset because you and your dad almost got hurt. All done eating?"

Zack nodded and she stood and held out her hand. "Then let's get you in the tub."

A low murmur of voices came from Quinn's room when they went by, and she frowned. Something was going on, and as soon as she got Zack settled, she was damn well going to find out exactly what.

Chapter Thirteen

Lanie waited a few seconds after Zack's eyes drifted shut, then closed the book she'd been reading to him. The more she thought about Quinn's failure to check on his son, the more concerned she became.

Standing, she brushed back the hair so like his father's, and dropped a kiss on Zack's forehead. He was going to be a handsome man when he was grown, just like Quinn. Tall, and strong and gorgeous. It made her heart ache a little to think of losing him to some woman, but she supposed all mothers felt that way. At least, thanks to Quinn and Cody, he'd have the chance to grow up. She'd already thanked Cody. Now it was time to see Quinn.

"Night, sweetie," she whispered, pulling the blanket around Zack's shoulders. "Love you." Flipping off the light, she headed down the hall.

The voices from Quinn's room had stopped, but there was a soft swish of movement from inside. She straightened her back and knocked firmly.

The sounds ceased. Abruptly, the door swung inward, Duncan blocking the opening with his body as he gazed stoically at her.

Lanie blinked. What was he still doing in there? She'd assumed Quinn would be alone. Her brow furrowed as she returned his stare, a kernel of anger growing in her stomach. She'd had about enough of this man's rudeness.

"I want to see Quinn."

Duncan's expression didn't change. "He's busy." With one hand he started to shut the door in her face.

Her anger exploded with volcanic force. Placing both hands on the door, she shoved with all her strength. The move caught Duncan off guard, and as he staggered back, Lanie pushed by him into the room.

"Too bad," she snarled. "This is still my house and he's still my husband. If you have a problem with that, you're welcome to pack your bags and leave."

He shrugged. "Suit yourself."

"I will." She turned to face the room. "Quinn?"

Her eyes widened in shock as she located him. "Oh, my God."

He was lying on his back, the blankets pushed aside to bare his left leg. Eyes closed, his skin was a pasty white, beads of sweat glistening in the light.

"What happened?" Her voice came out a whisper as she moved to the side of the bed. "Is he going to be okay?"

Duncan followed her. Reaching down, he removed the towel-wrapped bag of ice on Quinn's leg, exposing the horrible scars. Slowly, she sank to the bed, her gaze glued to the swollen flesh. Images tumbled through her mind. Quinn's odd gait the day they'd had the picnic. His refusal to go riding with her. Last night, only dancing to the slow songs.

Duncan replaced the ice before he answered her. "At best, he's undone all the hard work we've put in since his last surgery. Even worse, he may have torn the muscles."

"Have you called the doctor?"

"No."

"Why not?" She glared at Duncan, her anger building again.

"Because I wouldn't let him." The mumbled words came from the bed. Quinn's eyes were open a mere slit. "Didn't want you feeling sorry for me."

Her breath caught on a sob. "You're an idiot, McAllister. Don't you know I could never feel sorry for someone as hardheaded as you? You should have told me." She brushed his hair back, much as she'd done with Zack earlier.

"Couldn't." With a sigh, his lids dropped.

"It's the muscle relaxers," Duncan commented. "Normally, they pretty much knock him out, but the pain is keeping him from sleeping soundly this time. You don't have to stay. I can handle it." Moving to the other side of the bed, he lowered himself to a chair.

Anger forgotten, Lanie watched him curiously. "Are you some kind of nurse? Is that why you go everywhere with him?"

Duncan tore his gaze away from Quinn and glanced at her. "I'm a physical therapist."

She shifted, trying to find a more comfortable position without disturbing Quinn, and wound up sitting on the floor. She took Quinn's hand in hers and felt his fingers tighten. He wasn't totally awake, but he wasn't unconscious either.

"You hate me, don't you?" She faced Duncan with the question, keeping her voice low.

He hesitated only a second. "Let's just say that if I'd known he was going to do this trial marriage thing, I'd have done everything in my power to stop him."

"Why?"

"Why?" He spit the word, leaning forward in his chair. "Because I was there from the beginning, from the time they brought him into the emergency room, barely alive. I saw what you did to him, and I'll be damned if I let you do it again."

Lanie stopped breathing for a second. Was it possible she'd finally found someone who would tell her the truth about the accident? Duncan didn't like her, but he had no reason to lie.

"Tell me," she said. "What did I do to him?"

He hesitated again, and she continued desperately. "He's sent for his medical records, so I'll know soon whether you tell me or not."

His gaze sharpened. "Why did he send for his records?"

"Because I asked him to. I want to know the truth."

"Are you telling me you didn't know about the accident?" His lip curled in a sneer.

"I only knew what Edward told me. That Quinn had a minor accident. A cut on his head, a broken leg. He said he'd already been released from the hospital."

Duncan went still. "When did he tell you that?"

"About two weeks after Quinn left. I know now he lied to me. The other day, Quinn said something about a coma. Please, Duncan. Hate me if you want to, but I need to know what really happened."

He leaned back in the chair, his gaze on Quinn again. "Maybe you do." A sigh lifted his chest. "I'd worked late that night. I stopped in the ER on my way out to talk to a friend. That's where I was when they brought Quinn in. The accident occurred on the state line between Nebraska and Iowa. Lincoln was the nearest big city so they air-lifted him there. But Edward wanted him in Chicago. As soon as he was stable, they flew him in to Northwest Hospital."

Lifting a hand, he rubbed his eyes. "His heart stopped twice on the way. The second time, they almost didn't bring him back. He was in a coma from the head injury and his thigh had been crushed, almost torn off. The doctors in Chicago wanted to amputate. They thought the trauma was weakening his condition, and Edward wasn't making any attempt to talk them out of it. But by then, I'd seen the CT scans and X-rays of his leg. I knew that with half a chance I could help. It took a while, but I finally convinced the doctors to let me try."

"Why?" Lanie fought the tears that were threatening to spill over. "What made you fight for him? Most people wouldn't have."

He shook his head. "Edward. I knew someone like him once. A man who let someone I loved die for his own selfish reasons. I couldn't stand there and let them mutilate Quinn just because Edward didn't seem to care."

"Knowing Edward, he probably didn't," she said softly. "What better way to have complete control over his son than by making him an invalid?"

"Yeah, that's the impression I got."

"How long was he in the coma?"

"Two months. As soon as his leg was healed enough from the first surgery, I started working with him, keeping blood flowing to the muscles so they wouldn't atrophy. By the time he woke up, I felt like I knew him."

His heated brown gaze pinned hers. "The first word out of his mouth was your name. He could barely talk, but he kept asking for you. He was so sure you were there, that everyone was keeping you away from him. Until Edward showed up and told him you really weren't there, that you'd filed for divorce. It damn near killed him. He wouldn't talk to anyone, wouldn't eat. He just lay there and stared at the ceiling."

She lost her battle with the tears. They streamed down her cheeks, her body shaking at the force of the silent sobs. God, to know how betrayed he must have felt, how hurt. No wonder he'd hated her, could no longer trust her. She'd failed him when he needed her most.

A hand brushed the moisture from her face. "Don't." Quinn's voice still sounded drugged but his eyes were open. "Not your fault. I know that now."

"It was my fault." She gripped his wrist, pressing the palm of his hand to her cheek. "I should have realized Edward was lying about the divorce. I should have checked for myself. If I'd known what he was doing, I would have fought him, Quinn. Nothing could have kept me away from that hospital."

"Ssh. I know."

Duncan was frowning. "What do you mean, he lied about the divorce?"

Lanie kept her gaze on Quinn's. "I didn't file for a divorce, Duncan. Edward told me Quinn had. He lied to both of us. We found out the day you got here. That's why Quinn insisted on this trial marriage."

"Is she telling the truth?"

Quinn's eyes were closing again. "Yes. Was gonna tell you. Never seemed to be the right time."

Silence fell for a few minutes until Duncan broke it. "Guess I owe you an apology."

"No." She wiped her eyes. "You were only trying to protect him. In a way, you were as much Edward's victim as Quinn and I. If you hadn't been there for him all these years…" She choked on another sob. "I'll always be grateful he had you."

Duncan cleared his throat. "I'm going to get more ice. Can you stay with him until I get back?"

She nodded, understanding what he'd offered her. His trust, his approval. Holding back tears again, she smiled at him. "Just try and get rid of me."

* * * * *

Lanie woke instantly at the slight movement from the bed and lifted her head from the mattress to meet Quinn's amber gaze. "You're awake."

"Looks that way." He smiled at her. "Why are you sitting on the floor?"

She stretched, her bones popping with the action. "So I'd know if you woke up. How do you feel?"

His eyes unfocused for a second before clearing. "Better, I think. The worst of the pain is gone. It only aches now. Where's Duncan?"

"In bed. He said if you needed anything to wake him. Do you want me to get him?"

"No, let him sleep." He ran a hand down her arm, then abruptly flipped the blankets back. "Come on. You're freezing and you can't be comfortable down there."

A tingle shot through her. The thought of crawling into bed with him had her heart pounding against her ribs. She hesitated. After everything that had happened today, her emotions were in a state of turmoil. She wasn't sure she could resist him right now. If she were going to be honest, she wasn't even sure she wanted to.

"Quinn, I don't think that's a very good idea."

His gaze softened as he studied her face. "As much as I'd like to make love to you, Angel," he murmured, "I think you're safe for now. I'm in no shape to jump you, and you can't spend the night sitting on the floor."

She *was* cold and uncomfortable. A few more hours like this and she'd be too stiff to move. The bed was starting to look really good, and he was right. He was in no shape to seduce her.

Shifting a little, she put her hands behind her to brace as she toed her boots off, then stood and slid carefully under the blankets, trying not to jar the bed. Quinn moved his arm under her head and pulled her closer to his warmth. His other hand pulled the blanket up to cover her shoulders.

"That's better," he said. "I think one of the things I've missed most was sleeping with you. You never realize how big a bed can be until you're in it alone."

"I know. There were so many times after you left that I'd reach for you before I woke up enough to remember you weren't there."

Gently, he stroked her hair. "I'm sorry, Lanie. So sorry about so many things. When we got married I promised you I'd stay here, that I wouldn't go back to Chicago. But I let Edward get to me. I should have known better."

She flattened her hand over his heart, feeling the strong comforting beat. "He's your father."

"And you're my wife. Somewhere along the line I forgot that was supposed to be more important." He hesitated, then touched her forehead with his lips. "I'd spent my whole life trying to make him proud of me, to make him love me. Until you, it was all I ever wanted. When he started calling every day, telling me how much he needed me, how much the company needed me—well, I went a little nuts. He even had me believing that if you really cared about me, you wouldn't ask me to stay in Wyoming."

"And what about now?" She slid her hand up to curl around his nape, her fingers tangling in his dark hair as she lifted her face to see him better. "He's not going to leave you alone, Quinn. I'm surprised he hasn't called yet. How do I know you won't go running back the second he does?"

"I won't." His jaw clenched. "But I don't how to prove it to you. I guess you'll have to wait and see." He traced her lips with a finger, his gaze fixed on her mouth. "I love you. There's only one thing that can make me leave you again, and that's you."

His words, his touch, the warmth from his hard, muscular body, all combined with her inner confusion and stress from the near accident with Zack. Explosions of heat were detonating in the secret places of her body. Places he'd once known so well that the lightest caress could send her plunging into the whirling waters of ecstasy. Even while she knew she shouldn't, a small groan escaped her throat and she pulled his mouth to hers.

He tried to keep the kiss slow, but she wouldn't allow it. Desperately, she arched against him as she deepened the kiss. All rational thought vanished when his tongue touched hers. This was Quinn, the man she'd loved since she was a little girl. The man who'd always been able to set her body aching with desire by merely walking into the room. His taste was familiar and exotic at the same time, and it had been so long. She needed... Oh, God, how she needed.

Without quite knowing how it happened, her T-shirt was gone. Quinn's breath came in harsh gasps, a match for her own as his hand covered her breast, his thumb rasping over the nipple. She stifled a whimper as sensation streaked downward from the caress.

She shouldn't be doing this. There was a reason why, but it eluded her as his mouth traveled down her neck, his lips closing on a breast. Her hands were everywhere, delighting in the feel of his tight muscles, and flat stomach. His breath sucked in sharply when she moved lower, and his skin quivered as she reached her goal, pulling a groan from deep inside him.

His hands were shaking when he fumbled with the button on her jeans and pushed them down her hips, taking her panties with them. She wiggled slightly to get them the rest of the way off, pushing them aside with her foot.

It was her turn to shake when his fingers found her, parted her to allow him access. His mouth covered hers to capture her cry as he set her ablaze.

"Sweet Angel," he breathed. "I need you so much."

The heat in his voice was tinged with pain, and she suddenly remembered part of what had bothered her before. "Your leg."

"Forget my leg." He bit down gently on her bottom lip, then kissed her again, his fingers still driving her mad.

It took all her willpower to pull away from him, but she managed it long enough to push him onto his back. Before he had time to protest, she swung her leg over him and sat up.

Holding her breath, she closed her eyes and eased down his length. Quinn surged to meet her, his hands clamped around her hips. As she moved, the hot scent of desire assailed her and her head dropped back.

It had been so long, too long since she'd let herself feel these emotions. Now they took control, the blaze he'd started raging into an inferno that consumed her. Body burning, she danced higher and higher, like a spark caught in the winds from a bonfire.

Quinn's hands caught her, pulled her down to his chest and she opened her eyes to see the flames reflected in his.

"I love you, Lanie," he whispered, his voice hoarse.

Her mouth found his, kissing him frantically. The touch of his tongue on hers was more than she could stand. Pressure that had built with each contact shattered, her climax swamping her senses until she was barely aware of Quinn's cry as he joined her.

She didn't know how long it lasted. It felt like hours. Prisms of light shimmered behind her eyelids before she began to descend from the place they'd gone together. Exhausted, she went limp, her body humming from the rapture it had experienced.

But even as she drifted into sleep with Quinn's arms wrapped securely around her, a niggling question rose uneasily in her mind. Oh, God. What had she done?

Chapter Fourteen

The sound of someone moving around the room woke Quinn. Tentatively, he stretched. In spite of his leg, he felt good. Real good. Had he dreamed what happened last night, or had it been real? A smile curved his lips. That was no dream. He might not have been in any shape to seduce her, but she'd taken matters into her own hands. Lanie had made love to him.

"It's about time."

His eyes popped open at Duncan's words and his smile faded. A frown took its place as another memory returned. "You ratted me out to Lanie last night. Remind me to cut your salary."

Duncan grinned, his eyes sparking with amusement. "Unless you've had a few women stashed out of sight in the last five years, I think I deserve a raise."

Quinn's frown deepened. "What are you talking about?"

A pair of pink panties sailed through the air to land on his stomach. He stared at them a second before grabbing the silky material and shoving it under the blankets. "Damn. Was she still here when you came in?"

"Nope."

Quinn groaned. "That means she left so fast she missed part of her clothes. I have to get dressed and find her."

Duncan was around the bed in a flash, pushing him back down. "Oh, no you don't. I'll admit, it doesn't look like you did as much damage as I thought, but there's still some swelling. You need to stay off the leg for at least another day. We can do some massages and stretching to help the soreness."

"Dunc, I have to talk to her before she does something stupid, and I can promise you, she's not going to set foot near this room."

"Stupid like what?" He examined Quinn's thigh.

"Stupid, like call Harper and confess. I'd take bets that right now she's hiding somewhere, letting guilt eat her alive."

"Maybe you should let her call him." Snagging a bottle of liniment, he poured some on Quinn's leg and dug in with his fingers. "If Harper's any kind of man, he'll step out of the picture."

"That's just it. He doesn't deserve to find out that way. No one would. And if Lanie stays with me it has to be because she really wants to, not because Harper dumped her."

"It almost sounds like you feel sorry for the guy."

He winced as Duncan's fingers hit a particularly sore spot. "I guess I do, in a way. I know Lanie better than anyone else alive, and deep down inside she understands she doesn't love him. If she did, last night would never have happened. Her head just needs time to catch up with her heart. But Harper loves her, and I know what it's like to feel that way about someone who doesn't love you back."

Duncan sighed, then wiped the excess liniment off with a towel. "Fine. I'll get your clothes and we'll see if you can walk, but only if you promise me you'll hit the hot tub later today."

"I promise."

* * * * *

She was insane, a full-blown idiot. Lanie berated herself for the hundredth time since she'd snuck out of Quinn's room in a panic before dawn. The roan mare she was brushing turned to look at her questioningly as dust flew into the air.

"Sorry," she mumbled an apology to the horse and slowed her strokes. A quick check on Zack showed her he was still busy grooming his pony and hadn't heard her. All four pups romped around his feet while Daisy kept an eye on her brood from a short distance away.

God, she felt so guilty. Not only had she betrayed Jared, Quinn probably thought she'd decided to make this trial marriage a real one. And she couldn't even blame him. He hadn't forced her. She closed her eyes and leaned her forehead against the mare's neck, inhaling the comforting smell of horse.

Forced her? If anything, she'd forced him. Her cheeks flamed at the memory. He'd tried to slow her down to no avail. So what if her body felt more relaxed than it had in months, years even? Her mind was churning like a banana in a blender.

How could she ever face Jared again? One look at her and he'd know. Maybe she should simply find him and confess. After all, there could be consequences to what she'd done that wouldn't be apparent for months yet.

She lifted her head and took a deep breath. Why had she been so stupid as to have unprotected sex with Quinn? She knew better. A rapid calculation of the math involved had shown her she could be in big trouble.

The image of a little girl popped into her head. One with black hair and Quinn's eyes. Angrily, she shook away both the picture and the longing that filled her. One time didn't mean she'd get pregnant. It had taken months before she got that way with Zack. And there wasn't going to be another time. She'd make sure of that. Somehow.

She also wasn't going to mention the possibility of a surprise pregnancy to Quinn. Not unless she was sure her fears had come to pass. What she'd done last night had caused enough problems between them without adding more to the list.

"Dad!"

At Zack's delighted yell, the brush flew out of her hand and her gaze darted frantically to the stable doors. Abruptly, her heart was lodged in her throat, and she had to quell the urge to run.

Quinn was standing in the sunlight, dust motes glittering around him, one hand braced on the doorframe. He was dressed in black jeans and a white T-shirt that hugged his body lovingly. His hair was tousled, tumbling down onto his forehead, the white streak standing out starkly from the surrounding darkness.

His gaze was locked on her even as he caught Zack and swung him into his arms. "Hey there, champ. How ya' doin' this morning?"

"Okay. Mom is going riding with me."

"Is that right?" He hugged Zack before putting him down. "Guess you need to finish getting your horse ready."

He grimaced as he straightened, watching Zack run back to his pony, and for the first time she realized his face was pale, covered in a light sheen of sweat. Instantly, concern overpowered her other emotions and she hurried to his side.

"What are you doing out here? You should still be in bed."

"I wanted to talk to you." His grin looked labored as he released the frame and draped an arm over her shoulder for support. "Don't worry. The stairs were the hardest part."

"You could have sent Duncan to find me."

"Would you have come?" He arched a brow in question.

Heat flushed her cheeks. "I've been really busy this morning, and it's Martha's day off."

"That's what I figured." Reaching into his pocket, he pulled out a scrap of pink silk and offered it to her. "You left in such a hurry you forgot these."

She'd only *thought* her cheeks were hot before. Now they had to be three shades darker than the panties. Hastily, she snatched them and crammed the garment in her own pocket. There was a bench inside the door and she ducked her head as she led him to it.

"Sit with me." He patted the wood beside him.

"I really should get the horse ready. I promised Zack—"

"Lanie, you can't pretend we didn't make love last night."

It had been too much to hope he would let this slide. Weakly, she sank down next to him, trying desperately to gather her thoughts. "I'm not, but it shouldn't have happened. I don't blame you," she hurried to assure him. "It was my fault. I've been under so much stress lately—we both have—and what with Zack almost getting seriously hurt yesterday, and finding out what you went through after the accident, it was too much." She realized she was running her words together the way Zack did when he was excited, and took a deep breath. "That's why it happened."

He lifted his hand and curved it around her nape, forcing her to look at him. "Don't," he said gently. His other hand brushed her hair back. "Don't lie to yourself, Lanie, or to me. It's always been like that between us, like a match to dry grass, and it always will be. Last night was too wonderful to turn it into something bad, or to feel guilty about. We didn't do anything wrong."

"I did." She swiped at her eyes. "I promised Jared I wouldn't sleep with you, and I broke that promise. But it's more than that. How am I supposed to make a rational decision if I keep doing things like this? It's not fair to any of us."

"Damn." The curse was soft as he pulled her head to his chest. "You should never have made that kind of promise, Angel. We're still married, no matter how it occurred. What we do together is none of Harper's business."

"But it is." She tried not to let herself wallow in the comfort of his arms, tried not to remember he'd been her best friend long before he was her lover. "This will kill him, Quinn. He loves and trusts me."

"Then don't tell him."

"I won't have to," she whispered. "He'll know."

"Not unless you tell him. He might suspect, but he can't know for sure. Don't do that to him, sweetheart."

"It's so dishonest. And what if—" She bit her tongue to stop the words. He knew her too well, though.

"What if you're pregnant?"

With a sigh, she lifted her head to stare at him. "You thought about it?"

"Of course. I was pretty sure you weren't on the Pill." His eyes narrowed suddenly and his body tensed. "You weren't going to bring it up, were you?"

"Not unless I was sure. But I would have told you if it turns out I really am, Quinn. I never intended to keep Zack from you."

He glanced at his son before his body relaxed again. "Sorry. I know you didn't." His thumb traced her jaw as he gazed down at her. "Would having another baby be so bad?"

She hesitated before answering him, but she had to be honest. "Under the circumstances, it could be. I went through it alone the first time. I don't think I could stand doing that again."

"You won't have to, Lanie. When will you know for sure?"

"In a few weeks." Her lips curved in a wavering smile. "My timing really sucked."

A laugh shook him, and before she could brace herself, he kissed her. It was an easy kiss, but it still sent sparks shooting up her spine.

"I think your timing was great." He grinned at her. "And I wouldn't mind a bit having another one. Maybe a girl this time." His smile faded. "I missed so much with Zack. Missed seeing you get big as a house, missed feeling him move inside you. I'd like a chance to do all that now."

"Quinn, I doubt I'm pregnant, and last night can't happen again."

He sighed. "Not unless you're sure you can trust me, you mean. Just tell me one thing. Is there a chance for us at all, Lanie? Do you still care about me?"

"There's a chance," she murmured. "As for still caring about you, of course I do. You're Zack's father. But there's Jared, too." She rubbed her forehead. "Sometimes I feel like I'm going crazy."

"You're not crazy, just confused. Give it time and stop worrying so much. This will work itself out."

"Have you been talking to Sherry?" She smiled at him. "She told me almost the same thing."

"I knew she was smart." He pushed himself to his feet. "Guess I'd better head back and let you two get on with your ride."

Anxiously, she stood with him. "Shouldn't I help you? And you probably haven't had breakfast yet."

Slowly, he leaned down and gave her a long kiss. "Stop worrying," he commanded. "I made it out here, I can make it back. And Duncan does a pretty mean omelet. Besides, I promised him I'd spend some time in the hot tub."

She nodded. "Okay. We won't be gone long. I plan on riding out to the cabin to make sure Cody is settled, and then we'll head back."

Her heart clenched as she watched him limp slowly and painfully toward the house. If only she could be sure he'd stay. But even without Edward in the picture, there was that damn company. Five years ago she'd known he would never give it up, hadn't really wanted him to. It was as much a part of Quinn as his arm. All she'd wanted was some kind of compromise. With today's technology, was it so far-fetched to think he could run McAllister Pharmaceuticals from here, with only an occasional trip to Chicago?

She sighed. He'd brushed aside her suggestions then, and she couldn't bring herself to believe things would be any different now. Sooner or later the company would call him back.

"Mom?"

She glanced at Zack then hurried to help him lift the child's saddle onto the pony's back, pushing her troubled thoughts aside. This was her special time with Zack, something they did every Sunday, and she wasn't going to let anything interfere.

* * * * *

Quinn stopped inside the kitchen door and leaned heavily against the wall, taking deep breaths. Knowing Lanie was watching him had been the only thing that kept him moving across the yard.

"I hope it was worth it." Duncan poured another cup of coffee and set it on the table. "Because you look like death warmed over."

"It was." He grinned in spite of the pain radiating from his thigh. "She finally admitted she still cares about me."

Duncan snorted. "Can you make it to the table?"

Quinn straightened. "She doesn't love Harper," he insisted stubbornly. "She just needs time to realize it."

Beside him, the phone rang and he lifted it from the hook. "Hello?"

"Heard you nearly got yourself killed yesterday. You ready to give it up and come back where you belong?"

He stiffened at the familiar raspy voice, the pain in his leg suddenly forgotten. "It's not going to work this time, Edward. I said all I had to say before I left."

"I know what you're doing." Edward's voice was curt. "Do you really think the board is going to put up with a four-year-old boy owning controlling interest in the company?"

"They don't have much choice, do they? And since I'll be voting his shares until he's twenty-five, they can address any problems they have to me. Regardless, you're gone."

"Does your wife know you're taking over the company?"

Quinn lifted a hand and wiped the sweat from his forehead. "Lanie is none of your business and this conversation is over."

"Wait." There was a brief silence before Edward spoke again. "We can work this out, Quinn. If it's custody of the boy you want, we'll hire the best family lawyers in the country. We can even get the damn ranch back if you want it that much."

Anger curled inside him, and when he spoke it was through clenched teeth. "I don't need you to tell me what I can do, Edward, and the only thing I want right now is you out of my life. Don't bother calling again." He dropped the phone back into the cradle.

Duncan was still in the same spot, listening unashamedly to Quinn's side of the conversation. "I take it he knows you're buying up the stock?"

"Looks that way." He limped to the table and lowered himself to a chair. "Tom must have passed the five percent mark on the buy-up. Edward is not a happy camper right now. He even offered to help me get Zack."

"This surprises you?" Duncan slid a plate of eggs and bacon in front of Quinn and moved the coffee closer.

"No, I expected a reaction like this when it finally hit home that I'm not going to sit back and let him get away with what he's done." He paused. "What surprises me is he knows what happened with the bull."

"How the hell could he know that?"

"He couldn't. Not unless someone told him, and there were only a handful of people here."

Duncan joined him at the table. "Well, I didn't tell him, and neither did you."

"You can cross Lanie off the list, too. She hates him. That leaves Sherry, Cody Simmons or Harper."

"I don't know." Duncan looked doubtful. "Sherry seems pretty loyal to your wife. I can't see her spilling her guts to Edward."

Quinn nodded. "I agree. The Simmons kid showed up out of the blue yesterday. It's possible Edward sent him."

"Or it could have been Harper. He *does* stand to gain a lot if you leave."

"Yeah, or Harper."

He kept his gaze on Quinn. "Are you going to tell Lanie?"

"No." He shrugged. "If it is Harper, I couldn't prove it, and she wouldn't believe me anyway." Pushing the plate aside, he lifted the coffee. "I only wish I knew what he was going to try next. Edward won't give up until he stops breathing."

"Neither will you." Duncan scooted the plate back in front of him. "Whether you like it or not, you and Edward are cut from the same mold in some ways. When it comes to stubborn, you can match him dollar to dime. Now eat."

With a sigh, Quinn picked up the fork and dug in, his mind whirling. "Why hasn't Edward started buying up stock on his own now that he knows what I'm doing? It isn't like him."

"Maybe he is."

"No, Tom is watching the market closely. If anyone were buying up the stock, he'd know it. I'm missing something here, Dunc, and I don't like the feeling. I don't like it at all."

Chapter Fifteen

"Lordy, what a week it's been." Lanie plopped down on the couch next to Quinn. "I don't think I've had five minutes to sit down since last Sunday."

"I've noticed." He turned the TV off and smiled at her. "Got everything done?"

"For now. The new people I hired took over the riding groups today while Sherry and I worked on our booth for Frontier Days. It's all ready for tomorrow. And Cody is great. Not only with the kids, but with taking appointments and handling the customers. I don't know how I managed without him."

"Maybe things will slow down next week and you can take some time off."

With a sigh, she leaned her head back and closed her eyes. "Not a chance. Next weekend is our first trail ride and campout. It'll take most of the week to get ready for that, even if I have the kids take turns manning the booth."

"No wonder you're tied up in knots." He stood and pulled her to her feet. "Come on."

"Where are we going?"

"Outside."

She tried to free her hand but he hung on. "Quinn, I just put Zack to bed. What if he wakes up?"

"Duncan is here. He'll listen for him."

Across the den, Duncan looked up from the book he was reading. "Sure. No problem. I'm going to take my book upstairs to my room, anyway. If he even makes a peep I'll hear him."

Reluctantly, she let Quinn lead her through the house and down the back steps. They were almost to the bunkhouse when she blinked in surprise. "Your leg. I can barely tell you're limping."

"Duncan is good at what he does. It's still sore in a few spots, but nothing I can't handle. By next weekend I should be ready for the trail ride."

"You're going with us?"

"I wouldn't miss it for anything." Instead of entering the bunkhouse, he went around the side and onto the deck, pausing to flip a switch on the hot tub. Water spurted and gurgled in the darkness.

"Quinn, what are you doing?" A curl of anxiety mixed with anticipation suddenly tightened her stomach.

He leaned over to check the water temperature then stood and reached for the buttons on her shirt. "Thirty minutes in the tub and you'll feel like a new woman."

"But I didn't bring a swimsuit!" Even to her ears the protest sounded weak, and she cast a yearning look at the tub. Right now the thought of immersing herself in jets of hot water seemed heavenly.

"You don't need a suit. Its pitch dark out here and there's no one around but me." He lifted a hand and ran his fingers down her jaw. "Don't tell me you're bashful? What happened to the Lanie who used to go skinny dipping in the lake with me in broad daylight?"

"She grew up. Maybe." With a wry grin, she glanced at the tub again. "Okay, but I can take my own clothes off, thank you."

The only light came from the millions of stars brightening the sky, but it was enough to see his outline, to know he was also undressing. Her pulse rate jumped. She had tried not to think about last Saturday night, to block it from her memory, and she'd been so busy she had almost succeeded. Now it all came rushing back, heating her blood until her fingers shook.

Thanks to her fumbling, he made it into the water before she did. It swirled around his narrow hips as he waited. When she hesitantly reached the edge, he held out a hand and took hers.

"There's a bench under the water. Just step down."

She tested the water with a toe, then did as he suggested, taking another step down until she was standing beside him. He smiled at her gasp of pleasure as bubbles slid over her skin. A little embarrassed, she sank onto the bench until the water reached her chin. Her hair was getting soaked, but she didn't care. This felt too fantastic, like thousands of fingers were massaging every inch of her body. "Forget every disparaging remark I ever made about hot tubs," she murmured as the tightness eased from her muscles.

"We should have brought a bottle of wine with us." Quinn seated himself and stretched his arm behind her along the rim.

"The way I feel right now, one glass of wine and I'd fall asleep and drown."

"I'd save you." He pressed on her shoulder. "Lean back and relax."

Relax. Easy for him to say, she thought. He wasn't sitting in a pool with a sexy, naked man while geysers of water did strange things to certain parts of his anatomy. Things she had to get her mind off of right now.

Letting her head rest on his arm, she gazed up at the stars, searching for a topic of conversation that would be safe.

"What ever happened to Judith?" There, that should change the direction of her thoughts.

"Judith?"

"Yeah, you remember. Judith. Your fiancée. Auburn hair, nose turned up so much she'd drown in a light rain. Judith." The high-class hussy, she added mentally.

As though he'd heard her last comment, he chuckled. "Judith was never really my fiancée. We had an arrangement of another sort."

"I don't think I want to hear this after all," she mumbled.

She didn't have to look at him to know he was grinning. It was in his voice when he answered her.

"Actually, Judith was probably more attracted to you than she ever was to me."

"What!" She bolted upright.

Laughing, he pulled her back into her former position. "From the minute I regained consciousness in the hospital, Edward started parading women in for me to look over. Women he deemed 'socially suitable' for the CEO of McAllister Pharmaceuticals. It was driving me crazy. I'd met Judith at several parties and was aware of her inclinations. I also knew her parents were giving her a hard time about finding a husband and settling down. They were even threatening to cut off her money."

He shrugged. "When Edward started pushing me in her direction, I made a deal with her. We'd let everyone think we were engaged. It got Edward and her parents off our backs, and allowed her to pursue her interests safely. All we had to do was appear in public together occasionally. The truth is, we couldn't stand each other."

"What about all those women who showed up with you in the Chicago newspapers? Didn't being engaged put a damper on your dating?"

He turned his head to gaze at her, his arm curling around her neck. "Were you keeping an eye on me, Lanie?"

Heat rushed to her cheeks and she blessed the darkness. "Watson is a small town. Believe me, every time your name was in the papers, I heard about it."

He hesitated before tilting her face up to his. "Would it surprise you to know I wasn't interested in those women? I wasn't interested any woman except one, no matter how hard I tried to forget her."

She snorted. She couldn't help herself. "Are you trying to tell me you didn't sleep with any of them?"

"No, I'm not telling you that. I'm only human, Lanie. But there wasn't as many as you seem to think, and none of them mattered to me. Remember, I had a lot of operations on my leg stretched out over the last five years. Between my time in the hospital and the physical therapy afterward, I was usually in too much pain to even think about it. The other night was the first time for me in a long time."

Her gaze searched his face. "You're serious."

"Oh, yeah. Dead serious," he said fervently. "If it hadn't been for the dreams, there were times I'd have wondered if 'it' even worked anymore."

"Dreams?" She couldn't stop grinning, or stop the feeling of elation that swept her. All that jealousy when she'd read the Chicago papers had been for nothing. He hadn't cared about those women.

"They damn near killed me. And you starred in every one."

Before she knew what he was doing, he shifted her until she was on his lap, the hard length of his erection pressing against her thigh.

Quinn's voice went husky. "I'd wake up needing you so much that I hurt. That hasn't changed. I still need you."

Delicately, she cleared her throat. "How many surgeries have you had?"

A sigh escaped his lips. "Seven. The last was a few months before you came to Chicago."

Her eyes widened. "Do you need any more?"

"No. That was the final one. And stop changing the subject."

"I wasn't."

"Yes, you were." His hand slid up her side, halting just below her breast. "It's what we both want, Lanie. Stop fighting it. Last time, you made love to me. Now let me return the favor."

She twisted to face him, her hands moving up his chest until they twined around his nape. "I shouldn't," she whispered.

"You should."

"It will only create more problems."

"It may solve a few." He pulled her closer, his mouth coming down to cover hers.

"You brought me out here to seduce me," she said accusingly when they came up for air.

His hands were everywhere, stirring fires hotter than the water in the tub. "Guilty as charged," he murmured. "I had to do something. At the rate you've been working, I figured I'd be lucky to see you again before winter."

"I know, and I'm sorry. I promised to spend part of each day with you, but it's our busiest time of year."

"There's one thing that would help." He pushed a strand of wet hair away from her face. "Let me move into your room with you."

She shouldn't even be thinking about making love to him again. Tomorrow she'd suffer the agonies of renewed guilt. But right now, she wanted him and damn the consequences. He was her husband. And if he ended up leaving again, well, she'd deal with it the way she had before.

"Lanie?"

"For tonight," she whispered. "That's all I can promise."

"I'll take what I can get." He stood, letting her slide down his body until her feet found the bottom of the tub. "Unless you want to make love right here, we'd better get out. I can't wait much longer."

The thought of making love in the tub heated her blood even more. But this time she wanted to feel his weight, to hold him the way her heart ached to hold him. She wanted to forget the last five years had happened and simply love him. For tonight.

* * * * *

They left their clothes on the deck, slipping across the yard naked, and the trip took twice as long as usual. Quinn couldn't keep his hands off her, didn't even try. Every other step, they stopped to kiss, to tease. By the time they reached the darkened house, Lanie was giggling like a teenager. At this rate, they were going to wake everyone on the ranch, and company was the last thing he wanted right now.

Lanie was a step ahead of him as they reached the porch, and he caught her around the waist, pulling her back against his body. His hands splayed low on her abdomen, he leaned down to nuzzle her throat.

"Um." Her arms came up to circle his neck, the position arching her upper body as her head tilted to the side.

Slowly, he slid his right hand up her stomach. "Your skin feels like silk," he whispered in her ear.

"I'm still wet."

He let his left hand drift lower, into the tangle of curls, his fingers exploring gently. "Yes, you are. Very, very wet." He circled her ear with his tongue, eliciting a moan, and at the same time her legs shifted to allow him greater access. "I should probably dry you off before we go inside."

"Dry me off?" Her voice sounded dazed, drugged with desire.

"Yes. Slowly and carefully, until you can't breathe, can't think about anything but me." He skimmed a hardened nipple with his palm.

"Quinn." His name was a fevered gasp on her lips, her body trembling under his touch.

"God, if this is a dream I hope I never wake up," he groaned.

"Quinn, I'm going to—"

"Let go, Angel. I want to feel you."

She arched even more, her body pressing into his hands, clenching around his fingers. Silently, the climax shook her until she was limp. He supported her until it was over, then turned her to face him.

"I want to taste you," he whispered. "Here." His mouth descended on hers, drinking deeply, taking his time. Nearly crazy with need, he lifted her to the rail running around the porch.

"And here." His tongue trailed down her neck to a nipple. He teased it, made it peak into a hard pebble before he took it between his teeth. When her head dropped back, he moved to the other breast, showering it with the same attention.

She inhaled sharply as he lowered himself to one knee. "And here," he breathed against the swollen folds. With infinite tenderness, he lavished her with all the love he'd kept bottled up for five long years, tasting her the way he'd imagined doing. Tasted until her hands were fisted in his hair, until her breath came in ragged sobs.

When he could stand it no longer, he stood. Hands on her hips to brace them, he eased forward, sheathing himself inside her tight passage. Lanie's legs closed around his waist, and her arms circled his neck, pulling his mouth to hers as he moved. Tongues touched before lips met, battled together feverishly.

Teeth nipped, then lips soothed the pain away. The essence of love drifted around them, and he tasted salt.

"You're crying," he murmured.

"Yes."

"Don't." His lips moved to her eyes, drying the moisture. "Don't cry, Angel."

"Oh, Quinn." This time her mouth found his fully.

The kiss deepened, became frantic as he increased his movements. It took every ounce of his willpower to hold off, to wait for her. Even when she tightened around him, the tiny spasms caressing his length, he forced himself to wait, to catch her cries. He didn't want to miss a single sensation from her climax.

As it began to fade, he withdrew, then buried his length with one hard thrust, straining with the ecstasy of his own release. It felt as though he were being ripped in half, the climax was so strong. And he never wanted it to end, never wanted to be separate from her again. Colored lights exploded behind his eyes as he clung to her, and he barely recognized his voice calling her name.

For the first time since he'd left Wyoming so many years before, he felt like he belonged somewhere. Here, with her. He didn't give a damn about the ranch, he realized. Not unless Lanie came with it.

Silence reigned as they recovered, each holding onto the other. Somewhere in the darkness a night bird called to its mate.

Lanie gave a shaky laugh. "We didn't make it to the bed."

"We've got all night. We'll get there."

He leaned back and cupped her face in his hands, running his thumbs over cheeks. "Why were you crying?"

Moisture glinted in her eyes, and she nibbled her bottom lip for a second. "It's just... It was so beautiful, Quinn. You've never made love to me quite like that before. It was always wonderful, but this time." She sighed. "I don't know how to explain it. My feelings are all tied up with how much pain we've been through, how much we've missed. And it was for nothing."

"Maybe it wasn't, Angel. As much as I hate that I wasn't here for you and Zack, maybe it took losing you to make me realize what I had, how much I really need you. I will never take you for granted again, and I'll thank God for every minute we have together."

She leaned against him heavily and closed her eyes. "You fight dirty, McAllister."

A smile lifted his lips. "I'll do whatever it takes to make sure you don't leave me."

Her eyes opened and she gazed up at him intently. "Including lie?"

His smile faded. "No, Angel. I haven't lied to you, and I never will."

A shiver ran over her as she nodded. "I guess I'll have to take your word for it." She slid off the rail and caught his hand. "It's getting chilly out here. Why don't we try to make it to bed this time?"

"Sleepy?"

She grinned at him over her shoulder. "Not in the least. If I'm going to feel guilty tomorrow, I want to make sure it's worth it."

"That sounds interesting."

"You have no idea, McAllister. No idea at all. But you're about to find out."

Chapter Sixteen

The feeling of being stared at brought Quinn out of a sound sleep. Groggily, he opened his eyes, wondering if Lanie were awake. No, her warm body was still curled beside him and he could hear her soft, even breathing.

Neither of them had gotten much rest last night, both bent on making up for lost time. He smiled. They hadn't succeeded, but they'd sure gotten off to a great start. It was almost dawn before exhaustion had forced them to sleep. And from the dim light showing through the window, it wasn't much past that now.

"Did you have a bad dream?"

Quinn whipped his head around at the question, his startled gaze meeting the curious gray eyes of his son. Zack was sitting Indian style on the foot of the bed, his dark hair rumpled.

"Mama always lets me sleep with her when I have a bad dream," he explained.

"No." Quinn rose up on an elbow. "No bad dreams. Only very good ones."

Zack nodded wisely. "Billy's mom and dad sleep together all the time. Are you going to sleep with Mom from now on?"

Good question, Quinn thought. He certainly hoped so, but he doubted Lanie was ready for that yet. Last night had been nothing short of a miracle and he didn't want to push his luck.

"I don't know, Zack. Guess we'll have to wait and see. Your mom isn't used to having someone in bed with her. It might take a while before she gets accustomed to the idea."

Zack glanced at his mother. "Does Mom like you better now?"

Lanie shifted, the blanket sliding down a bare shoulder, and Quinn hurriedly adjusted it. Once she was decent, he patted the bed beside him.

Zack didn't need a second invitation. He scrambled up the bed and settled in Quinn's arms.

"Why do you think your mom didn't like me?"

One small shoulder lifted in a shrug. "'Cause she acted mad when you first got here. I was scared she'd make you leave again and I don't want you to go."

"I'm not going to leave, Zack." He smoothed his son's hair down. "A long time ago, before you were born, your mom and I lived together here on the ranch. But something bad happened and I left. It hurt your mom because she wanted me to stay. Now she feels a little like you do. She's afraid I'll leave again, and this time it would hurt you, too."

"Didn't you tell her you were staying?"

"Yes, but it's hard for her to believe me when I didn't stay last time. Pretty soon she'll know I'm telling the truth. Your mom and I are still married, Zack. I love both of you, and I'm never going to leave you."

"Not even if you get busy again?"

"No, not even then."

"Okay." He sat up and leaned across Quinn to shake Lanie. "Mom?"

Lanie groaned but kept her eyes closed.

"Hey, Mom!" He shook her again. "Martha said if you were going to open the booth on time, you better haul your bottom out of bed."

One eye opened a slit. "What time is it?" she mumbled.

"Six-thirty," Quinn supplied after a glance at the clock.

Cursing under her breath, Lanie sat straight up, then frantically clutched the sheet to her chest. "I'm late! Zack, run downstairs and tell Martha I'm awake. And tell her to forget any breakfast for me. I won't have time."

Zack bounded out of bed, slamming the door behind him when he ran out of the room.

"What time are you supposed to be there?"

"Seven." Her gaze swept over him. "You're still here."

A grin twitched at his lips. "Where did you think I'd be?"

"I don't know. I guess I thought you'd leave when I fell asleep."

"And miss holding you? Not a chance." He ran his hand down her bare back. "Feeling any guilt this morning?"

"No— Yes." She buried her face in her hands. "I don't know!"

"I love a decisive woman." His grin turned to a chuckle. "There probably isn't too much guilt if you can't make up your mind."

She raised her head and stuck her tongue out at him. "It's too early to be thinking about things like that, and I've got too much to do. I'll worry about it later."

With a flick of the blankets, she stood and headed for the adjoining bathroom. Quinn watched the view with a great deal of interest, then followed her. Having a baby certainly hadn't hurt her. In fact, her shape was fuller now in all the right places.

She looked up in surprise when he entered the bathroom. "Quinn, what are you doing?"

"I thought I'd help with your shower. A job always goes faster when two people are working on it." He caught her around the waist and kissed her soundly. "Besides, I figure it will give you something else to think about today. Staying in that booth must get awfully boring."

* * * * *

Lanie leaned her elbows on the booth counter and took a deep breath as another group of tourists drifted on down the street. Boring? She grimaced. Like she'd had time to be bored. The booth had attracted a steady stream of people all morning. And thanks to Quinn, she hadn't made it to town until eight. Luckily, she'd done most of the setting up yesterday. The only thing remaining had been putting out the brochures and the entry forms for the drawing.

Quinn had been right about one thing, though. Every time she thought about his ministrations in the shower, her stomach lurched and heat flashed through her body. It had been hard to concentrate on answering questions. Right in the middle of a conversation, she'd catch herself eagerly scanning the crowds for sight of his dark hair, that tall, sexy body.

She was treading on dangerous ground here. Somehow, she'd let herself get caught up in Quinn's seductive web, and the worst part was, she didn't regret a second of it. Oh, the guilt was there, and the fear of being hurt again. But to her surprise, spending the night with Quinn had been so wonderful that guilt took a backseat to the rest of her emotions.

All these years with Jared she'd told herself the physical side of a relationship wasn't important, that what really mattered was caring and shared goals. Suddenly she found herself rethinking that idea. Was she really ready to settle for a life without fireworks? Could she, in all honesty, marry Jared knowing she'd be cheating them both? Because deep in her soul she knew no man alive could do to her what Quinn could accomplish so easily.

With something akin to horror, she realized she'd barely thought of Jared all day. Dear Lord, had she agreed to marry him only to give Zack a father? How had she fooled herself so badly?

She took a deep shuddering breath as the truth hit her. Even if Quinn left again and they continued with the divorce, she couldn't marry Jared. She'd rather spend the rest of her life alone than be tied to a man she didn't love. It wasn't going to be easy, but she had to tell him. Soon.

Her brow furrowed. Where was Jared? She would have expected him to drop by the booth before this. It wasn't a meeting she was looking forward to, but now that he hadn't appeared, her curiosity was aroused. Especially since she hadn't heard from him all week. He must have had an emergency call this morning.

A small group of tourists stopped at the booth, distracting her as they filled out the entry form for the contest. She was giving away two tickets for the upcoming trail ride and campout.

The crowds were beginning to thin out as noon neared, people moving toward the picnic area where a bar-b-que was in progress.

As she chatted with the couple looking over her brochures, her gaze scanned the streets again. It was Zack's laughter that captured her attention first. He was perched high above the crowd, sitting astride Quinn's shoulders as they moved down the street.

Smiling at her son's obvious delight, her gaze dropped to Quinn face. Their eyes met and her heart turned over in her chest when he returned her smile. Even without touching her, he made her feel as though she'd been kissed, caressed. The sensation had goose bumps chasing each other up and down her spine.

Almost as though he knew what she was thinking, his amber eyes darkened while he stepped around the counter, stopping in front of her. "Hi."

"Looks like you two have had fun this morning." She gestured at the bags in Quinn's hand.

"Not as much as we'd have had if you were with us." He lifted Zack from his shoulders and deposited him on the counter, along with his packages, then leaned down and brushed her lips with his. "Miss me?"

"Yes," she breathed. "Both of you."

"Hey, Mom. Guess what?"

"What, sweetie?"

"Dad got you a present."

"Oh, really?" She arched a brow at Quinn.

"Can we show it to her now, Dad?"

"Sure. It's in that white bag." He picked it up and handed it to her.

Feeling like a kid on Christmas morning, Lanie reached inside and pulled out a belt. A gasp escaped her lips as she saw the buckle. Made from polished silver cut in an ornate pattern, it was inlaid with bits of turquoise in the shape of a cornflower. More raised flowers adorned the leather and her name was done in block letters on the back.

"Quinn, it's beautiful. I've never seen anything like it. Thank you."

"Sam Two Crows says it's gen-u-ine leather," Zack piped in. "And he made them by hand. We watched him put the names on." He pointed to his own waist. "Me and Dad got one, too."

"So I see." Quinn's was a more masculine match for the one she held, but Zack's buckle was silver with a gold cowboy riding a bucking horse.

Quinn's hands were already working her current buckle lose. "Let's see if it fits. Sam said he could adjust it if we needed him to, but it looked right." He pulled her old belt free and dropped it into the bag.

Instead of having her turn so he could thread it through the loops on her jeans, he reached around her, making sure her body was leaning against his. Helplessly, she put her hands on his chest to brace herself and gazed up at him.

"I'll take any excuse," he murmured. He dipped his head and kissed her again. "There. A perfect fit."

From the look in his eyes, she had the impression he wasn't talking about the belt. "It does seem that way." She smiled at him. "Thank you, again."

Two women had stopped at the booth and she turned to talk with them. They appeared to be more interested in Quinn than in the contest or the ranch, but he wasn't paying attention to them. He had shifted to study the back of the booth. Instead of bare wood, it was covered with an oil painting of the ranch in vivid colors designed to draw interest.

As soon as the women moved on, he glanced at her. "Who did this?"

"One of the local artists. She's really good. We have an art festival every fall and her work always sells out."

"An art festival." He shook his head. "I still can't believe how many tourists are here. We actually saw someone with dreadlocks and a nose ring talking to a guy wearing chaps and spurs."

Lanie chuckled. "Tourists winter a lot better than cows, McAllister, and these days, we can make more money on them."

"Why do you even keep cows?"

She shrugged. "The tourists we take on the campouts expect to see them." She picked up a brochure and handed it to him. "See? We advertise that they get to live like the cowboys did, which basically means we round up the herd beforehand, and they get to ride herd on it. You'd be amazed at how seriously these people take the job."

He was thumbing through the brochure with a great deal of interest. When he saw the name on the front, he gave a low whistle. "This travel agency is nationwide. And you're listed with them?"

"Yes." She couldn't keep the smug tone out of her voice. "They contacted me a few months after I started the trail rides and offered to list us. It really did wonders for the business. Until then, the only advertising we'd done were some posters nailed up in all the surrounding towns. They even print up the brochures every year."

"Doesn't it eat into your profit? Something like this must be expensive."

"Nope. We haven't spent a penny. They said the cost is made up through their clients."

A frown briefly furrowed his brow, then he shrugged. "I guess they know what they're doing."

"They sent a guy out to take pictures last year." Zack commented. "There's even one of me and Mom."

Lanie ruffled his hair. "Mrs. James, their local agent, would like me to turn the ranch into a real dude ranch, but running a hotel isn't my cup of tea. I'd rather keep the ranch private." She checked her watch. "Have you seen Sherry? She's supposed to take over at noon."

Quinn put the brochure back on the stack. "She's with Duncan. They went to grab some food before they headed in this direction. Hungry?"

"I passed hungry two hours ago. I'm starved."

"Tell you what. Zack and I will go hustle them along and save a table for us. What do you want to eat?"

"Everything."

He laughed. "You got it. Ready to go, champ?"

When Zack extended his arms, Quinn swung him back to his shoulders. "See you in a few minutes."

* * * * *

Quinn and Zack hadn't been gone more than ten minutes when Sherry and Duncan showed up. The scent from the bags of food they carried had Lanie's stomach growling.

"You can take off," Sherry told her. "We passed Quinn and he said you were about to collapse from hunger."

"He's right. God, that smells good."

"Here." The blonde reached into a bag and handed over a few French fries. "That should give you enough strength to make it to the picnic grounds."

Munching on the windfall, Lanie strolled down the board sidewalk, pausing when some jewelry caught her eye, then moving on. Food first. She'd have time to see all the displays this afternoon.

All the food booths had been set up in the park at the far end of town, the hundred or so trees offering shade to the diners. And from the look of the crowd, everyone was taking advantage of it. Each table was crammed to capacity, and she scanned faces rapidly searching for Quinn.

Stepping off the walk, she stuck the last of the fries in her mouth. He had to be here somewhere. It was simply a matter of finding him.

She'd started toward a heavy line in front of a concession booth when someone gripped her arm. Smiling, she turned. "I was starting to think you'd—" Her smile faded abruptly as she stared into Jared's angry face.

"Jared. I thought..."

"I know what you thought." His grip on her arm tightened. "I may not be Quinn, but I want to know what's going on, Lanie. I was watching you with him earlier."

Disbelief widened her eyes as she stared at him. "You were spying on us?"

"It wasn't hard to do when you weren't making any effort to hide it," he snapped. "You were acting like a couple of lovesick teenagers."

Running a hand through his hair, he made a visible effort to calm down and failed. "You're sleeping with him, aren't you?"

Every muscle in her body stiffened. "Jared—"

"No, don't lie to me. I could tell by the way you touched each other." His fingers dug in as he gave her a tiny shake. "How could you do that to us, to me, after you promised?"

"Jared, you're hurting me." She struggled briefly to free her arm but he didn't seem to hear her. "Please. We need to talk, but not here, not like this."

"God, McAllister warned me but I didn't listen. I should never have stayed away from you this last week." A look of panic flashed across his features, gone so fast she wasn't sure she'd seen it before he lowered his head.

"I'm sorry." He took a deep, shaky breath. "I shouldn't have tried to talk to you now. But I almost went crazy when I saw you together, Lanie. I miss you and Zack. You're the only family I have here, and I don't want to lose you."

Guilt streaked through her. How could she tell him it was over between them when he was hurting so badly, when all this was her fault? She couldn't. Not now. It would have to wait until they were alone, until he'd calmed down.

"It's okay," she murmured quietly. "Just let go of me."

"I think you better listen to her, Harper." Quinn's voice came from behind them, his words edged in steel. "Unless you want all your fingers broken."

Jared dropped his hand as though she'd burned him. All the blood had drained from his skin, leaving his face white. His jaw clenched and released spasmodically. "Stay out of this McAllister. It's none of your business."

"Now that's where you're wrong, Harper." Amber flames kindled in his eyes. "Anything that happens to my wife is my business, and you'd be smart to remember that."

"Quinn." Lanie put her hand on his chest. "Please. It's okay. He wasn't hurting me. Don't cause a scene."

He gazed down at her for a moment, then gave a curt nod. "Get out of here, Harper, while you still can. And if you can't be civil, then stay away from Lanie."

Without a word, Jared turned on his heel and stalked off. Lanie watched him until he vanished amid the throng of people, her heart aching for him. If he was this hurt now, what would he feel when she told him it was over? Abruptly, she turned away from the thought.

"Where's Zack?" She scanned the crowd anxiously, praying he hadn't overhead any of the conversation.

"With Buck and Ruby, saving our seats. Are you okay?" He curved a hand around her nape. "If he hurt you—"

"He didn't. Really, I'm fine." Gingerly, she rubbed her arm. "Can we forget this happened?"

He studied her a second longer. "What set him off?"

She sighed. "Us. He was watching us earlier. I guess it doesn't take a rocket scientist to figure out we're sleeping together. He was just so upset and hurt, Quinn. I don't think he knew what he was doing."

"Well, you said he'd figure it out as soon as he saw you. Looks like you were right."

"Being right doesn't help." She tilted her head and looked up at him intently. "Did you warn Jared to stay away from me this last week?"

"No. I haven't talked to him at all. Why?"

"Just something he said. It didn't make much sense."

"What did he say?"

"He said that McAllister warned him but he didn't listen. Are you sure you haven't talked to him?"

Quinn's eyes narrowed, and he turned to gaze in the direction Jared had gone. "Positive."

Chapter Seventeen

Lanie glanced at her watch, then checked the people still milling on the street. The crowd had thinned out as darkness fell. Another thirty minutes and she could close the booth down and go home.

If possible, today had been even busier than yesterday. Or maybe it only seemed that way because she'd pulled the afternoon shift. Thank heavens there were only two more days left of the four day event. It would take the rest of the week to get ready for the trail ride and campout.

At least all this work gave her an excuse for avoiding Quinn. She lifted a hand to her upper arm, wincing at the resulting pain of her touch. The bruise had gone from an angry red to a deep purple and black, and she was terrified of what he'd do if he saw it. The last thing she wanted was for him to find Jared and do something rash. Jared was her problem and she'd handle him her own way.

Leaving a few brochures out, she gathered up the rest and locked them underneath the counter so they'd be handy in the morning. Two of the girls she'd hired would be manning the booth for what was left of Frontier Days, but she would have to stop by and check on them periodically.

"Lanie?"

She spun at the familiar voice, her eyes widening. "Jared. What are you doing here this time of day?"

"I hoped I'd find you alone." He sighed and stepped closer to the counter. "I'm leaving, Lanie, but I had to talk to you first, to apologize for yesterday."

"You're leaving?"

"Only for a week." He gave her a sad smile. "I wouldn't get to see you anyway, and I need some time to think. The vet in Jackson offered to take my calls while I'm gone."

"When will you be back?"

"Sunday morning." Gently, he touched her arm. "I hurt you yesterday, Lanie, and it's killing me. I can't let anything like that happen again."

"Don't, please. You didn't intend to hurt me, Jared." She covered his hand with hers. "I know that. This whole trial marriage thing has been harder on you than it has on the rest of us combined, and I hate that. You don't deserve to go through this." She took a deep breath. "When you get back Sunday, we need to talk."

He stared at their hands for a second, then turned his palm up and curled his fingers around hers. "I guess we do. There's something I should have told you long ago. Maybe it's time." He kissed the back of her hand then released it. "I have a plane to catch. I'll see you Sunday afternoon."

A dull ache settled in her middle as she watched him walk away, shoulders slumped. He already knew what she was going to tell him. For the first time in four years he hadn't told her that he loved her.

* * * * *

"Well?" Duncan arched an eyebrow as Quinn walked into the kitchen.

"It was Tom." Quinn couldn't stop the grin on his lips. "As of market's close Friday evening, I own fifty-four percent of McAllister Pharmaceuticals. Tomorrow, I'll have Franklin add it to Zack's trust fund. By the middle of the week, he'll be the richest four-year-old in the country."

"And you'll be nearly broke." Duncan scowled at him. "What are you going to do if this," he waved a hand in the air, "doesn't work out?"

"It will." He shrugged. "But either way, as the executor of the trust fund, I'll be president of the company until Zack is old enough to take over. That includes a decent salary so I won't starve by any means." He laughed. "I may even be able to afford you."

Duncan looked down studiously at the cup of coffee in his hands. "About that. I've been doing some thinking, Quinn. You really don't need me anymore. All your surgeries are done, and whatever work your leg still requires, you can do on your own."

Shock rippled through him. Whenever he'd thought about the future, Duncan had always been there. He was the brother Quinn had never had. The idea that he would leave was inconceivable. "You're quitting?"

A smile lit Duncan's eyes. "Yes. But not right this minute. I have to stick around long enough to see how everything works out." He sobered. "Just because I don't work for you doesn't mean I won't be there if you need me, Quinn. But you've got your own life to live now. You've got a wife, and a son, and a company to run."

There was a slight hesitation before he spoke again. "The truth is, I've been hiding behind you to keep from having to make a decision about my own life. When Tracy died, I didn't know what to do, how to keep going. You gave me a reason. But it's been five years now. It's time for both of us to stand on our own two feet."

"What will you do?" The sadness that washed over Quinn made it hard to speak.

"I've saved almost everything you paid me and invested a lot of it. I think I'd like to settle down in a small town, maybe even here in Watson, and open a business. I've been looking the place over and they don't have a sporting goods store. With all the tourists and the winter sports, I could probably make a good living at it, and there's an empty building on Main Street that's the right size. And I won't give up physical therapy entirely. I'm sure once I send my credentials to the area doctors I'll be able to pick and choose the cases I want."

"You wouldn't miss Chicago? All your family is there."

"I suppose there are some things I'd miss. But not all my family is there. You'll be here, and the others can visit." He grinned. "I'd love to get my sister on a horse."

"You'd better learn how to ride one yourself before you do." Quinn laughed. "I'll be glad to teach you," he added innocently.

"Thanks, but no thanks. I'd rather have Lanie teach me. At least that way I might survive the experience."

They both looked around as the back door opened.

"Teach you what?" Lanie smiled at them as she entered the kitchen.

"To ride a horse," Duncan told her.

"Sure. Any time."

"Duncan is thinking about opening a sporting goods store in Watson," Quinn told her. "What do you think?"

"I think it's a great idea. We really need one. Most of the tourists have no idea what the winters are like in Jackson Hole, so they're never prepared for the cold. Be sure to stock lots of parkas, gloves, caps and boots. You'd even get the locals' business. Right now we have to drive to Jackson for things like that."

"You've convinced me. I'll call the real estate company tomorrow."

Quinn barely listened to the conversation. Instead, his gaze searched Lanie's face. She was pale and appeared exhausted. And she was avoiding looking at him.

He stood and pulled out a chair. "We left your food in the oven. Why don't you sit down and I'll get it for you?"

She shook her head. "Thanks, but I'm not hungry. Where's Zack?"

"Watching a cartoon video in the den."

"I think I'll go visit him for a while. It feels like I haven't seen him in days."

"Want to go for a walk later?"

She paused in the hall doorway. "I'm sorry, Quinn. I can't. I have a phone call to make and then bills to pay so I can get them in the mail. It's going to take most of the evening."

"Who do you have to call this late?"

"Pete and Ollie Garner. They do all the cooking on the trail ride. They'll start stocking the chuck wagon tomorrow and I need to go over the supply list with them tonight. So, I'll see you in the morning."

"Sure." He waited until she was gone, then sat back down.

"What was that all about?" Duncan asked.

Quinn rubbed his eyes tiredly. "If I had to guess, I'd say she had another run-in with Harper today. You don't know how badly I wish this was over with so life could be normal again. I hate to see her torn like she is now."

Duncan toyed with his cup. "Have you told her about the trust fund yet?"

"No."

"Are you going to?"

"Yes. As soon as it's finalized. Probably this week."

"How's she going to take it?"

Quinn smiled grimly. "Knowing Lanie, she'll be mad as a rattler with his tail caught between two rocks. But she'll get used to the idea. Especially when she realizes it's the only logical solution to my staying on the ranch. I'll still have to go to Chicago occasionally, but most of what I'll be doing can be taken care of from here."

"What about Edward?"

His jaw tightened. "Edward can handle his own problems. The company is no longer one of them. As long as he leaves us alone, he can rot in hell for all I care."

* * * * *

Lanie hung up the phone and nibbled her bottom lip as she stared at the large, bulky package on her desk. All during her conversation with Pete, the brown manila envelope had distracted her.

When he'd sent for his medical records she'd thought it was the only way to find out about what had happened to him. Now that she knew the truth, she was torn about reading the information. It felt too much like an invasion of Quinn's privacy to look at them.

Not that she could wade through it in a few hours. From the size of the package it would take months to read it all. And even then, she doubted much of it would be understandable to anyone not in the medical field.

She reached out and touched it with one finger, tracing the return address of the hospital. No, she couldn't do it. Not without making sure Quinn didn't mind. He'd only sent for them to prove he couldn't have signed the ranch over to her. Now that she knew he was telling the truth, she really didn't need to see the records.

Pushing her chair back, she walked out of the office. The house was quiet, but a light still showed from the den. Duncan glanced up from the book he was holding when she paused in the door.

"Where's Quinn?"

"He went to bed about ten minutes ago. Something wrong?" He carefully marked his place and closed the book.

After a brief hesitation she moved farther into the room and sat down across from him. "His medical records arrived."

"You need someone to interpret them?"

"Probably, but I don't want to open them unless I'm sure Quinn approves."

"He knows they arrived. He's the one who got them out of the mail and put them on your desk."

Heat flushed her cheeks. "He doesn't mind if I read them?"

"Not at all. I think he was happy you're interested in knowing what he went through. It makes up a little for all the years he thought you didn't care."

"Not enough," she said softly. "Nothing can ever make up for my not being there when he needed me so badly. I'm surprised he'll even speak to me."

"Quinn loves you. Don't beat yourself up for something you couldn't help." He glanced down at his book before looking up to hold her gaze. "I admit, I didn't like you much at first. I thought you were going to hurt him all over again and I wasn't sure he could stand it. But just being here has changed Quinn. He's more relaxed, happier. Stronger. I hope things work out for the two of you, but if you decide you can't live with him, he'll survive."

Lanie leaned back in the chair. "You think I'm going to choose Jared, don't you?"

"Are you?"

"No." She stared into the empty fireplace. "If nothing else, Quinn has made me realize that I never loved Jared the way I should have. Marrying him would be the biggest mistake of my life. But that doesn't mean I've decided to stay with Quinn, Duncan. Not unless I can be absolutely sure he won't leave us again."

"He won't."

She gave him a wry smile. "There was a time when I trusted Quinn with my life. It never occurred to me that a day might come when he wouldn't be there. But that day came, Duncan, and if it happened once, it can happen again.

Especially with Edward in the picture. For Zack's sake and my own, I have to be sure of him before I make any promises."

"Your marriage was that bad?"

"It was wonderful. For a while, anyway. Until Edward started calling every day, pushing Quinn's buttons. Each time, Quinn would get a little tenser. He'd stay silent for hours on end. I could see it happening, but I didn't know how to stop it. Then he started dropping comments about the benefits of living in Chicago."

She took a deep breath. "I finally confronted him, reminded him that we'd agreed to make the ranch our home. That's when the fights started. He said I was being unreasonable, that I'd fit in with his high society friends just fine. It was a lie, though, and we both knew it. I'm not cut out to wear fancy clothes, or sit around a country club sipping tea all day. Ranching is all I know, all I've ever wanted to do. I could have given in, moved for his sake, but it would have killed our marriage as surely as Edward did."

Duncan nodded. "He's changed, Lanie. Nearly dying can do that to you. Edward doesn't have the power over him he had before."

"I'll have to see it for myself before I trust him again."

"You will. Have you told Harper you aren't marrying him?"

"No, he's gone for a week. I'll tell him when he gets back Sunday. In the meantime, I'd appreciate it if you don't say anything to Quinn. Jared deserves to hear it first."

"You got it."

She stood. "Thank you for listening, Duncan. I can see why Quinn thinks so highly of you. I'm glad you're going to be staying in Watson."

"So am I. And I hope we can be friends, too."

"I'd like that very much." She smiled at him. "Goodnight, Duncan."

"Goodnight." He picked up his abandoned book and opened it.

Lanie made her way down the hall, and quietly up the stairs. For a moment, she stopped outside Quinn's room and lifted her hand to the door. "I hope Duncan is right and this time you stay," she whispered.

Instead of going to her own bedroom, she crossed to Zack's and eased the door open to slip inside. A small nightlight cast a dim glow over the room, and its light picked out a tall figure standing by Zack's bed. Startled, her hand flew to her mouth.

"It's me," Quinn's voice came out of the shadows.

"What's wrong?" She moved quickly to his side, her eyes straining to pick out Zack from among the blankets.

"Nothing." He slipped an arm around her waist. "I was watching him sleep. Sometimes it's hard for me to believe he really exists. I have to keep checking to make sure I didn't dream him."

"I still feel the same way, myself," she whispered, leaning her head against his shoulder. "I suppose we always will."

"Do you think we'll be sneaking into his room, checking on him, when he's twenty?"

She let out a soft chuckle. "Probably, but we can't let him know it. He'd be humiliated."

"It's strange. I never really thought about having kids, except in an abstract sort way. I had no idea I'd feel so much. Now I'd like a whole house full."

"Let's not get carried away," she murmured wryly. "One or two more would be plenty."

His head turned in her direction, and even in the weak light she could feel his gaze on her. "That sounds promising. I guess I could settle for two more. As long as it's with you."

She stepped away from him, but took his hand. "Come on. Let's get out of here before we wake him up."

Outside her room she stopped and faced him. Abruptly, she reached a decision as she studied his face. She'd stopped lying to herself. Maybe it was time she stopped lying to him.

"I'm not going to ask you in tonight, Quinn. I still need some time to think about all this. It feels like everything is hitting me at once. But there is one thing I need to tell you."

"What?" His amber eyes studied her warily.

She lifted her hand and cupped his cheek. "I love you. I don't think I ever stopped."

He inhaled sharply, then pulled her into his arms. "God, I've waited so long to hear you say that. I love you, Lanie. I'll go to my grave loving you." His mouth covered hers.

Chapter Eighteen

It was nearly June, Lanie mused, carrying her second cup of coffee to the office. The nights were warming up nicely, and the weather reports for this weekend were perfect. Her guests would get their money's worth.

Putting her cup on the desk, she sat down and picked up her list of things to finish before the trail ride. Pete and Ollie were ready. They would leave with the chuck wagon tomorrow and get the camp set up. The next day, Friday, the guests would arrive and the groups would head out at ninety-minute intervals. She would lead the first group, Sherry the last.

No rides were scheduled the day before a campout, so she made a note to send Cody and the others out tomorrow to round up the cows and get them settled down. As summer wore on, the animals became so used to the campouts that they rarely strayed too far from the area. But this early in the spring, with new calves at their sides, they could be almost anywhere on the twelve-hundred-acre ranch.

Her gaze wandered to the desk Quinn had set up across the room, and she smiled. Things had been different since she'd told him she loved him. They both seemed more relaxed, laughing and teasing each other.

He looked so good she had to stifle a sigh each time he walked into a room. Not once since he'd been back had he worn a suit. He was dressed this morning in faded jeans, boots and a black T-shirt that hugged his body snugly. His hair had grown a little too, making the white streak at his temple even more visible. She hadn't been able to take her eyes off him until he'd vanished inside the old bunkhouse with Duncan.

It was getting harder and harder to keep him out of her bed. Not because he was pushing her, but because *she* wanted him there. She wanted the freedom to touch him, make love with him, and wake up in his arms every morning.

The problem was, her conscience wouldn't let her. Not until she'd had a chance to talk with Jared, to tell him it was over. Only then would she feel free to be Quinn's wife again on every level.

Sunday wasn't that far off, and she wavered between anticipation and dread. The only solution was to stop thinking about it. With everything she had to do between now and then, it shouldn't be too hard to keep her thoughts off the confrontation with Jared. It was more difficult to keep her mind off Quinn when she saw him every day, when he looked so damn sexy.

She shook her head in disgust. Her libido seemed to be running in high gear these days. All she wanted to think about was getting Quinn back into bed.

Forcing her mind off her husband, she turned back to the list. The camping gear and sleeping bags had all been cleaned and aired, and were ready to go in the second wagon first thing in the morning. The couple who had won the drawing she'd held during Frontier Days had been notified and were ecstatic over the chance to go on the trail ride.

Everything was shaping up nicely, but she still needed to call Mrs. James at the travel agency's branch office and make sure there had been no last-minute cancellations. Just as she reached for the phone, it rang, and her brow furrowed in annoyance at the interruption.

"Hello?"

"You think you've won, don't you, girl?"

The voice was raspy, and sounded older than she remembered, but she recognized it immediately. Her body stiffened and her grip on the receiver tightened.

"Hello, Edward. Quinn isn't here. If you want to browbeat him, you'll have to call back later."

"It's you I called to talk with."

Her chin lifted, squared. "Too bad. I don't want to hear anything you've got to say."

"What has he promised you? That he'll stay in Wyoming and never leave? He's lying to you, girl, and it's time you found out the truth."

"Oh, right, Edward." Sarcasm laced her tone. "And you've always been so honest with me. Do you really think I'm going to believe anything you say?"

"Has he told you he owns controlling interest in the company now?"

It felt as though her heart was suddenly lodged in her throat. "You're lying."

"It's easy enough to check. His takeover has been in all the Chicago newspapers. Now where do you suppose he'll have to live while he's running the company?"

Her stomach churned and she was desperately afraid she was going to be sick. "I don't believe you. Why wouldn't he have told me?"

Edward gave a raspy laugh followed by a deep cough. "Because he didn't want you to know the truth, girl. Our lawyers told him you could wind up with half the company if you claimed he'd abandoned you, that he needed to establish residency before continuing with the divorce or a custody fight. He even went so far as to put all his assets in a trust fund for the boy so you couldn't touch them. Ask him. Let's see if he denies it."

"Goodbye, Edward." She dropped the phone into its cradle then stared at it, her body chilled. It wasn't true. It couldn't be. Edward had simply switched tactics. Quinn couldn't have made love to her like he had if he planned on betraying her.

But it hadn't felt like a lie.

She took a deep, shaky breath, then stood. No, she'd learned her lesson with Edward. She wasn't going to believe him this time. Not without proof.

The trip to Quinn's desk was the longest of her life, each step taking all her energy. Sweat beaded her forehead and coated the palms of her hands when she reached her goal.

The computer sat by itself to the left. The fax machine was on a separate table to the right. In the middle lay several stacks of neatly sorted papers.

Slowly she picked up the first stack and thumbed through it, her gaze scanning each page. There were production schedules for drugs with long names, reports from research and development, a thick sheaf of forms that had been filled out for the FDA, and a cost projection on yet another drug.

None of it made much sense to her. She only knew it wasn't what she was looking for. Without trying to be neat, she put the first stack down and picked up the second.

The top sheet was an e-mail printout, and she sank into the chair as she read it. According to his stockbroker, as of last Friday evening Quinn owned fifty-four percent of McAllister Pharmaceuticals. Edward had told the truth. And if he'd told the truth about this, what about the rest of it?

Bone deep pain surged through her along with a simmering anger. Yanking the first e-mail off, she wadded it into a ball and tossed it to the floor.

She wasn't even surprised to discover the next item was a thick legal document. The rest of the papers slid off her lap unnoticed as she read every word. It didn't take a lawyer to see what Quinn had done. It was spelled out clearly. All of his assets, including the company stock, were tied up in this trust fund. It left him virtually penniless.

Of course, as executor of the fund, and acting president of the company until Zack turned twenty-five, Quinn would draw a large salary. And there was still the ranch. He could make a small fortune by selling it, she thought bitterly.

How could she have believed him? Hadn't he proved she couldn't trust him five years ago? It felt as though her whole world had crumbled around her, the acrid dust of pain filling the air.

Well, he wasn't going to destroy her this time. She had a son to protect. The anger that had simmered became a boiling cauldron, threatening to scald any it touched. She'd be damned if she let him do to Zack what Edward had done to him.

Adrenaline propelled her out of the chair, the papers still clutched in her hand. Martha said something to her as she went through the kitchen, but the words didn't register on her consciousness.

The trip across the yard to the bunkhouse was made in a red haze of fury. She yanked the door open so hard it slammed against the wall, leaving a dent where the knob hit.

Inside, both men jumped at the loud bang, turning quickly to face her. Quinn dropped the weights he was holding and took a step in her direction.

"Lanie? What's wrong?"

"You bastard." She ground the words out through tightly clenched teeth. "You've been lying to me since the day you got here. And the pathetic thing is, I almost bought it. Was three months what your lawyers thought it would take to prove you didn't abandon me, Quinn?"

"What are you talking about?"

"This so-called trial marriage of yours. Are you going to deny your lawyers told you I could win half the company in a divorce settlement because you abandoned me? Or that I couldn't touch anything you owned if you tied it up in a trust fund for Zack?"

His face went white under the bronze of his tan. "No, but I didn't—"

"Just shut up! I don't want to hear any more of your lies." Her breath caught on a sob as she waved the papers at him. "This tells the whole story. Well, you want to know what I think about your trust fund?" Savagely, she ripped the papers into small pieces and threw them in his face.

"I never wanted your money or your company, and neither does Zack. We've made it fine on our own." She took a backwards step toward the door. "I can't make you leave the ranch, but Zack and I will be gone as soon as I can arrange it. Until then, stay away from me, Quinn."

Before tears could blind her, she bolted, Quinn's frantic voice following her as she ran.

Instinct led her to the stable. Several horses were saddled, waiting on a group of riders. She leaped onto the back of the closest, ignoring Sherry's alarmed questions. By the time they went through the open stable door, the chestnut mare was running flat out.

* * * * *

Quinn watched helplessly as Lanie raced away on horseback. Her face was buried in the mare's neck as she spurred it to greater speeds. It didn't take much imagination to know she was crying.

He had to find her, explain. With her head start, there was only one horse on the ranch capable of overtaking her. Xan. He knew the horse was kept in a separate pasture away from the mares, and it would mean taking the time to saddle the fractious stallion, but he'd have to risk it.

Even as he moved toward the stable, he gave a piercing whistle, praying the horse hadn't forgotten him. There wasn't time to chase him down.

For an instant there was silence, and he held his breath, waiting. Then in the distance he heard the shrill scream of the stallion, followed by the thundering of hoofs.

He watched long enough to see the black soar over the shorter inner fence, clods of dirt flying into the air when he landed. Quinn dashed into the stable, his gaze searching frantically. Several saddles were out, ready for use, and he grabbed one, hoisting it to his shoulder as he snagged a bridle from a hook.

Sherry blocked his return path into the corral. "Quinn, what are you doing? No one has ridden Xan in five years!"

"Then he should be well rested. Either help me, or get out of the way."

Xan was prancing nervously outside the door, his neck arched as he danced sideways. A cross between an Arabian and an American Saddle breed, the black was huge. His delicate ears twitched forward as Quinn crooned to him softly, and he took a hesitant step toward his owner. Cautiously, he extended his long neck, wide nostrils flaring as he checked Quinn's scent.

"That's a good boy," Quinn murmured. He caressed the satiny hide with one hand, and with the other slipped the bridle over the horse's nose. When it was buckled, he handed the reins to Sherry. "Hold him while I get the saddle on."

"Quinn, please." The blonde was clearly agitated. "Xan isn't one of our trained riding horses. Even if he's willing to let you on his back, it won't be from the right side. He's too excitable."

"I'll manage." He got the saddle on in record time, acutely aware of each passing second.

She snorted. "Sure you will. Okay, if you're determined to do this, try climbing up on the fence and mounting from there. I'll hold him until you're seated. At least that way you won't hurt your leg again."

His feet barely hit the stirrups before Xan exploded. The bridle was ripped from Sherry's grasp as the big horse raced across the corral. There wasn't even time to open the gate. Quinn braced himself when he felt the muscles beneath him bunch and tighten. Grinding his teeth against the strain to his thigh, he shifted his weight forward. And then they were airborne, Xan's front legs tucked to his body as they cleared the fence.

It almost seemed the horse had been waiting for this chance. Taking the bit in his teeth, he shot across the pasture like a bullet fired from a high powered gun. Quinn wrestled the black's head around until he was pointed in the direction Lanie had gone, then let him run.

Tears formed in his eyes as the wind created by their speed battered them. With every step, Xan's stride lengthened until they were flying across the ground, and the surrounding area became a blur of green.

He had no idea where Lanie might be. All he could do was hope she would continue in the direction she'd been going. The mare had been a quarter horse. Good for a brief burst of speed over a quarter-mile stretch, but lacking the stamina for a prolonged run. Xan could go on like this for miles.

Even then, it seemed like hours before he caught sight of Lanie. Without continued guidance, the mare had slowed, sweat still dripping from her chestnut coat after her forced exertion.

Lanie's head was down, her shoulders slumped, so lost in thought that the mare became aware of their presence before she did. The chestnut whinnied nervously, stepping sideways as she scented the stallion.

The movement brought Lanie out of her stupor. Quinn saw her glance over her shoulder, her eyes going wide at the black bearing down on her. Abruptly, she dug her heels into the mare's flanks, but it was too late. Quinn was beside her. Xan had slowed on his own as he reached the mare, and with no hesitation, Quinn plucked Lanie from her saddle.

For a moment she struggled, her hands beating his chest, then she went limp. "Damn it, I told you to stay away from me."

She may have stopped fighting, but her eyes were still molten with anger and pain. Tears had left tracks in the dust on her cheeks.

His arms tightened around her, and his own heart pounded with fear. What if she didn't believe him?

He cleared his throat. "Yeah, well, I don't take orders any better than you do. Did you really think I'd sit back calmly and let a bunch of lies ruin what we have together?"

She turned her face away. "They weren't lies. You own the company. You put all your money in that trust fund because you were afraid I'd try and take it away from you."

"That's not true, Lanie. Edward took the facts and twisted them around to his benefit. And he got exactly the reaction from you he was hoping for. Do you really want to play his games again?"

"I saw the papers with my own eyes."

He barely restrained the urge to shake her until her teeth rattled. The woman's middle name should have been "Stubborn". "Yes, you saw the papers. And yes, I did buy up controlling interest in the company. But I don't own it. Zack does. It all went into the trust fund. I don't want it, Lanie. And I don't want the ranch unless you come with it."

Xan danced restlessly at the added weight and Quinn shifted Lanie so she was sitting more comfortably on his lap.

"And I suppose you're going to tell me your lawyers didn't suggest you live with me?"

"No, they didn't. It was the day after you left Chicago. I kept telling them you had no reason to fight us, that you were the one who wanted a fast divorce. But Franklin Delaney, our lawyer, was having a nervous breakdown over the situation. He started listing all the legal problems that could crop up, and abandonment was one of them. He never suggested I live with you. What he suggested was that I come to Wyoming and get you to sign releases on all my finances."

She still wouldn't look at him, but he could tell she was listening. "Edward was dead-set against me coming back here. At first I thought it was because he was afraid if I came back, I'd want to stay. When Franklin insisted it was the only way, Edward dropped his bombshell. He finally told me about Zack."

Quinn took a deep breath and rubbed his forehead. "I can't describe the way it made me feel. To say I was mad wouldn't even begin to cover it."

She finally looked at him, her gaze searching his face.

"I wanted to hurt him, Lanie. The way he'd hurt me. But the only thing Edward cares about is that damn company. That's when I decided to acquire controlling interest. It wasn't just revenge, although that was part of it. I wanted the company to be there for our son, but there was the possibility that Edward would try to manipulate him the way he has me. I had to prevent that at all cost. I got the idea for the trust fund from my mother. She set one up for me that Edward couldn't touch. That's what I did for Zack. It had nothing to do with keeping you from getting it."

She was still searching face, trying to determine the truth of his words. "And what if Zack doesn't want the company, Quinn? Are you going to force him to take it anyway?"

"Of course not. Zack will be free to do whatever he wants. If he doesn't want the company he can sell it. At least this way he has a choice." He gave her a weak smile. "I was kind of hoping that by the time he was twenty-five we'd have a few more kids. Maybe one of them will be interested in the company if he's not."

"But as president, you'll have to run the company. That means you lied about staying here."

"No, Lanie. I'll be acting president, certainly, and I'll have to make trips to Chicago occasionally, but my CEO will handle most of the business. Anything that needs my attention on a daily basis, I can do from an office on the ranch. I won't have to be there in person. I'm not going to leave you and Zack again."

"I don't know." She shook her head. "Oh, God, I don't know what or who to believe anymore. I'm so tired of having my life torn into pieces. I can't do this right now, Quinn."

"You don't have to," he soothed, running a hand over her hair. "It will all be over in a few days. Edward's call to you was a last-ditch effort to cause problems. Franklin is filing the trust fund with the court this morning and notices will be sent to the board members this evening. Edward will have to leave and he knows it.

"Just promise me you won't do anything rash until you've had a chance to calm down and think things over. I love you, Lanie."

Her bottom lip quivered and she bit down on it before replying. "I guess if I didn't love you I'd be home packing right now. And I can't leave until after the trail ride, anyway." She wiggled off his lap and slid to the ground. "That gives me a few days to make a decision. We better get back before they send the whole ranch out to look for us."

It wasn't a promise, but he'd take what he could get at this point. He couldn't stand to lose her again.

Chapter Nineteen

Quinn sipped the hot coffee cradled in his hands, his gaze moving over the dark campground, searching for Lanie in the light from the bonfire. She'd been avoiding him since they had returned to the ranch Wednesday.

Not that it had been hard to do, he thought ruefully. He'd wound up on the phone with Franklin most of that afternoon, getting things in order. The man had been euphoric when Quinn offered him the CEO position. But there was no one he trusted more than Franklin. The lawyer knew the business almost as well as he did.

By Thursday morning, everyone had heard about the changes taking place, and he'd been swamped with phone calls from frantic board members. It had taken all his powers of persuasion to soothe them, plus a promise that a board meeting would be convened sometime in the next two weeks.

Now he had to figure out how to convince Lanie he would only be gone a few days. With the mood she was in, he was afraid to tell her about the board meeting at all. But he'd learned his lesson. Never again would he keep anything from her. Tomorrow was Sunday. As soon as they got back to the ranch and a little privacy, he'd sit her down and explain what was happening.

And then he'd make her go to bed and get some rest. A frown furrowed his brow as he checked the group again. For the first time since they had started on this trail ride, Lanie was nowhere to be seen.

He was really getting worried about her. She'd been like a dynamo, doing enough work for three people, never taking five minutes to rest. And while she laughed and talked to the guests, he'd seen the underlying tension she hid from the others. Dark circles had formed under her eyes and she hadn't eaten enough to keep a worm going. Now she'd vanished.

At the bonfire, one of the kids Lanie had hired pulled out a guitar and began to strum a tune. Quinn checked Zack's location, then stood resolutely. His son was sitting on a log between Sherry and Duncan, ready to join in the singing. That should keep him occupied long enough for Quinn to find Lanie. He had a pretty good idea where she was.

Stopping behind the small bathhouse, he let his eyes adjust to the darkness before moving toward the path leading into the woods. The moon was bright, and that helped guide his way. But even without the moonlight, the sound of gurgling, tumbling water would have led him in the right direction.

The small waterfall nestled in a rocky glade had been one of their favorite spots on the ranch when they were young. There was something almost mystical about the place at night. The water seemed to glow with a light of its own, and he wouldn't have been surprised to see fairies dancing in the clearing.

Instead, he saw Lanie. She was perched on a rock facing the falls, knees drawn up to her chest with her chin resting on them as she stared into the water. Half afraid she'd run, he moved to her side, sitting gingerly.

"It's still beautiful," he commented softly.

Lanie didn't even glance at him, and for a second he wondered if she was aware he'd joined her. When she finally spoke, her voice was low.

"I've always thought Zack was conceived here, that last time." Her chin quivered and a single tear glistened on her cheek. "I'm not pregnant, Quinn. I started about an hour ago."

She brushed the tear away with the heel of her hand. "I'm such an idiot. A baby is the last thing we need right now. I should be happy I'm not pregnant. But it feels like I've lost something special and I can never get it back again."

"Sweetheart." Through his own disappointment, he reached for her, pulled her onto his lap. "You aren't an idiot. I wanted you to be pregnant, too." Her arms curled tightly around his neck and he could feel her body trembling against his. Instinctively, he rocked her, his hands moving slowly over her back.

"I love you, Angel, and there's nothing I want more than to have another baby with you. But there's no rush. It will happen sooner or later."

"If you're here." Her voice was muffled against his shoulder.

"I'll be here, Lanie. Like I told you before, there will be times I have to go back to Chicago, but it will only be for a few days. I'll always come home again."

"Do you promise?"

A sweet ache of joy filled his soul and he smiled. "Not only do I promise, I cross my heart."

The tension drained from her body, leaving her soft and warm in his arms.

"Okay," she whispered. "I guess I'll stay. I didn't know what I was going to tell Zack, anyway."

"Is that the only reason you want to stay? Because of Zack?"

She hesitated, then shook her head. "No. I'm tired of fighting my feelings, Quinn. I may be taking a chance, but it's time I started trusting you."

He buried his face in her hair, a lump the size of a fist in his throat. Did this mean she was finally ready to call it quits with Harper and make a life with him instead? God, he hoped so. But he didn't dare ask her. Not right now. He would have to be happy with what she was willing to give.

"I think you're just tired, period." He brushed his lips across her temple. "I know you haven't been eating. Have you been sleeping?"

"Not much. Maybe a few hours a night."

"Then it's time you did. You can't keep pushing yourself like this, Angel. As soon as we get back to the camp I want you to eat, then go to bed."

She sighed. "I can't. I have to take care of the guests, and then there's Zack. If I don't put him to bed he'll stay up half the night."

"I'll take care of Zack. As for the guests, let the people you hired do their job. They don't need you every second."

"I'm not sure I can sleep. Every time I try, I just lie there with my mind spinning from one thing to another." She pushed a lose strand of hair away from her face and hesitated. "Will you stay with me tonight? I don't want to be alone."

"You know I will. I'll always be there when you need me." He stood and lowered her feet to the ground, catching her hand. "Come on. The sooner we get back, the sooner you can get some sleep."

He led her straight to the chuck wagon. Ollie, the younger of the two brothers who served as cooks for the trail rides, was rummaging through the items on the lowered side of the wagon. He glanced up as they stopped, then smiled, his eyes nearly disappearing into his whiskered cheeks.

"I was hoping you could get her to eat." He took a covered plate off a shelf. "Saved her supper just in case."

"Good." Quinn watched Lanie take the food. "Now make sure she eats it even if you have to sit on her." The threat wasn't a mild one, considering Ollie's size.

Lanie rolled her eyes, but obediently took the cover off the plate and sat down. Quinn leaned over and brushed her cheek with his lips. "I'll put Zack to bed while you finish."

He wound his way through the guests who were singing "Sweet Betsy from Pike" with more enthusiasm than talent, until he reached Duncan and Sherry. He squatted near the blonde, his voice low when he spoke to her. "I've convinced Lanie to get some sleep. Can you handle things without her?"

"Sure." She glanced at Zack before leaning closer. "I've been worried about her. She's running on nerves and not much else. If anyone ever needed a vacation, she does."

"That's not a bad idea. I'll see what I can do." He put his hand on Zack's shoulder. "Hey, champ. Ready to hit the sack?"

"Aw, Dad! Do I have to? I want to listen to the music."

"You can still hear it from bed. Pete and Ollie have the canvas raised on the wagon, so it'll be just like sleeping outside tonight."

Zack gave a long-suffering sigh. "Okay. Can I sleep with my clothes on like everyone else?"

Quinn ruffled his hair then picked him up. "If you want. But you have to take your boots off."

"Where's Mom?"

"Eating. Do you want to tell her goodnight?"

"Yes." Zack put his head on Quinn's shoulder, his small arms looping around his father's neck. He was already half-asleep.

Lanie looked up as they stopped, then put her plate aside. It wasn't empty, but Quinn could tell she'd made some headway on the food.

"I think I'd like to put him to bed, if you don't mind." She stood and took Zack from his arms, hugging her son close. "It feels like days since I've seen him. Why don't you get your sleeping bag and put it in my tent?"

He waited until she carried Zack into the back of the wagon, then walked to the truck Cody and Duncan had brought in case of accidents. A small city of pup tents was scattered around the camping area, but last night he'd slept in the open. Lanie's tent was set up near the wagon so she could hear Zack if he needed her.

Quinn crawled inside with his sleeping bag, then paused, eyeing Lanie's bag. Quietly, he zipped the two together to make one larger bed, listening to Lanie's voice as she murmured to Zack.

"Now remember, if you wake up tonight and need anything, all you have to do is call me. I'll be right outside."

There was a pause and then Zack's hesitant voice. "Mom, are you still scared Dad will leave? You've been acting funny."

"I'm sorry, sweetie. I didn't mean to worry you. It's just that sometimes grown-ups can have a lot of different problems. I promise to do better, okay?"

"Do you miss Jared? He hasn't been over in a long time."

Quinn sat up straighter, his head tilted as he listened for her answer.

"Jared has been gone all week. That's why he hasn't been by to see you. He'll be home tomorrow."

"Where did he go?"

"On vacation. Now, it's time for you to go to sleep. I love you."

"Love you, too." His words ended on a yawn.

While Lanie climbed down from the wagon, Quinn mulled over the information he'd heard. He'd wondered why Harper was making himself scarce. He had hoped it was because the man had finally accepted the fact that Lanie would never be his wife. Now it looked like the last week had only been a brief hiatus from the battle.

Lanie didn't even blink at the doubled sleeping bag. She merely pulled her boots off and climbed inside. Quinn mimicked her actions, then wrapped his arms around her, pulling her back into the curve of his body. "Comfortable?"

"Yes. Unfortunately, I'm not sleepy."

"You need to relax. Turn over on your stomach."

Obligingly, she shifted, laying her head on her crossed arms.

He pushed her T-shirt up and gently massaged the tight muscles in her back, feeling them loosen as his fingers worked. "Sherry thinks you need a vacation."

"Sounds heavenly. Some place hot, with sand, water and no horses."

"The Bahamas?"

"Too crowded. I'd rather go somewhere that wasn't overrun with people."

"There's a place on St. John that fills the bill. Exotic, luxurious, and cabins with private beaches."

"You're serious?"

"Of course. We could make it a honeymoon. You didn't have one the first time."

"I don't remember it bothering me," she said softly. "The lake seemed the perfect place for our wedding night. You turned the radio on in the truck and we danced for hours, barefoot in the grass."

"And then made love under the stars."

She sighed. "It was wonderful. I don't see how an island could have topped it."

Her voice had grown drowsy and Quinn stopped massaging to gently rub the soft skin on her back. It wasn't long before her even breathing told him she'd drifted off to sleep.

With a smile, he pulled her shirt down and lay beside her, breathing in her fragrance. Just as soon as he got the board members settled down, he was buying two tickets to St. John. And he would make sure she enjoyed it as much as she had their wedding night.

* * * * *

Bright sunlight woke Lanie, and she lay still a moment trying to figure out what was missing. Quinn. Eyes closed, she stretched a hand out to discover the other side of the sleeping bag was empty. But she knew he'd stayed with her all night. The vague memory of his arms holding her clung even now that she was awake.

A smile curved her lips as she extended her toes and stretched. She felt better than she had in a long time. Rested and free of the tension that had been her constant companion for the last few weeks.

"Hey, sleepyhead. Are you going to stay in bed all day?"

She opened her eyes to find Quinn kneeling at the opening of the tent, a plate in his hands.

"I brought you some breakfast."

"What time is it?"

"Nine-fifteen or so. You slept almost ten hours."

She sat up abruptly, searching frantically for her boots. "Why didn't you wake me up? My group should have started back to the ranch an hour ago!"

"Don't panic. Sherry changed the order. Your group will go last. You've got plenty of time."

"Zack?"

Quinn grinned. "He's watching what's left of the tourists try to rope cows."

She laughed and reached for the food. "Are they having any luck?"

"Not a bit."

"Probably a good thing. I doubt any of them would know what to do with a cow once they dropped a loop on it."

She made short work of breakfast, then together they packed the tent and sleeping bags in the wagon. By the time the horses were saddled, her group was the only one left. She stood in the stirrups and counted heads to make sure no one was left behind, then headed toward the ranch in a more direct line than they'd taken on the trip out.

Unlike Friday, Quinn rode beside her with Zack's pony on his other side. While the two chatted away, she unabashedly admired her husband, aware of the change in attitude she'd undergone since yesterday. When she'd told him last night that it was time she trusted him, she'd meant it. And the relief that had come with her decision had been too enormous for words.

Part of her wondered if she were only seeing what she wanted to see, fooling herself into believing he'd stay. But he had promised her, and she couldn't stop herself from thinking he meant it this time. As soon as she got back from Jared's, she'd tell Quinn that she wanted to make their trial marriage a real one.

The thought of Jared made her nibble her bottom lip, and tension edged its way back into her muscles. She dreaded the meeting with him, telling him it was over between them. Hurting him was the last thing she wanted, yet there was no way around it. Maybe he didn't have her love, but he deserved her honesty.

"What's the frown for?"

She glanced at Quinn then made herself smile. "Thinking about things I shouldn't be thinking about on a beautiful day like today."

It was true, in a way, she decided. There was one painful chore to get through, and then she and Quinn could start a new life together. They would finally be a real family.

Happiness welled inside her. Never again would she doubt Quinn. He was really going to stay on the ranch with her and Zack. And maybe there would be another baby soon. She went all soft thinking about it.

"If you don't stop that, I'm going to be forced to drag you off the horse and make love to you right here in front of everyone."

"Stop what?" Lanie blinked at him innocently.

"Looking like that."

A laugh erupted from her lips. "That would sure give them their money's worth." She shook her head. "As much as I normally love these trial rides, I'd like to get this one over with. Think we could coax them into a gallop?"

"Unless they want to get left behind. After you."

With a brief warning to those following her, Lanie urged her horse into a slow canter. There were a few squeals, but everyone seemed to be hanging on.

What was that saying? Today is the first day of the rest of your life. In her case, she felt it really was true.

Chapter Twenty

Quinn slid from the horse with a feeling of relief when they reached the stable. While his leg had improved amazingly, it was a little stiff after sleeping on the ground for two nights, and two long rides. He flexed it a bit, and saw Lanie watching him as she undid the girth on her saddle.

"Is it bothering you?"

"Not really. Just some tight muscles."

"That's bad enough. Why don't you go take care of it? I'll have one of the kids unsaddle your horse."

His jaw clenched. "I'm not a damned invalid. I can handle my own horse."

"I didn't mean. . ." Her gaze clouded over. "I'm sorry. Of course you can. I was only worried about you." She glanced at the people surrounding them. "We need to talk, Quinn. There's something I have to tell you."

A feeling of dread washed over him, leaving a hollow ache in his stomach. Suddenly, he wasn't too sure he wanted to hear what she had to say. What if she'd lied about trusting him, loving him? What if she'd made her choice and it was Harper?

He took a deep breath and nodded. "Now?"

"No, I've got too much to do this afternoon and I don't want us to be interrupted. How about tonight, after supper?"

"Okay." His nervousness increased. He felt like a Thanksgiving turkey waiting for the axe to fall across his neck, and he knew the feeling would grow stronger before tonight.

Trying to remain calm, he finished unsaddling the horse and turned it out to the pasture. On his way back through the stable he stopped beside Lanie.

"Anything you need me to do?"

"Thanks, but it's under control." She smiled at him. "All that's left is making sure everyone leaves with the right luggage."

"Then I guess I'll head for the house."

"Okay." To his surprise, she stood on her tiptoes and gave him a quick kiss. "I'll see you later."

Maybe he'd been wrong about why she wanted to talk to him. She certainly wasn't acting like a woman about to dump her husband for another man.

His emotions wavered as he crossed the yard. He had to believe this would all turn out right. If he didn't, if he didn't trust that she loved him, he wouldn't make it through the day.

Duncan was standing at the kitchen counter slapping together some ham and cheese sandwiches when Quinn came through the door. "Want one?" He arched an eyebrow in question.

"No thanks. I'm still full from breakfast." He got a cup from the cabinet and filled it with coffee before sitting at the table. "So, how's it going with you and Sherry? You seemed pretty cozy last night."

Duncan shrugged. "She's nice."

Quinn studied his back. "Why do I hear a 'but' in there?"

His friend slid the sandwiches onto a plate and carried them to the table, straddling the chair across from Quinn. For a moment he toyed with the food. "I don't know, Quinn. I'm not sure I'm capable of having a real relationship anymore. Sherry is a friend, but that's all she is."

"Dunc, it's been five years since Tracy died. You have to get on with your life. Sherry may not be the woman you want to spend forever with, but that doesn't mean you won't find someone someday. At least, you will if you start looking."

Duncan grimaced. "You make it sound like buying a new truck."

Quinn laughed. "Well, you sure wouldn't wait until the truck came to you, now would you?"

"I guess not." He took a bite of sandwich then spoke around the food. "How's it going with Lanie?"

Quinn's smile turned into a frown. "I don't know. One minute I think everything is wonderful, and the next I'm convinced it's all but over. She said she wants to talk tonight and there's only one reason I can come up with as to why."

Before Duncan could respond, the door flew open and Zack carried a squirming pup inside.

"Dad, can I bring Spot in to play for a while?"

Daisy had finally weaned the pups and, with a steady diet of puppy chow, they had doubled in size the last few weeks. Even Spot, the runt of the litter, now sported long gangly legs that nearly touched the ground when Zack held him.

"What does your mom say?"

"She's not here. She went to see Jared and she told me to stay with you until she gets back, so can I bring him inside?"

Quinn's heart twisted, but he tried not to let it show. "If you promise to keep an eye on him and take him outside if he needs to go to the bathroom."

"Yippee!" Zack dropped the pup to the floor and ran across the kitchen, Spot at his heels.

"Don't jump to conclusions."

Quinn looked up at Duncan's quiet words. "It's hard not to. She's obviously made up her mind. Her going to see Harper first doesn't look good. Right now she's probably telling him that by tomorrow I'll be out of her life."

"Or she could feel like she's not free to make a life with you until she's called it off with Harper. Give her a chance, Quinn."

Tiredly, he ran a hand through his hair. "You're right. But that doesn't make the waiting any easier."

The shrill ring of the phone interrupted him, and he waved Duncan back into his seat. "I'll get it. You're eating."

* * * * *

Lanie pulled the truck to a stop at the end of Jared's drive and shut off the motor. In spite of the bright sunlight, the scene was eerily similar to the last time she'd been here. The only thing missing was Sara's car.

Her feet felt like lead as she climbed out and started up the walk, and her palms were sweating. She'd made it up the stairs to the porch when she realized Jared was standing in the open doorway watching her.

"Come on in."

Nervously, she stuck her hands in her pockets. Under the circumstances, the thought of being alone with him in the house made her uncomfortable. "If you don't mind, could we take a walk instead?"

"If that's what you want." The smile he gave her was edged in sadness, but his voice was calm.

He knew, she realized. But that didn't let her off the hook. She had to tell him herself.

They walked toward the grove of trees at the far side of the yard and Lanie cleared her throat. "How was your vacation?"

"Fine. I stayed on my brother's boat and did a lot of thinking."

"The one in Florida?"

"Yes."

She nodded, then fell silent. God help her, she didn't know how to do this. They reached the shady area, and she still couldn't force the words out.

Almost as if he sensed her difficulty, Jared stopped. "Why don't I go first?"

"Okay." She leaned her back against a tree trunk and faced him.

"When I decided to become a vet, I knew it wasn't going to be easy. My family couldn't afford to help me pay for it, so I had to survive on loans and part-time jobs. By the time I finished I was up to my ears in debt. There was no way I could open my own clinic. So, for a year I worked with another vet. Almost every cent I made went toward the loans, and there wasn't much left for rent or food. I knew that at the rate I was going I'd never get it all paid off."

Lanie's brow furrowed. Why was he telling her this? She'd expected him to talk about them.

Jared saw her puzzlement and smiled. "Bear with me a bit and you'll understand." He lifted his gaze to the horizon and continued.

"One day, I got a phone call. This man told me he owned a clinic in a small town in Wyoming and they were desperate for a vet. He said he'd checked with the school I went to and they'd told him about me. And then he offered to pay off all my loans if I'd be willing to relocate and take over this clinic. He even knew of a house I could rent, a small ranch where I could treat larger animals if I wanted."

He closed his eyes briefly. "It sounded like a dream come true, but I told him I had to think about it. For the next few days I found out everything I could about this man, and he seemed legitimate. Not only was he rich, he owned a drug company that was listed in the Fortune Five Hundred."

Horror curled through her as she stared at him. "Oh, my God," she whispered. "Edward."

"Exactly." His expression was grim. "I managed to convince myself that what he wanted was no different than the programs offered to medical doctors. The ones that forgive their loans if they work in small towns for a few years. That's why I accepted. It wasn't until the day I left that I found out he wanted more than a vet."

He rubbed his forehead with one hand. "He said his ex-daughter-in-law and grandson lived in the area and he wanted me to keep an eye on them, to make sure they were okay and didn't need anything. He said his son was pretty much a bastard who had gotten you pregnant then abandoned you. But I wasn't supposed to let you know what I was doing because you wouldn't accept help from him. Even then, I didn't see anything wrong with his request. He just sounded like a lonely old man who wanted to make up for what his son had done, make sure his grandson was all right."

His tone lowered and he touched her cheek. "What I didn't count on was falling in love with you the first time I saw you. I thought I could check on this daughter-in-law occasionally and get on with my life. But you became my life, you and Zack."

He shook his head as though to clear it and his hand sank to his side. "Over the last four years, I've sent him dozens of pictures of Zack, and even a video or two. When you decided to take a shot at a riding stable, Edward was the one who contacted the travel agency and had them call you. He's even been paying their advertising fee for the ranch."

She couldn't believe what he was telling her. Shock after shock rippled across her mind. "Why didn't you tell me?"

"Because I was in love with you, and scared to death you'd hate me if you found out. I knew you'd think I'd only been pretending so I could get closer to you. Besides, it all seemed perfectly natural. Until Quinn showed up."

He sighed. "That's when Edward's calls increased, and he started making more demands on me. He wanted to know every move you both made. There hasn't been a day gone by that he hasn't called wanting information. Until last Sunday, he was driving me out of my mind."

If she hadn't been leaning against the tree, Lanie was pretty sure she would have fallen. Her knees were too shaky to support her weight. "What happened last Sunday?" she whispered.

"I called Edward and told him it was over, that he could find himself a new spy. And I told him what he could do with the clinic. If it takes the rest of my life, I'm going to pay him back every cent of my loans."

Her head was spinning, but there was one more thing she had to know. "That Saturday at the food court when you said McAllister warned you, you were talking about Edward, not Quinn."

"Yes. He kept telling me if I didn't want to lose you, I'd better not leave you alone with Quinn." The sadness was back in his smile. "But I lost you the minute he came back, didn't I, Lanie? I think I knew it the first time I met him. He was nothing like Edward had led me to believe."

Tears filled her eyes as she gazed at him. He was so handsome, so dear. And she was going to hurt him so badly. "I'm sorry, Jared. This is all my fault. I know now that I never loved you the way I should have, and you deserve so much more from the woman you marry. You deserve to be the center of her world. Even if Quinn hadn't come back, it would have been a mistake for us to get married."

He used his thumb to brush away the moisture that spilled onto her cheek. "I've always known you still loved him, Lanie. I guess I thought if we were married I could make up for whatever was missing. But I was wrong. If we'd stayed married for a hundred years I still wouldn't have been him. I finally realized that last week. And I love you too much to stand in your way."

"Oh, Jared. You'll find someone else to love, I promise."

He shook his head and stepped away from her. "There will never be another woman for me, sweetheart."

Slowly, she reached into her pocket and pulled out the small diamond she'd kept in the truck's glove box. "I know it doesn't feel like it now, but there will be. And when you find her, she'll wear your ring with joy and pride."

A suspicious hint of moisture filled his eyes as he tucked the diamond into his shirt pocket. "Just tell me you forgive me for believing Edward and I'll be satisfied. I couldn't stand thinking you hated me."

"Of course I don't hate you. You had no way of knowing what Edward was like." She hesitated. "What are you going to do now?"

"I'm not sure yet. My family wants me to move back to Montana and open a clinic there, but I haven't decided for sure." He shrugged. "It will take me a few weeks to settle things at the clinic here in Watson. I guess I'll figure it out as I go."

"I wish you'd stay, but I'll understand if you can't. If you do leave, will you stop and see us first? It would kill Zack if he couldn't tell you goodbye."

"I'll stop by."

He walked her to the truck and opened the door for her. "I hope McAllister knows how lucky he is."

"So do I." She reached for the key, then hesitated. "I do love you, Jared. I only wish it could have been more."

Leaning into the truck he brushed her forehead with his lips. "No you don't," he whispered. "He's the one you've always wanted. Be happy, Lanie, and know I'll always be there if you need me. All you have to do is call." Gently, he closed the truck door and lifted his hand. "Goodbye, sweetheart."

She fought her tears until she reached the end of the long, winding drive, then pulled over. With sobs shaking her frame, she buried her face in her hands and let them come. He'd looked so devastated, so miserable. But even after she'd torn him in half, he'd only thought about her, what would make her happy. Men like Jared Harper didn't come along every day, and she prayed he'd find some kind of peace.

The sun was sinking low over the mountains to the west when she finally dried her eyes and straightened. It was time to go home, home to her husband and son. And it was way past time to start the life Edward had denied them.

Edward. As she drove, she mulled over what Jared had told her about him. Why on earth had the man wanted to help her with the riding stable? Was he afraid she'd hit Quinn up for child support and thus spill the beans about Zack? He certainly wouldn't have wanted that to happen. But that didn't explain the pictures and videos Jared had sent him. Was it possible that Edward had been curious about his grandson after all? Or maybe Jared had simply assumed Edward would want to see Zack and sent them on his own.

The closer she got to the ranch, the more determined she became to get to the bottom of the mystery. She'd have her talk with Quinn tonight, and first thing tomorrow morning they would call Edward and find out exactly what was going on.

* * * * *

Quinn lifted the phone to his ear then winced at the nearly hysterical voice on the other end. It took him a second to identify the caller as Franklin.

"For God's sake, Franklin. Slow down. I can't understand a word you're saying."

"Where the hell have you been? I've been calling every hour since Friday!"

"On the trail ride. I told you about it."

"Don't you have a housekeeper or something?"

Quinn glanced at Duncan. He'd put his sandwich down and was listening to Quinn's end of the conversation. "Yes, but since no one was on the ranch, she went to visit her sister this weekend. What's up?"

The sudden silence from Franklin had his nerves standing on end. "Franklin?"

"God, Quinn. I don't know how to tell you."

"Just spit it out."

The lawyer took a deep breath. "It's Edward. He had a heart attack some time Thursday night. His housekeeper found him Friday morning and called an ambulance. You have to come home, Quinn."

Fear had adrenaline pumping in his veins. "Are you sure this isn't another one of his tricks?"

"It's no trick. The doctors don't know how he's held on this long. He's been slipping in and out of consciousness, but the times he's aware are getting shorter. If you don't leave now, it may be too late. I think he's only hanging on until you arrive. I can send the jet to pick you up."

"No." He tried to think, make a decision. "It would only take twice as long. We'll take a commercial plane. I'll call your cell phone from the airport and let you know the flight number. Tell him I'm on my way, Franklin. Don't let him die." He hung the phone up and turned to Duncan as his friend pushed his plate aside and stood.

"Edward had a heart attack. You call the airport and see if we can get on a flight. I'll pack."

Duncan reached the phone then paused. "What about Zack?"

"Damn." Quinn took the receiver from his hand. "I'll see if Lanie is still at Harper's." He found the vet's number on a list by the phone and punched it in. After six rings, he hung up. "They aren't answering. Sherry?"

Duncan shook his head. "She said she had a hundred errands to run this afternoon. I doubt if we can find her."

Quinn ran a hand through his hair. "We can't wait. He'll just have to come with us and I'll leave Lanie a note." He handed the receiver to Duncan. "Hurry."

As Duncan dialed, Quinn turned and ran down the hall. "Zack?"

"I'm in here."

In the den door he stopped and forced calm into his voice. "Hey, champ. How would you like to go on a trip with me? You'll get to ride on a plane and everything."

"Really?" Excitement lit his son's eyes. "Will I have to go to daycare?"

"Not until we get back. Want to help me pack your clothes?"

Zack bounded to his feet and raced up the stairs. Quinn wasted no time following him. He was cramming clothing into a suitcase when Duncan called up the stairs.

"Forget packing our things. We've still got clothes at the penthouse. If we rush, we can make the next plane, but we have to leave now."

Quinn slammed the lid on the case and snapped the locks closed. "Come on, champ. Let's get out of here."

They were going out the door when he remembered Lanie. Shoving the suitcase at Duncan he turned back to the house and grabbed a piece of paper and pen.

Lanie,

Gone to Chicago. Zack is with me. I'll call when I can.

"Quinn! We have to go!" Duncan's yell rang through the room.

Cursing under his breath, he signed the note "Quinn" and propped it on the table before running out the door.

Chapter Twenty-One

Lanie climbed out of the truck, her gaze fixed on the house. It was strangely quiet, with not a single light showing from any window. Only the stable was lit, and she doubted Quinn would be there. A glance showed her the Jeep Quinn had rented wasn't parked in its usual spot and her shoulders slumped.

Where could they have gone at this time of the evening? She wanted so badly to talk with Quinn, to feel his arms holding her. She needed the comfort he offered. Now it would have to wait a little longer.

Maybe they had driven into Watson for takeout. If so, they would probably be back soon. Feeling better, she reached for the back door only to stop abruptly at the sound of whining coming from inside.

"Spot?"

The pup scratched eagerly at the frame, his black coat nearly invisible in the dark room.

"What in the world are you doing in there?" She stepped through the door and picked the pup up. "I'm going to have Zack's hide if he snuck you in and then forgot about you."

Spot tried frantically to wash her face, wiggling so much she nearly dropped him.

"Poor baby," she crooned. "Were you scared? Come on. Let's get you outside."

She set him on the porch, watching as he darted down the steps and made a beeline for the stable. As soon as he disappeared from view, she flipped the kitchen light on. And froze.

A plate sat forlornly on the table with the half eaten remains of a sandwich, and the smell of burnt coffee drifted from the pot on the countertop.

The fine hair on her arms sprang erect. Something was wrong. Neither Quinn nor Duncan would have left the coffee pot on when they were leaving.

She turned it off and took the glass carafe from the heat. It wasn't until she faced the table again that she saw the paper propped against the salt shaker.

A note. Quinn had left her a note. The relief that flowed through her was short-lived as she picked it up with a trembling hand and read the message.

The muscles in her legs went lax and she groped for a chair. Dear God. He had left her again, and this time he'd taken their son with him.

* * * * *

The plane glided to a gentle landing, then taxied to terminal one at O'Hare and came to a stop. Impatiently, Quinn undid his seat belt and reached for Zack's. In spite of the late hour, his son was filled with boundless enthusiasm over his first airplane ride.

"Are we here?" Zack's eyes were wide as dinner plates.

"Yes, we're here." He scooped the little boy into his arms. "I'm going to carry you so we can go faster, okay?"

"Okay. Don't forget my suitcase."

"Duncan has it." He took a second to hug his son before stepping into the aisle, hoping it would calm his screaming nerves. The need to run, to get to the hospital as quickly as possible was fighting with his common sense. They couldn't afford to be detained for any reason, and these days, running through an airport was a sure path to disaster.

As they left the gate, a short man dressed in a chauffeur's uniform blocked their path. "Mr. McAllister. Mr. Delaney sent me to drive you to the hospital."

Quinn searched his mind and finally came up with a name to match the man's face. "Thank you, Charles. Where did you park?"

"Outside the luggage terminal, sir."

"This way." Duncan gestured down a hall. "It will be faster if we take the tunnel."

They pushed their way though the crowd heading in the same direction, Quinn taking little notice of the blue, pink and purple lighting lining the tunnel. In the background, "Rhapsody in Blue" played softly, but the music only increased his anxiety.

He glanced at Charles. The man was making a valiant effort to keep up with them, his shorter legs churning. "Is Franklin still at the hospital?"

"Yes, sir. They took your father to Northwestern and Mr. Delaney has never left his side. I'm sorry, sir, but he said to tell you that Mr. Edward's condition is deteriorating rapidly."

They went by the luggage turnstile at a near jog, and Quinn hit the outer door with the palm of his hand, slamming it open as he made straight for the shiny black limo at the curb.

Zack stared around the interior as Quinn fastened his seat belt. "It's got two back seats. Is it yours, Dad?"

"In a way." The truth was, it belonged to Zack now, but he couldn't tell his son that. It would only confuse him, and the trip alone was enough for him to deal with.

As the limo pulled into the traffic, Quinn turned on the speaker to the front. "Charles? Go as fast as you can."

"Don't you worry, sir." The chauffeur's voice sounded mechanical and far away. "I'll have us there in no time."

Quinn leaned back and closed his eyes, wishing desperately that this was simply another of Edward's schemes.

But he knew it wasn't. His insides were twisted into painful knots, and sweat beaded his forehead.

He couldn't even imagine his stubborn, strong father lying in a hospital bed. Other than the bouts of arthritis, Edward had always been healthy as a horse. Was there some sign he'd missed, something that should have warned him his father was ill? Now that he thought about it, Edward had been paler than normal the last time he'd seen him. He had chalked it up as a reaction to the fight they'd had.

Beside him, Zack's weight increased as his eyes drifted shut. Quinn shifted him into a more comfortable position, then glanced at Duncan.

"What if this is my fault, Dunc? What if the shock of losing the company caused his heart attack?"

"It's not your fault. Don't even start thinking it is. If Edward's heart was bad, this would have happened anyway. You only did what you had to for Zack's sake."

"I hope you're right," he murmured. "I'm not sure I can live with myself otherwise."

* * * * *

Lanie's heart pounded so hard she could barely hear her ragged breathing. Standing was impossible. Instead she stared blankly at the note crumpled in her hand. Her baby was gone, stolen by the man she loved, the man she'd promised to trust.

Trust. She shut her eyes tightly and took a deep, painful breath. She had promised to trust him, and until she found out what was going on, she would do just that. There had to be an explanation, and she had to quit panicking and think logically.

Carefully, she spread the note out again and examined it. The handwriting was Quinn's, but it looked as though he had written it in a terrible rush. The letters were all jumbled together making the words barely legible.

Her gaze shifted to the plate. That and the coffee pot were another thing. Both men were invariably neat, always picking up after they made a mess.

She forced herself to her feet and went through the house, realizing for the first time that the TV was on in the den. The volume was turned down low enough that she hadn't heard it before.

Upstairs, she checked Quinn's room. All his clothes were in exactly the same place she'd last seen them. The same proved true of Duncan's room.

Zack's was a different story. Clothes were slung across the bed, some drooping toward the floor. A quick scan told her several outfits were missing, as was the small suitcase he used when he spent the night with Billy.

Her first assumption had to be right. Something had happened. Some emergency that forced Quinn to return to Chicago and take Zack with him. He had vowed he would never leave her again and she had to believe he'd meant it. The alternative was too horrible to contemplate.

But she couldn't sit and wait for him to call. Not without going crazy. What if she were wrong? What if he really had stolen Zack?

Running, she raced to her closet and pulled out her leather carry-on bag, cramming clothes in haphazardly. She knew where his penthouse was and where the company offices were located. Somehow she'd find them.

A bra strap dangled from the bag and she shoved it back inside as she took the stairs two at a time. Her headlong flight came to a halt when she saw a shadowed figure moving inside the stable. Tossing her bag in the truck, she stopped in the door, squinting in the light.

"Sorry. Didn't mean to disturb anyone." Cody's voice came from right next to her and she jumped.

"What are you doing here?"

"Cleaning tack. I didn't have anything else to do so I thought I'd get started on it."

"You haven't seen Quinn have you?"

The young man smiled at her. "He was pretty hard to miss, the way they tore out of here. Slung gravel for a hundred feet."

"How long ago did they leave?"

He tilted his hat back, thinking. "Probably about thirty minutes after you left. Is something wrong?"

"Listen, I have to catch a plane to Chicago. Can you call Sherry for me? Tell her she's in charge of the ranch until I get back."

"Sure thing. How long are you going to be gone?"

Lanie edged toward the truck, impatient to get going. Quinn already had a two-hour head start on her. "I don't know for sure. I'll call when I find out."

Without another word, she jumped in the truck and sped out of the drive, praying she'd be able to get a flight tonight.

* * * * *

The CICU waiting room was full, but Quinn spotted Franklin immediately. The lawyer was pacing from one end of the room to the other, his brown hair in disarray. Even as they approached him, he ran a hand through it, doing more damage to the normally impeccable style. Exhaustion and worry lined his face.

"Quinn! Thank God. They only let you go back to see the patients every few hours, and only for fifteen minutes. But I arranged for them to let you see him as soon as you got here."

"How is he?" Gently, he shifted Zack to Duncan's arms. His son hadn't wakened even when he'd carried him through the hospital.

"Not good. Come on. I'll show you where to go in."

A nurse looked up from her station outside the double wooden doors. "Mr. McAllister?"

"Yes."

She nodded. "Only one person is allowed in at a time. Mr. Delaney will have to wait here. Your father is in bed three."

A man in a white jacket sat beside Edward's bed checking monitors and typing into a computer, but Quinn could only gaze helplessly at his father.

Edward seemed to have shrunk to less than half his normal size, and even through the green of the oxygen mask Quinn could see how blue his lips were. He was so still that if it hadn't been for the erratic beep of the heart monitor Quinn would have thought he'd gotten there too late.

Choking on fear and pain, Quinn got his shaking limbs under control and moved to the side of the bed. "Dad?" Tenderly, he brushed back a stay wisp of white hair from Edward's forehead, noting how dry the skin was.

"Dad, I'm here."

Other than the monitors, the only sound in the cubicle was Edward's raspy breathing. It came in short bursts followed by a long pause that terrified Quinn.

"Dad?" He picked up the gnarled hand lying so still on the sheet and clasped it in both of his.

"Don't do this to me, Dad," he whispered, his eyes blurring with moisture. "Don't leave me. I need you. Oh, God." He lowered his head as tears flowed unheeded down his cheeks.

When the fingers he held curled weakly around his, Quinn's head shot up. "Dad, can you hear me? I came as soon as I could."

Edward's eyes opened slowly, with a great deal of effort. For a second he stared at Quinn as though trying to identify him.

"Got...you to...come back, didn't...I?" Each word was a struggle, more of a pant than real speech.

"Don't try to talk, Dad. I'm here now." He leaned over the bed and cradled his father's face.

"Waited...for you. Had to...tell you..."

Quinn's body shook with the force of the sobs he was holding back. "What? You had to tell me what, Dad?"

"Letter...on my...desk...for you." The last words were spoken on a sigh of air, and his body went limp. The line on the monitor went flat and alarms screamed. Suddenly the room was full of people, pushing Quinn outside as he fought frantically to stay with his father.

"Dad! No!"

* * * * *

Lanie gazed up at the building as the cab pulled away from the curb. From this angle, she couldn't see the penthouse. Someone brushed by her, and she clutched her bag tighter. She didn't remember the streets being this crowded last time she was here, but then she hadn't been paying much attention.

Bright light spilled through the glass doors, and she took a deep breath before pushing them open.

"May I help you?" The rotund doorman all but lifted his nose in the air as he surveyed her dirty jeans and wrinkled T-shirt.

"Yes, you can. I'm Mrs. McAllister and I need the key to my husband's penthouse."

One of his eyebrows vanished into his hairline. "I'm sorry, but we don't give clients keys to strangers without their permission. There's a phone on the desk if you'd like to call him first."

Now what? She didn't know the number to the penthouse and if she told this man that, he'd toss her out on the spot. Her chin squared as she rummaged through her purse and came up with her driver's license. "Here. You can check my identity yourself."

He glanced at the card, then handed it back. "Just because you have the same last name doesn't mean Mr. McAllister would want you to have his key."

Propping her hands on her hips, Lanie glared at him. "Listen, Buster. I can rope, throw, hog-tie and brand a five-hundred-pound cow in twenty seconds. You wouldn't even make me breathe hard. Now, I've had a very bad day, and if you're smart, you'll give me that damn key. Because if you don't, when I get through with you, my husband will take over and finish the job."

"You keep saying he's your husband, but I've known Mr. McAllister since he moved in." His eyes narrowed as he stared at her. "He's not married."

"Now that's where you're wrong. He's married to me and has been for five years. We have a four-year-old son."

The man's gaze swept over her again, and he hesitated. "Weren't you here a month or so ago?"

"That's right. I was wearing a red dress and my hair was done up."

He hesitated a moment longer. "Well, I guess it wouldn't hurt to let you in. If Mr. McAllister doesn't want you there, he can handle it himself."

"Exactly." With a great deal of satisfaction, she followed him to the elevator and watched him insert a key into a slot.

"That will take you straight up, Mrs. McAllister."

"Thank you." Relief flowed through her until the doors opened again on the penthouse. The apartment was cold and dark, with no sign anyone had been there in weeks. The same metallic smell she'd noticed on her first visit was more pronounced and she wrinkled her nose. The place could definitely use a good airing out.

And a cleaning, she decided as her fumbling fingers found the light switch. A light coating of dust covered the glass-topped tables.

Her shoulders slumped with despair as she moved farther into the room. They should have been here, and she had no idea where to look now that they weren't.

Feeling like an intruder, she checked each room in the huge apartment. Signs that Quinn had once lived there were everywhere, from the cluttered office to the spacious master bedroom with an adjoining bath.

Tired, hungry, dirty and scared out of her mind, Lanie dropped her bag on the king-sized bed in Quinn's room and headed back to his office. There had been a Rolodex on the desk. Maybe she could find the phone number of someone who would know why her husband and son had vanished.

Thirty minutes later, she slammed the phone back into the cradle, frustration fighting her anxiety. She'd tried Edward's number as well as the one listed for Franklin Delaney. There had been no answer at either place. A call to the company had only garnered a recorded voice telling her the office hours.

She was out of options. All she could do now was wait, and pray they would show up here before the night was over.

Chapter Twenty-Two

Lanie pushed her wet hair back and turned off the tap, her gaze sweeping the shower. There was no stall door, simply a wide opening at one end of the clear glass blocks separating the shower from the rest of the bathroom.

It was strange. She knew Quinn had been through numerous surgeries, and knew there had been times when he doubted he'd ever walk again, but the reality of what he'd gone through hadn't sunk in until she'd stepped into that shower.

Not only was it large enough for a wheelchair to maneuver in, there were odd looking brackets on the walls. They could only have been for handicapped bars. There were also two showerheads, the one she'd just used, and another above a ceramic tile bench.

Her heart twisted as she imagined Quinn, stubborn independent Quinn, unable to shower without assistance. He must have hated it. If only she'd been there for him when he needed her none of this would be happening now.

She squeezed the excess water from her hair and picked up a towel. There had to be a good reason he'd left again and taken Zack. Especially after his promise last night. And as soon as she got dressed, she was going to call every number in his file even if it meant waking up half of Chicago. She *would* find him, and when she did, he was going to get a piece of her mind for scaring her like this.

Draping the damp towel over the rack to dry, she rapidly braided her hair. She was tying the end off when she heard the quiet hum of the elevator doors opening. Frantically, she looked around the room. Her clothes were on Quinn's bed, but there was a dark blue terrycloth robe on a hook behind the door. She grabbed it and shoved her arms through the sleeves, listening to the voices from the front of the apartment. One was Quinn's, but the person doing most of the talking was a stranger to her.

"I sent Charles to restock your refrigerator this morning. He must have left the lights on. I didn't think to call Delores. I'll do that first thing tomorrow. Looks like the place could use a cleaning."

"There's no rush."

Lanie paused in the act of belting the robe. That last voice had been Quinn, but he sounded so tired, so defeated. She gave the belt one final yank and made her way through the bedroom. Before she reached the hall, Zack spoke. Her son sounded as though he were nearly asleep.

"Is this your home, Dad?"

"No, champ. The ranch is home. This is just where I stay when I come to Chicago. What do you say we try to give your mom a call again? Maybe she'll be home by now and you can talk to her."

Lanie gripped the door frame, her eyes closing in sheer relief. She'd been right to trust him after all. Smiling, she started down the hall. "She's not home. She's right here."

"Mom!"

Zack ran to meet her and she swooped him up into her arms.

"Guess what? I got to ride on an airplane and a lady gave me a set of wings and sodas and there was this tunnel with weird lights and music playing and a car with two back seats." He stopped to yawn.

"That sounds like a lot of excitement for one little boy." Her gaze met Quinn's over Zack's head and her smile faded. He was looking at her blankly, as if he'd never seen her before. But it was his face that made fear curl in her stomach. His skin was pale and lines of grief were etched around his mouth.

Slowly, she lowered Zack and took a step into the living room. Duncan brushed by the other two men and picked Zack up, his eyes meeting hers. "I'll show him his room and get him in bed."

Absently, she nodded.

"Lanie?" Quinn's voice was low, filled with doubt. "What are you doing here?"

"Looking for you." She stopped in front of him and lifted her hand to his cheek. "What's wrong, Quinn?"

"Didn't you find my note?"

"Yes, but it didn't tell me much. Only that you'd gone to Chicago and you were taking Zack with you."

"I see." He swayed on his feet then caught himself. "You thought I'd left again. I tried to call you at Harper's but there was no answer, and I couldn't leave Zack by himself."

Abruptly, she was in Quinn's arms, his face buried in her neck as his body trembled uncontrollably. Alarmed, she glanced at the man standing to Quinn's right as she held her husband protectively. The stranger looked helpless and worried.

"What's going on?" she demanded.

"I'm Franklin Delaney, Mrs. McAllister." He partially extended his hand, then drew it back and ran it over his mussed hair. "Edward—" His chest lifted as he took a deep breath. "Edward had a massive heart attack. He died about an hour ago."

Shock ripped through her and her arms tightened convulsively around Quinn. "Oh, God. I'm sorry, Quinn. I'm so sorry."

Franklin shifted from foot to foot then gestured down the hall. "I should make some calls. I'll be in the office if you need me."

As soon as the lawyer was gone, Quinn released her and moved to the wide bank of windows looking down on the city.

"Dad rented this place for me while I was still in the hospital the first time." His voice was low. "I hated it. Stupid, huh? He knew I was in no shape to do it myself, but I never even thanked him."

Lanie followed him and ran her hand over his back. "He didn't expect thanks, Quinn. Edward wasn't that type of person."

"That's no excuse." He lifted a hand to his forehead and rubbed. "This is my fault, Lanie. I knew what the company meant to him. That's why I took it away. I wanted to get even for all the things he'd done, to hurt him the way he'd hurt us. I wanted it so badly I fooled myself into believing I was doing it for Zack. But I wasn't. It was revenge, pure and simple, and now my father is dead and I'm no better than he was."

"No." She gripped his arms and turned him to face her. "No, Quinn. You're nothing like Edward. You're good, and decent, and loving, but you're only human. You were reacting to the hurt he'd caused you."

He was staring down at her as though he hadn't heard a word she'd said.

"I'm sorry I scared you," he murmured. "I tried to call from the airport, and again from the plane. There was never an answer."

"It's okay," she soothed. "I was only a little scared at first. Then I remembered your promise. I knew something must have happened or you'd never have left me again."

He slid his hands up to cup her neck, his thumbs moving gently over her jaw. "There was no answer, Lanie," he repeated. "I know I gave you three months to make a decision and it's only been half that time. But if you've made a choice, I have to know what it is. As much as I need you right now, I don't think I could stand to find out you're only staying out of some sense of duty."

"Oh, Quinn. Don't you know that for me there never was a choice? I've loved you since the first time I saw you. The night after that fund-raiser, when you brought me here, part of me knew I could never marry Jared. If you hadn't shown up at the ranch I would have found a way to call it off on my own. There's never been anyone else for me but you, and there never could be. That's what I was going to tell you tonight, but I thought I owed it to Jared to tell him first."

"You're sure?" A spark of hope replaced the sorrow in his amber eyes.

"I've never been more positive of anything. I love you, Quinn, and I want to spend the rest of our lives together."

For the second time that night she was swept into his arms, his lips moving over her face.

"I love you, Lanie. God, I was so scared when I couldn't reach you. Zack told me you'd gone to Harper's and I thought I'd lost you. Then when you walked out of the bedroom, wearing my bathrobe, I thought I'd dreamed you here because I wanted it so badly. I'm never letting you out of my sight again."

"You're going to have to." Duncan's voice came from across the room. "Zack wants her to tuck him in."

* * * * *

Lanie shifted on the seat of the limo as the long car pulled away from the cemetery. Quinn, sitting beside her, seemed to be holding up well. He'd accepted the condolences of everyone with stoic dignity, even comforting those who were most distraught.

But she knew appearances were deceiving. He'd eaten almost nothing since Sunday, and she doubted he'd slept more than a few minutes. She'd lost count of the times she'd awakened to find him on the bedroom balcony, staring into the night. He was hanging on by a thread, and it was only a matter of time before it snapped.

She reached for his hand and he returned the grip, holding on to her tightly. In a way, she wished he would snap. It would let him finally grieve. She knew from her experience with her own parents that without that cleansing, he couldn't begin to heal.

"Where are we going now?" Zack was fidgeting again, the way he had all through the funeral. She'd explained what was going on in the simplest possible terms, but he was only four, too young to really understand.

"We're going to your grandfather's house."

"Why can't we go back to Dad's?"

"I told you, sweetie. Because there are going to be lots of people there, and your dad's apartment isn't big enough to hold them all."

"Will there be other kids?"

"I'm sure there will. I saw a few earlier."

"Okay." He settled back on the seat.

"There's a swing set and jungle gym in the backyard." Quinn spoke for the first time since they'd entered the limo. "Dad had someone build it for me when I was little. I don't know why he never took it down."

Lanie glanced at him. "Maybe because it reminded him of you."

Quinn shook his head. "I doubt it."

"Can I play on it?" Zack was showing a bit more enthusiasm.

"Sure. But let Duncan check it first to see if it's still in good shape."

The car made a left turn onto a long driveway and Quinn's grip on her hand tightened until it was painful. "We're here."

The house came as a pleasant surprise to Lanie. Knowing Edward, she'd expected it to be big, and it was. What she hadn't expected was the style. It looked like a Swiss chalet, like something out of a fairy tale. The outside was white stucco with bare wooden beams showing through, and the windows on both floors were divided into leaded glass panes. Above the second story, the peaked eave extended outward, more exposed beams supporting the roof.

And the flowers. Not even the cars lining the drive could conceal the riotous blooms. Some were as common as roses, but others she'd never seen before. She'd love to have the time to wander among the beds and take a closer look.

"It's beautiful, Quinn."

"Yes, it is. Dad was so proud of this place." His voice was husky. "He'd laugh and talk about how the neighbors' noses were out of joint when the son of an immigrant moved into the area. I suppose it will have to be sold now."

Lanie's brow furrowed as they climbed out of the limo. She'd never considered the disposal of Edward's property, but it was obvious Quinn had. A trace of regret had been in those words.

It had to be sentimentality, she decided. He'd told her the ranch was his only real home. If it were true, there was no reason to keep this house.

The front door opened as they reached it, and an elderly woman greeted Quinn with a hug.

"Mr. Quinn. I'm so sorry about your daddy."

"Thank you, Enid." He put his hand on Lanie's back. "This is my wife, Lanie. Lanie, Enid was my father's housekeeper for longer than I can remember."

The woman's pale blue eyes swept over her before she smiled. "I'm happy to finally meet you, Mrs. McAllister, even under the circumstances. I've heard a lot about you." She leaned over to put herself on a level with Zack. "You don't have to tell me who this is. You look just like your pictures, Mr. Zack. I've got some cookies in the kitchen I made especially for you. Would you like to go have one?"

Quinn's gaze sharpened as the woman straightened and took Zack's hand. "What pictures?"

"Why, the ones in your father's bedroom. There must be a dozen of them." The housekeeper headed for the kitchen with Zack following her eagerly.

Quinn turned to look at Lanie. "You sent him pictures?"

"No, but I know who did." She saw Franklin approaching and shook her head. "I'll tell you about it later when we have more time."

She barely recognized this Franklin as the one who'd worked beside Quinn the last few days. His suit was crisp and every hair was in place. He exuded calm dependability and she blessed him silently for taking most of the arrangements from Quinn's shoulders. It was clear why Quinn had made him CEO of the company. He looked apologetic as he spoke.

"Quinn, several of the board members are waiting to speak with you. I know this is a bad time, but I think they need a little reassurance. It shouldn't take long."

Quinn rubbed his forehead tiredly then put his arm around Lanie's shoulders. "Okay, let's get this over with."

As they crossed the room, she leaned in closer. "Tonight you are going to get some sleep if I have to slip a sleeping pill in your drink."

"You'd probably do it, too." He smiled down at her. "But I don't need a pill, Angel. All I need is you."

* * * * *

Lanie breathed a sigh of relief as she slipped quietly from the room. If the house had been a surprise to her, the people now filling it had been an even bigger one. She'd always insisted that she would never fit in with Quinn's circle of rich acquaintances. But everyone had made a point to speak with her, make her feel welcome.

Had her grandfather's hatred of the wealthy colored her own opinion? A few days ago she would have said no. Now she wasn't so sure. Maybe they dressed a little better, but these people seemed no different than her friends at home.

Curiously, she glanced around the hall she found herself in. The house was so large she'd only seen a small part of it so far. The front of a wide staircase curved near the entry, and she made her way toward it, pausing to run a finger over the shiny surface of an antique table.

Edward may have been the son of an immigrant, but he'd certainly had good taste in furniture. Every piece she'd seen had been an antique, sturdy and comfortable. Unlike Quinn's apartment, this felt like a real home, one that should have been filled with the laughter of children.

At the top of the stairs, she hesitated a moment then turned left. The first room was a guest room. While decorated beautifully, there were no personal touches. It wasn't until she opened the door of the last room that she found signs of occupancy.

This must have been Quinn's room, she realized as she stepped inside. Partially used bottles of cologne still sat on the dresser and his familiar scent lingered in the air. On a chair in the corner lay a pair of sweats, looking as though he'd just stepped out of them.

A vague feeling of unease settled on her as she wandered around the room, examining an old tennis racket here, a trophy there. On one wall hung a picture of a younger Quinn with three other boys. All were sweaty and laughing, dressed in football jerseys, their arms draped around each others shoulders.

Every item in the room catalogued Quinn's growing up years. Years when she hadn't known him, and later, years when he'd lived here while he went to college. It was the room of someone who had been happy in this house.

Oh, God, what had she done? How could she have been so self-centered?

"I see you found my lair."

Lanie spun toward the door, her stricken gaze falling on Quinn. He'd undone his tie, leaving it loose around his neck. His voice had a raw, husky quality, and his eyes were rimmed in red.

"Don't sell it," she whispered.

His brow furrowed. "Don't sell what?"

"The house. Oh, God, Quinn. I was so wrong. All this time I've thought of the ranch as your only home. I could never picture you here. It was like this place didn't exist for me. But I was wrong. This is your home, the house you grew up in. I shouldn't have forced you to stay in Wyoming. You tried to tell me, but I wouldn't listen. It's no wonder you left me. I was stupid; stupid and naive, and blind."

"You weren't blind, Angel." His arms closed around her, pulled her tightly against his body. "The ranch is my home. I've always loved it. But I didn't understand until a few weeks ago that it was home because of you." He stroked her hair with one hand. "If you don't want to sell this house, then we won't. At least it will give me somewhere to stay when I have to come back."

She tilted her head back and stared at him. Somehow, he seemed different than he had earlier. "Are you okay?"

"I'll be fine." He reached into his shirt pocket and pulled out several sheets of paper. "Right before Dad died, he told me he'd left a letter on his desk. I found it about twenty minutes ago."

She took the letter he was holding out to her, hands shaking. "Are you sure you want me to read this?"

"Yes."

Hesitantly, she opened the pages, her gaze dropping to the first line.

Quinn,

If you're reading this, it means time has finally caught up with me. My doctors told me a year ago that my ticker was bad and nothing short of a transplant would help. I chose instead to live what was left of my life on my own terms. Which brings me to the reason for this letter.

If you think I'm going to apologize for everything I've done, you're wrong. I did what I had to do, and I've no regrets.

Laughter bubbled in Lanie's throat, pushing past the tears. "Typical Edward. Stubborn to the end."

Quinn put his arms around her from behind, and she suddenly realized the tension was gone from his body.

"Keep reading."

She nodded and leaned back against him.

There are things I should have told you long before now, but I could never bring myself to speak them out loud. A letter seemed easier for both of us.

We never talked much about your mother and I know you think I married her for her money. Well, you're right. When you've known the kind of poverty I grew up in, you'll do anything to get out of it. Again, I'm not apologizing. Love is weakness you can't afford when your future is on the line. Your mother understood that, and in our way we served each other well. She had you and her social functions, and I had the company. We were content.

There's one final thing I have to tell you before I go. I'm afraid your inheritance will consist of what money I have in my bank accounts and the house. You see, the stock in the company that would normally have gone to you, I no longer own. When I realized you were buying up company stock for my grandson, I ordered my broker to sell my shares to you. Zack has them all now.

It's ironic in a way. The only thing I ever wanted was to see you at the head of the company, continuing the heritage I started. Now, I've got exactly that, and you did it yourself. So, you see, in the long run, I've at least won that battle.

The battle over your wife goes to you, however. I still think you could have done better, but I'm willing to admit she's doing a fine job raising my grandson. Just make damn sure he knows everything he needs to know about my company before you turn it over to him.

Edward

Chapter Twenty-Three

☙

Lanie folded the letter carefully. "How do you feel about this?"

"Well, at least I know I didn't cause his death."

She turned in his arms, her own coming around his waist. "I never doubted that."

"You know, right now I just feel sorry for him. He never knew what real happiness was. He was too driven to succeed. It seems like such a waste of the time we're given."

"I know, but it was his choice, Quinn. He didn't have to be the way he was." Her head settled against his chest. "And I know this has been hard for you. When my parents died I was numb. Nothing seemed real anymore. I kept thinking it was a mistake, that any second they'd walk through the door. As long as I believed that, they weren't dead. It was a month before I finally accepted they were gone and let myself say goodbye."

"But you were only thirteen."

"Age doesn't matter. When we lose a parent, even a bad one, we're all children," she said quietly. "It's time for you to say goodbye to Edward now, and realize there's nothing you can do to change the past."

"I think you're right. But I'm so damn tired. I feel like I could sleep a week."

"That's natural. And it will probably be good for you…"

Her words trailed off as someone knocked on the door.

"Come in." Quinn kept his grip on her as Duncan stuck his head inside.

"Edward's lawyers are ready to read the will. They need you downstairs."

"Tell them we'll be there in a few minutes."

Duncan hesitated. "We have an unexpected guest. Harper is here." He shot Lanie a glance, then closed the door.

Quinn studied her face, noting the puzzled look. "You weren't expecting him?"

"Why would I be? He was—" She halted abruptly, nibbling on her bottom lip. "I was going to tell you later, when things calmed down a bit. He was working for Edward, Quinn. He has been the entire time. That's where Edward got the pictures of Zack. He confessed the whole thing to me last Sunday."

"I know."

Her eyes widened. "You knew? And you didn't tell me?"

"Well, let's say I suspected. Edward knew everything that happened on the ranch. He had to be getting the information from someone. Harper seemed the most likely candidate."

Quinn cupped her cheek. "I didn't have any proof, Angel, and I knew you wouldn't believe me without it. That's why I didn't tell you."

He hesitated then took a deep breath. "There's something else you should know. When I had the accident, I wasn't going to Chicago, Lanie. I was coming back to Wyoming, to you. The farther I went that night, the more I realized I'd never be able to live without you. So I turned the truck around and headed home. If I hadn't had the accident we'd have been together all these years."

Gently, he tilted her face up and searched her eyes. "We both have to stop blaming ourselves. Those years are gone and we can't get them back. But we can go on and make a life together from here on out." He dropped a kiss on her lips. "Now, let's get downstairs. Dad's lawyers are waiting."

* * * * *

Lanie was reeling with shock when they finally left the sitting room. She couldn't even begin to comprehend the amount of money he'd had in his bank accounts, the "only inheritance Quinn would get". It was more than most people could earn in ten lifetimes, and her husband hadn't even blinked.

Zack had been gifted with yet another trust fund, this one earmarked for his education. And it was big enough that he could go to Oxford if he wanted.

Even Jared hadn't been forgotten. Edward had left him the clinic in Watson. She glanced in her ex-fiancé's direction. He was standing by himself in a corner, looking lonely and uncomfortable and she couldn't help feeling sorry for him.

"Quinn..."

"I know." His knuckles skimmed her cheek. "Let's go talk to him."

Jared straightened as they approached, his eyes wary. "Sorry to intrude, McAllister. The lawyers insisted I be here."

"Don't worry about it. I'm glad Dad left you the clinic. You deserve it after what he put you through."

The vet's gaze drifted to hers, then he nodded curtly. "I agree with you. But knowing Edward, he only did it because he hoped I'd keep making trouble for you. You don't have to worry, though. I won't. And if it's any consolation, I think in his own warped way, Edward cared about Zack. He couldn't have been all bad."

Lanie threaded her arm through Quinn's. "Does this mean you'll be staying in Watson after all?"

"It looks that way." He cleared his throat. "When you get home I'd like to talk to both of you about buying your grandparents place."

She smiled at him. "You don't have to wait. I'd be happy to sell it to you."

"Guess that means we'll still be neighbors then."

"For a few months of the year, anyway." Her grip tightened on Quinn's arm as he looked at her in surprise.

"Lanie?"

"Excuse us, Jared. I need to talk to my husband."

She pulled Quinn away from the others, leading him to a window that overlooked the backyard. Zack was on the swing set, yelling in glee as his feet reached for the sky. Several other children and a few mothers were with him.

"He'll start school in the fall," she mused. "It really wouldn't be good for him to drag him back and forth from here to the ranch every few weeks. And I'm afraid I'm a little selfish. I don't want to be away from you for even a day."

She turned from the window to gaze up at Quinn. "When I was in your room, I knew how wrong I'd been to force you to stay in Wyoming. This is your home, and it always will be. And you were right about something else. For me, home is wherever you are. I think we should live here."

He looked as stunned as she'd felt after hearing the will read. "Lanie, I can't ask you to do that. You love the ranch."

"You aren't asking me." She touched his cheek. "I'm volunteering. As for the ranch, we'll still have it. We can spend every summer there, and every holiday. I'm sure Sherry will jump at the chance to run it herself."

"But you always said you'd die spending your time cooped up in a house. And you hate the idea of country clubs."

The cleft in her chin became more prominent as she grinned. "Who said I was going to stay cooped up? I think it's time the McAllister Riding Stable expanded. Some of these people sure look like they could use the exercise."

Quinn threw back his head and laughed. "I won't tell them you said that." His gaze sobered as he put his arms around her. "Lanie, are you sure?"

"I've never been so sure about anything. I want Zack to grow up in the same house you did, in the same room. I love you, Quinn."

His arms tightened and he buried his face in her hair. "And I love you. I promise you, Angel. The second time around is going be a lot better than the first. I'll never leave you again."

"I know," she whispered. "And even if you did, I'd come after you."

Epilogue

Lanie leaned against the fence in the bright afternoon sun, watching Quinn put Xan through his paces. Beside her, Sherry shifted restlessly. There was something on her foreman's mind and she waited patiently, knowing Sherry would tell her sooner or later.

Zack ran by on his way to the stable. Now that he was six, he'd decided he was too big for his pony, and Lanie had promised him he could choose his own horse. Spot, almost as big as Zack, trotted at his side, tongue lolling in the heat.

"I can't get over how Kate has grown," Sherry commented. "Or how much she looks like Quinn."

"She acts like him, too." Lanie smiled at mention of her year-old daughter. "I'm afraid she's spoiled rotten, thanks to her father and brother. And now Martha has joined her fan club. She hasn't let Kate out of her sight since we got here yesterday."

She glanced at Sherry, noting the blonde wasn't meeting her eyes. "So tell me all the news. How's Duncan doing with his store?"

"Wonderful. Between the tourists and the locals, he's really making a killing. And he fits into the community like he was born here. Everyone loves him. I think he's planning on dropping by tonight. He misses Quinn when you're in Chicago."

"Quinn misses him, too."

Sherry crossed her arms on the top rail. "Have you heard from Jared?"

"Not in quite a while. What's up with him?"

"He's seeing someone, and you'll never guess who it is."

Lanie smiled. "Sara Carson?"

"How did you know?" Sherry gaped at her.

"I could say it was a lucky guess, but I always got the feeling Sara was a lot more interested in Jared than she let on."

"You don't mind?"

"No, I'm happy for them. They're more alike than Jared and I ever were."

Sherry turned to face her, her expression intent. "What about you? Are you happy in Chicago?"

Lanie arched her brow in surprise. "Sherry, you know I am. I've got Quinn and the kids, and the riding stable is doing great. I've never been happier in my life. Now, are you going to tell me what's on your mind, or am I going to have to pry it out of you?"

The blonde's face turned three shades of crimson. "Well, I was just wondering if you might be willing to rent me one of the bunkhouses. I mean, I love gramps, and everything, but he doesn't really need me living with him. And since I'm running the ranch anyway, I thought it might be easier if I lived here."

"I don't know why you're even asking me." Lanie studied her face. "You're in charge here. If you want to live in one of the bunkhouses, just move in. And forget the rent."

Sherry looked down, apparently finding the toe of her boot very interesting. "What if I won't be living there alone?"

Lanie's smile turned into a full-fledged grin. "Who is it? Anyone I know?"

A sigh lifted Sherry's chest. "Cody asked me to marry him."

"Cody? Cody Simmons? Our Cody?"

"You don't have to sound so shocked." Sherry glared at her. "I know he's a few years younger than I am, but grandpa is crazy about him."

"What about you?"

The blonde's gaze softened. "I'm nuts about him too. I haven't given him an answer yet, but I can't even think straight when he's around. Then, when I see you and Quinn together with Kate and Zack... I want the same thing. I want a family of my own, with kids and everything. Do you think I'll make a lousy mother?"

"I think you'll make a wonderful mother." Lanie hugged her. "Now go find Cody and put him out of his misery. Then, we've got a wedding to plan. Good thing we're going to be here all summer."

Sherry returned her hug with a whispered, "Thank you," then hurried off in the direction of the brood mare barn.

Lanie watched her go, until Quinn stopped next to the fence and slid from Xan's back.

"What was that all about? It looked pretty serious."

"It was. Cody asked Sherry to marry him."

"And?"

"She's on her way to tell him yes."

He stepped closer and draped an arm around her shoulders. "I guess I should be happy for her, but I was hoping her and Duncan would work things out between them."

"I know." She stood on tiptoe and gave him a quick kiss. "But you can't push him, Quinn. When he's ready, he'll find someone."

"You're right, as usual." He got back on Xan, and with no warning, leaned down and lifted her over the fence, eliciting a squeal of surprise.

"Quinn! What are you doing?"

He gave her a lecherous grin. "Taking you for a ride. There's this waterfall I know about, and you have been hinting it might be time to give Kate and Zack some competition. I can't think of a better place to get started on it."

She went soft against him. "Neither can I, McAllister. Neither can I."

Also by Katherine Allred

For the Love of Charley

Sweet Revenge

The Sweet Gum Tree

What Price Paradise

About the Author

In real life, I'm Kathy to those who know me, since Katherine has always sounded snooty to my ears. Physically, I'm 5'5" with brown eyes. The rest of me is subject to change at the whim of my caloric intake, exercise regimen (or lack thereof), and Miss Clairol. I've worked at everything from killing bugs to telephone operator. I have a degree in journalism that is stuffed in a drawer somewhere. I've been writing for seven years now and have sold seven novels, five most recently to Cerridwen Press. The Sweet Gum Tree won the PASIC Book of Your Heart contest in 2002 in the single title category. I've been a member of Romance Writers of America since the day I started writing, and serve as judge for numerous chapter contests. I've been married to the same man for thirty-eight years now. We got married when I was two. That's my story, I'm sticking to it.

Katherine welcomes comments from readers. You can find her website and email address on her author bio page at www.cerridwenpress.com.

Tell Us What You Think

We appreciate hearing reader opinions about our books. You can email us at Comments@EllorasCave.com.

Why an electronic book?

We live in the Information Age—an exciting time in the history of human civilization, in which technology rules supreme and continues to progress in leaps and bounds every minute of every day. For a multitude of reasons, more and more avid literary fans are opting to purchase e-books instead of paper books. The question from those not yet initiated into the world of electronic reading is simply: *Why?*

1. *Price.* An electronic title at Ellora's Cave Publishing and Cerridwen Press runs anywhere from 40% to 75% less than the cover price of the exact same title in paperback format. Why? Basic mathematics and cost. It is less expensive to publish an e-book (no paper and printing, no warehousing and shipping) than it is to publish a paperback, so the savings are passed along to the consumer.

2. *Space.* Running out of room in your house for your books? That is one worry you will never have with electronic books. For a low one-time cost, you can purchase a handheld device specifically designed for e-reading. Many e-readers have large, convenient screens for viewing. Better yet, hundreds of titles can be stored within your new library—on a single microchip. There are a variety of e-readers from different manufacturers. You can also read e-books on your PC or laptop computer. (Please note that

Ellora's Cave does not endorse any specific brands. You can check our websites at www.ellorascave.com or www.cerridwenpress.com for information we make available to new consumers.)

3. *Mobility.* Because your new e-library consists of only a microchip within a small, easily transportable e-reader, your entire cache of books can be taken with you wherever you go.

4. *Personal Viewing Preferences.* Are the words you are currently reading too small? Too large? Too... ANNOYING? Paperback books cannot be modified according to personal preferences, but e-books can.

5. *Instant Gratification.* Is it the middle of the night and all the bookstores near you are closed? Are you tired of waiting days, sometimes weeks, for bookstores to ship the novels you bought? Ellora's Cave Publishing sells instantaneous downloads twenty-four hours a day, seven days a week, every day of the year. Our webstore is never closed. Our e-book delivery system is 100% automated, meaning your order is filled as soon as you pay for it.

Those are a few of the top reasons why electronic books are replacing paperbacks for many avid readers.

As always, Ellora's Cave and Cerridwen Press welcome your questions and comments. We invite you to email us at Comments@ellorascave.com or write to us directly at Ellora's Cave Publishing Inc., 1056 Home Avenue, Akron, OH 44310-3502.

Cerridwen Press
Monthly Newsletter

News
Author Appearances
Book Signings
New Releases
Contests
Author Profiles
Feature Articles

Available online at
www.CerridwenPress.com

Cerridwen Press

Cerridwen, the Celtic goddess of wisdom, was the muse who brought inspiration to storytellers and those in the creative arts.

Cerridwen Press encompasses the best and most innovative stories in all genres of today's fiction.

Visit our website and discover the newest titles by talented authors who still get inspired—much like the ancient storytellers did...

once upon a time.

www.cerridwenpress.com

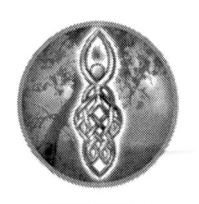